Advance Praise
MY YEAR AT THE GOOD BEAN CAFE

Luetkemeyer works with the fine art of fragmenting reality so that the reader experiences several planes simultaneously: imagination, hidden dark forces, synchronicities, time travel, personal psychology, non-ordinary states of consciousness, substance-induced perceptions, speculation, pure fiction, pieces of consensual reality and more. To say his writing is mind-tweaking is an understatement. His fiction is like reality jazz. The theme can go in many directions, most of them non-linear.

– Frank De Luca, PhD
A Field Guide to Humans:
Enriching Relationships Through the Enneagram

My Year at the Good Bean Café...catches the reader's imagination and interest from the first page...and it does not let the reader stop reading until the very last page.

– Bernadette Longu
Readers' Favorite (5-Star Review)

This is the strangest novel I have read (and enjoyed) in many a year... a compelling read... every story within the book is skillfully plotted and highly unpredictable...trust me when I say you'll never be bored reading this.

– *The Wishing Shelf Awards*

[Luetkemeyer's] personalizing of the reader draws the reader in and makes the stories seem like a fireside chat with the characters...[He] has an innate ability to convince you that even if these events didn't happen, the characters themselves are convinced they did.

– Grant Leishman
A Drop in the Ocean

My Year at the Good Bean Café is an intense, beautiful, often dark, but wonderful read. It has everything: love, hate, violence, drugs, altered states, joy and pain. It takes every twist and turn into unknown worlds. I loved it, even though there were times I would have closed my eyes, had it been a movie.

– Ginna BB Gordon
Bear Me Away to a Better World

The twelve stories are loosely interlinked, with the characters from one narrative frequently gatecrashing another. Stories such as *The Two Wives of Frederico Ricci* and *Ten Thousand Hours in Shadowland* had a joyful vibe, while *Born Again* and *The Migration of Plastic Pink Flamingos* possessed an inherent sadness. The October story, *Travelling Man*, came with a disturbingly dark undertone. *Becoming Nobody* was the most thought-provoking story I have read in a while. I recommend *My Year at the Good Bean Café* to anyone who loves magical realism, especially those who appreciate Haruki Murakami's works.

– Shrabasty Shakraborty
Readers' Favorite (5-Star Review)

MY YEAR AT THE
GOOD BEAN CAFÉ

OTHER BOOKS BY EA LUETKEMEYER

Memoir

The Book of Chuck

Fiction

Inside the Mind of Martin Mueller

Penitentiary Tales: A Love Story

MY YEAR AT THE GOOD BEAN CAFÉ

A NOVEL

EA LUETKEMEYER

Laughing Buddha Books
Jacksonville, Oregon

Published by Laughing Buddha Books
Jacksonville, Oregon

www.ealuetkemeyer.com

Cover painting by the author
Cover painting photographed by Dr. Richard Handler
Author photograph on back cover by John Mazzei

ISBN: 9798218186616

Book and cover design by Lucky Valley Press
www.luckyvalleypress.com

Printed in the United States of America on acid-free paper

Global distribution by Ingram

For the patrons and staff
of the Good Bean Café
and the artists and entrepreneurs
of Jacksonville, Oregon

ACKNOWLEDGMENTS

Thanks to my early readers for their encouragement, comments, and suggestions. I heard you.

Gratitude to Dr. Richard Handler for his guidance on all things medical; to attorneys Tom and Barbara Roberts for their legal expertise; to David Gordon and John Mazzei for their insight into the music industry; to Terry and Paula Erdmann for permission to simulate their column *The Unfettered Critic*; to Hannah West for the regeneration of my long-dormant website; to Ginna and David Gordon of Lucky Valley Press for crafting these pages; and, as always, to my lovely wife, Leslie, for her patience, and frequent and welcome visits to The Creepy Room. Love you all.

'Tis strange but true; for truth is always strange;
Stranger than fiction: if it could be told,
How much would novels gain by the exchange!
How differently the world would men behold!

– Lord Byron

CONTENTS

PROLOGUE

UNLIKELY AND INEXPLICABLE

If you look into the camera
and you see something you recognize,
don't click the shutter.
– Yasuhiro Wakabayashi, Photographer

DEAR READER: YOU SHOULD KNOW up front with whom you'll be spending the next few hundred pages exploring the nature of unlikely and inexplicable events and how they affect our lives. Adrian Lomachenko here, to whom unlikely and inexplicable events have occurred with such frequency they have come to be expected. I sometimes spend days on end doing nothing but waiting for something strange to happen. I am rarely disappointed.

The first such event occurred to my five-year-old self. I was sleeping alone in my own bed in my own bedroom for the first time, having spent the entirety of my young life in the same bedroom as my parents. They had tucked me in and said goodnight. You'll be fine, they assured me but I was not convinced. Alone with my stuffed monkey, Miranda, I closed my eyes against the writhing water stains on the disintegrating wallpaper and my ears against the tiny voices that came from behind the closet door. I chewed on my monkey's left ear, having long since chewed off the right. When I opened my eyes, the room was bathed in soft blue light. A man sat on the edge of my bed. He looked at me and smiled. I felt safe in his presence.

Hello, he said.

Hello, I said.

What's your name? he said.

Adrian, I said.

That's a very nice name, Adrian, he said.

What's your name? I said.

I'm Adrian, too, he said. We have the same name.

My young mind was perplexed. How could there be two Adrians?

What's your monkey's name? the man said.

Miranda, I said.

Miranda! Very nice! Why did you name her Miranda, Adrian?

She told me her name.

Did she now!

He looked around the room.

So…this is your room, huh?

Yes.

It's a very nice room, Adrian. You're a lucky boy. You'll be happy here, you and Miranda. You should sleep now.

I closed my eyes. He touched my face with his fingers. I fell fast asleep.

Twenty years later, I had a dream. I sat on the edge of a small bed in a small room bathed in soft blue light. In the bed was a child holding a stuffed monkey. He was afraid to sleep alone and I reassured him. When I woke up, I remembered the conversation in my dream, and I remembered the incident from my childhood, and I realized they were one and the same.

I WAS BORN AND RAISED in Chicken Ranch, Arkansas, where scarcity was the rule: little money; not much to think about; nothing to do. I was bussed to a high school that served the lower quarter of our rural county and I graduated at the top of my class of thirteen. That and my ACT scores and my documented state of poverty were sufficient to grant me a scholarship to the University of California, Berkeley, which probably satisfied their quota for applicants from Chicken Ranch, Arkansas.

While my peers spent their lazy Arkansas days catching catfish in the Buffalo River, I read books and painted pictures. My taste in literature ran to the Southern writers: Faulkner, Penn Warren, O'Conner, Lee; the science fiction masters: Asimov, Heinlein, Bradbury, Ellison; the magical realists for their playful spinning of reality: Marquez, Allende, Murakami, Foos. With my brush and palette, I mimicked the fabulous imagery of the Surrealists. You might think, with my predilection for prose and paint, I would have majored in literature or fine art but, no, my soul was torn by two opposing forces: creativity and greed. I wanted *money*. I would fashion a life of middle-class comfort and privilege and erase the memory of an impoverished childhood.

So, I majored in finance.

I graduated Magna Cum Laude from Berkeley and landed a position at the headquarters of a major bank in the Financial District of San Francisco. I had an office with a view on California Street, my own parking space (a prized piece of real estate in San Francisco), wore a tailored suit, and carried a briefcase crammed with other people's important documents. I had a girlfriend who studied Real Estate Law and wanted us to become wealthy together…and I was miserable. The restless, demanding forces of creativity, long repressed, rose up to challenge the cynical forces of acquisition and greed, and I was torn between them. Here I was in the West Coast literary mecca of the world—and I wore a suit!

SOME EVENTS ARE SO UNLIKELY AND INEXPLICABLE your life does an about face and you go to where you were truly bound. I skipped the morning meeting at the office and took Uber to City Lights Bookstore in North Beach. When I die, friend, spread my ashes down its labyrinthine aisles. I wandered them for an hour and, such was my habit, filled my basket with more books than I would find time to read. I would be missed at the office but didn't care.

I stood on the corner of Broadway and Columbus Avenue awaiting my ride back to the Financial District. At my side stood a tall man in a yellow silk shirt with puffed sleeves over baggy crimson trousers tied at the ankles. His long black hair was parted in the middle. Golden hoops hung from his ears. He carried an umbrella though there wasn't a cloud in the sky. The white flashing pedestrian sign cycled through twice, but he didn't cross. He turned and looked down upon me from his height. His eyes were dark pools with points of light at their centers, like the light at the end of a tunnel. A cunning smile curled his lips.

Good morning, brother, he said.

His voice was resonant, seeming to come from far away after a long journey.

Same to you, friend, I said.

I felt an inexplicable kinship with the man. His eccentric appearance so contrasted with mine that I was sorely reminded of the sacrifice of personal freedom that the pursuit of material gain demanded.

How is your day? he inquired.

There are things I'd rather be doing, I confessed.

He nodded shrewdly.

Don't wait too long, he said. Tomorrow never comes.

With that, he turned and stepped off the curb into the path of a cable car, somersaulted through the air like a red and yellow bean bag, and was impaled on the iron foot peg of a telephone pole. His arms hung limply at his sides. One hand yet held his umbrella. Before he closed his eyes, he winked and smiled his canny smile at me. I swear he did.

I QUIT THE BANK AND TOOK a part-time job at an oyster bar. I parted with my girlfriend. She would not have liked what I became. I wore what I felt like wearing, and let my hair grow. I was accepted into the MFA Program in Creative Writing at San Francisco State University. I would come away saddled with a mountain of student loan debt like a million other aspiring intellects but that's the price one pays for higher educa-tion in the U.S.A. I became intimate with the nooks and crannies of San

Francisco and spent two years in pursuit of my degree making up stories about its various and sundry characters, a few of which found print in literary journals, the collection of which became my thesis, and was later published as *Baghdad by the Bay Again*, after Herb Caen's far better collection of essays, *Baghdad by the Bay*, written thirty years before I was born. My humble version was well received but a good review and four dollars will get you a medium mocha at Starbucks. My true reward is that a copy can still be found on a shelf of City Lights Bookstore.

On the strength of its publication, and my MFA from San Francisco State, I was invited to interview for a teaching position at Rogue Community College in Medford, Oregon. My drive north was filled with apprehension. What if they hired me? Why ever would I leave San Francisco, the literary mecca of the Western World, to live in the hinterlands of Southern Oregon?

THE FOLKS AT ROGUE COMMUNITY COLLEGE liked my southern roots. They liked my modest publication history. They liked the circuitous route by which I'd arrived at their doorstep. They offered me the position. I accepted. My modest salary would cover my student loan payment, rent on a room in town, and put food on the table. But Southern Oregon?

Argh! What had I done?

Returning to San Francisco in a dubious state of mind, I stopped in the quaint historic town of Jacksonville for lunch. The instant my feet hit the ground I felt a certain energy suffuse upward through the soles of my shoes. A salutation. An invitation. I did a walking tour of the town. Not a traffic light nor parking meter in sight, only old brick and ivy and smiling people being led about by their dogs. I visited its festival grounds, its galleries, its eclectic shops, its bookstore, Rebel Heart Books, its welltended cemetery. I sat at the Good Bean Café and marveled at the diversity of its patrons: young and old reading novels, reading the bible, playing chess, typing at their laptops, and having lively conversations. I perused its bulletin board, replete with flyers advertising theater and music and holistic health. I read the engaging columns in the *Jacksonville Review*. Clearly, this was not your typical, well-preserved historic western town of a few thousand people. There was artistry and intelligence and entrepreneurship in the very air. More creative types *per capita* than even in San Francisco.

What do you think, Miranda? I thought. Have we arrived?

SOMETIMES AN OTHERWISE INCONSEQUENTIAL event can trigger a revelation. I wrapped up my business in San Francisco and headed north to Oregon. I took the slow coastal route, a leisurely passage into my new life. I rolled down the window and let the salty air wash over me. I reveled in the blue sky, the ribbon of surf, the pavement un-scrolling beneath my wheels, and contemplated my next book. My teaching load would be light, and I would have plenty of time to write. But about what?

In Ft. Bragg, 170 miles north of San Francisco, I took a room at the Noyo Harbor Inn, an extravagance given my dwindling funds, but I was in the mood to celebrate the turn of events my life had taken. I dined on the patio of the Harborview Bistro & Bar. Lights twinkled on the lapping water like distant stars, and the masts of small craft rocked to and fro like metronomes in slow motion. After dinner, I lingered over a crisp Chardonnay and Haruki Murakami's short story collection *Blind Willow, Sleeping Woman*. I was midway through the story *Chance Traveler,* which examines the nature of coincidence, when the woman at the next table approached with a timid smile.

Excuse me, she said. May I ask what you're reading?

I held up the book. She read the cover.

What's it about? she said.

It's a work of *magical realism*, I said.

When she failed to respond, I added, A genre of fiction wherein fantastic occurrences are treated as normal.

Oh, she stammered, thank you.

She returned to her table, seeming embarrassed by her boldness or else by her faltering response. I resumed reading *Chance Traveler* where I'd left off. In the very next paragraph, the protagonist sits in a restaurant reading a book. The woman at the adjacent table approaches him—and asks what he's reading!

It came to me in a flash: my next book would explore the occurrence of unlikely and inexplicable events and how they affect our lives. I would sit at the Good Bean Café in Jacksonville, observe its patrons, engage in conversation, and with a little help from Miranda devise a story, real or imagined, around a watershed moment in the lives of each of twelve characters, one for each month of the year. The challenge: to finish each story in the month in which it was begun. I would call my book *My Year at the Good Bean Café*. I would write the first word in January of the new year.

A BIT ABOUT MIRANDA: SHE CEASED BEING a stuffed monkey when I ceased being a timid child in Chicken Ranch, Arkansas. Thereafter, she was merely a cherished recollection of a childhood companion, and though I had no illusions she was anything else, I would sometimes appeal to her for inspiration when my writing faltered. But she became more than a memory the night I spent on a houseboat moored off the coast of Sausalito, Marin County, California.

Earlier that day I'd bought a hit of acid off a street dealer on Telegraph Avenue in Berkeley outside a Tibetan curio shop where I'd purchased a pendant, seven charms on a chain, thought to stimulate mystical insight. I dropped the acid in the evening when alone on the boat I was tending for a friend out of town. I fingered the pendant as I sat on the deck in a rocking chair watching the sun go down, and the seagulls dip and soar over white-capped waves on the bay, and across the bay the lights of the San Francisco skyline as they blinked silently and twinkled like fairy dust. As the acid took hold of me, I became obsessed with the number seven. I saw a group of seagulls cavorting in the salty air off the bow of the boat and there were seven of them. I saw a cluster of sailboats make their way in the rough waters from Alcatraz to the Embarcadero and there were seven of those, too. Even the cottony moan of a foghorn emanating from the roiling sea smoke beyond the Golden Gate Bridge sounded in groups of seven. There was something mysterious going on and I was seized by the notion that I should capture its meaning in a poem of seven lines. But as I sat at the typewriter on the desk in the main room of the boat which served as study, parlor and boudoir, my fingers poised on the keyboard in rapt anticipation of cosmic revelation…nothing happened; the doors of perception had slammed shut rudely in my face.

I went out to the deck and searched the sky, where the stars had arranged themselves neatly into clusters of seven.

Miranda! I called out. Miranda! I need you!

My supplication was met by silence. I called again and again until I had called out seven times, then I heard a voice behind me.

I'm here.

I turned, and there in the dark interior of the boat, glowing softly like a Luna Moth in moonlight, stood Miranda.

Come closer, she said.

Her voice was soft and sweet. I seemed to float across the distance between us. She put a hand on my arm. I put a hand on hers. She was real, alright, ephemeral as a fairy, yet her fleshly presence no less corporeal than that of any woman I had been with, and the comeliness of her carriage no less alluring than that of any nymph conjured by the lurid imagination of the artist Botticelli.

Miranda!

Her eyes were like nothing I had seen before: portals onto an imponderable swirling cosmos. I would have left my wife and children for her if I had had them to leave.

Your need is very great, she said: a poem of seven lines that unlocks the secrets of the Universe!

I put my hands on her hips. I stroked her willowy torso.

My need is great indeed, I said, but not for lines of poetry.

When dawn broke over the bay, I was alone. I untangled myself from the twisted blankets and the sweaty sheets and went to the deck of the boat. Off the bow, five seagulls dipped and soared in the salty air. A trio of sailboats leaned their sheets into the wind. A foghorn sounded twice. If Miranda had bestowed the secrets of the Universe upon me that night, they were lost to me now, but I would never forget the pleasure of carnal knowledge raised to the level of rapture by a stuffed monkey morphed into my muse and mystic paramour.

OH, AND ONE MORE THING: We'll dispense with the *Dear Reader* device. Your name is Sam. I need to feel I'm addressing a real person, not a mass of anonymous readers *out there* somewhere. I hope you don't mind. I promise you won't lose your identity by sharing it with others. You'll remain a unique individual, just like everyone else. Besides, it's only for a year.

Well. It's you and me and Miranda, Sam. Can we do this?

JANUARY

GEOMETRY OF THE EXTERNAL WORLD

Roses are red, violets are blue
I'm schizophrenic and so am I
                    – Oscar Levant

Friday, January 1st, 2019

GOOD AFTERNOON, SAM! THANKS FOR BEING here on the first day of my year at the Good Bean Café. I'm comfortably settled into a modest studio apartment above a garage on South Oregon Street, a short walk away. Fortuitous.

And what a day of writing it has been! An author's delight! I arrived at the Café promptly at 6:00 a.m. and took a table that gave me a view of the entire room: the kitchen, the counter, the toilet, the two front doors. It will be my table of choice for the duration of this book. I plugged in my laptop, ordered coffee, and returned to my table.

Hey, Miranda, I said to myself, what do you have for me today?

Total silence. She's that kind of muse: arbitrary and capricious. She makes her appearance when it pleases her. But never mind. I have my methods.

Patrons arrived singly and in pairs: a white-haired man with a kind smile, accompanied by a youth with a serious inward look, each with a bible in hand; a forty-something woman in denim trousers, scuffed black velvet boots, and a plaid jacket, who opened her laptop and immediately began scrolling; a young couple with sleepy eyes and tousled hair and desultory conversation; an unkempt solitary man with a bowed back and a halting step, who muttered to himself; a middle-aged man dressed for a day's labor, soon joined by others. I examined each in turn for telling details that might prompt a story but drew a blank. Sometimes I am dull for no particular reason.

At 7:00 a.m. the cook arrived. Tall and slender. Just out of his teens. His straight black hair gathered in a knot at the top of his head. He scrutinized the patrons, then looked quickly away. There was about him an air of contempt combined with suspicion bordering on paranoia. I imagined he employed an arcane vocabulary when simple words would suffice, to demonstrate his superior intelligence and further distance himself from others. I imagined he fancied himself descended from royalty.

I now had the prototype for the protagonist of my January story. I would deposit him in another time and place, foreign and fanciful. I would examine his psychology and have the tone of the story reflect the interior of his troubled mind. I would call him Lucian, a name that came to me just now, from where I couldn't say. I spent the next several hours composing the following fanciful tale, which I will fine tune by and by.

Enjoy the read, Sam.

GEOMETRY OF THE EXTERNAL WORLD

HIS HIGHNESS, THE YOUNG LORD LUCIAN, heir apparent to the Kingdom of Sandu, would tell you he was nobody's fool. That the devious lot of his malefactors believed for a minute their treachery might escape his intelligence only proved their lack of it. The insidious sideways glances, the furtive whisperings in the hall, the sudden silence at his approach—all evidenced the perfidious plot afoot!

Determined to conceal his suspicion, Lucian feigned an air of heedless disregard, that the perpetrators might think him oblivious, but the strain of his efforts betrayed him. He was one moment buttoned up tight as a maiden's corset, the next as chatty as a drunken monkey. Get a grip! he admonished himself. Be one and the same person at all times!

His fitfulness did not escape the attention of the Royal Family. The services of his uncle, Court Physician and Mathematician Sir Tomasz Sandu, were called upon. Sir Tomasz promptly diagnosed *Chronic Bifurcation of The Soul* and prescribed an excursion into the wilds of the Unclaimed Territories, the outermost region of the known world, *to engage the boy's senses and align the cosmos of his inner space with the imperturbable geometry of the external world.* A most suspicious remedy, Lucian thought—a holiday in the hinterlands where all manner of foul play might befall him! He would have to be on guard.

Lucian's other uncle, Sir Borodine Sandu, an explorer of renown often commissioned by the Court to map the Unclaimed Territories, agreed that Lucian might accompany him on his next expedition. The Queen gave her imprimatur—with a suspicious readiness, it seemed to the young Lord: it was clear he could trust no one but himself!

TRULY THE FANCIFUL LANDSCAPE of the Unclaimed Territories, with its alien flora and fauna, where boulders thrummed like far-off thunder and water ran uphill, was engaging to the senses and Lucian might have become *aligned*, as it were, but for the slyness of Borodine, who seemed delighted to compound his disorientation. The passage he plotted seemed so meandering, such a patchwork quilt of latitude and longitude, that one might wonder if they were not lost, a possibility Lucian posed to him one blustery day as they stood upon the peak of a craggy range.

Not at all, Borodine said, seeming pleased with the question, if only to prove it preposterous.

He un-scrolled the map he had composed en route. He looked at his compass. He scanned the horizon. He pointed.

Look there, he said. Do you see that range opposite us, across the intervening valley?

I do, Lucian said.

And do you see the uppermost peak on the left whose shape is that of a dunce's cap?

I do, Lucian said.

And the peak beside it whose shape is that of a sleeping camel?

I do.

Borodine smiled, a little smugly, Lucian thought, and said: That is where you will find us!

Lucian laughed derisively.

And *what*, dear uncle, do you suppose *we* are doing on yonder peak?

I suppose, dear nephew, that *we* are gazing *this* way wondering what *we* are doing on *this* peak. Therefore, I propose that *we* descend and cross the valley, on the assumption *they* will do the same, and *we* will encounter *them*, that is to say *us*, in the middle.

THE NEXT DAY, FOLLOWING A FITFUL night's sleep in which Lucian dreamt if he crossed his legs and puckered his sphincter just so, he might levitate and float blissfully above the pitchforks of the howling masses, he and Borodine approached the valley's mid-point. Nothing more had been said of the absurd notion of encountering themselves but, lo, approaching in the near distance, were two astoundingly familiar figures: Lucian and Borodine! Lucian halted, too stunned to proceed, as did his replica, whereas Borodine and his likeness embraced and exchanged greetings as old friends and colleagues might.

Borodine!

Borodine!

Lucian was introduced to himself: Lucian, meet Lucian.

The two Lucians extended their hands but withdrew them and settled for a pair of wary nods.

My dear Lucian, said one or another of the Borodines to one or another of the Lucians, I suggest you take a stroll and become acquainted with yourself. Sir Borodine and I have matters to discuss. A brief respite, then we'll be on our way.

Lucian and Lucian strolled to a log beside a gully and sat like bookends. They gazed out over the expanse of valley that receded to the distant mountains. Overhead, scudding clouds blocked the sun, casting a shadow that seemed to permeate Lucian's very flesh. He shivered and folded his arms about his torso. He glanced at his double, then looked quickly away. Had the Universe sent him an ally? he wondered. A confidant he could trust indubitably in all matters of the heart and mind? Or had this alter ego been sent by the Universe to betray him? He would question the lad but feared he might lose sense of which Lucian he was: the one who queried or the one who replied. He thought to regard himself as *Lucian The One* and his counterpart *Lucian The Other.*

Friend or foe? he asked.

Pardon me? replied Lucian The Other.

Are you my friend or are you my foe?

Must I be one or the other?

Yes! You must be *The Other* if I am *The One*, but are you my friend or are you my foe?

Lucian The Other shrugged. He raised a palm to the sky.

I am who I am, he said.

Lucian The One found this answer evasive. He would try a different approach.

Do you have a scar, he said.

I do, said Lucian The Other.

Where is it?

On my calf, below the knee.

May I see?

Lucian The Other pulled up his trouser leg, pushed down his stocking, and pointed.

There, he said.

Lucian The One pulled up his own trouser leg, pushed down his stocking, and placed his leg alongside that of Lucian The Other, revealing a matched pair of moth-shaped scars.

How did you get it? said Lucian The One.

I was bitten by a rabid Honey Badger when a young boy, said Lucian The Other.

And did you then spend a fortnight bound to your bed and foaming at the mouth?

So I'm told, said Lucien The Other.

As did I, said Lucian The One.

He held out his arm.

Pinch me, he said, pinch me hard and tell me if you, too, feel the pain.

Lucian The Other pinched the arm of Lucian The One.

Aiee! said Lucian The Other. I felt the pain as well!

Excellent, said Lucian The One. Now hold out your arm that I might pinch you.

Lucian The Other complied. Lucian The One pinched his arm.

Ouch! he exclaimed. I, too, felt the pinch in the self-same spot! Tell me, have you been circumcised?

I have, said Lucian The Other.

Well, I won't ask to see, said Lucian The One, satisfied that in matters of the flesh he and Lucian The Other were synonymous. But were they kindred spirits in matters of the mind and heart? He would hasten to the point.

Tell me, he said, is your mother the Queen?

She is.

And you are heir apparent to the Kingdom of Sandu?

I am.

And Sir Borodine and Sir Tomasz are your uncles?

They are.

And your Uncle Tomasz, Mathematician and Court Physician to the Kingdom of Sandu, has determined that you suffer from *Chronic Bifurcation of the Soul*?

He has, yes.

And you now accompany your uncle on this expedition to *align the cosmos of your inner space with the imperturbable geometry of the external world*?

That is the prescription, yes.

And do you suspect, as I do, that some nefarious conspiracy is in the making, involving the whole of the court, the subject of which is yourself?

I have considered that possibility, said Lucian The Other, stroking his chin and nodding.

Oh…but you have not concluded it?

I have not, replied Lucian The Other. I am inclined to believe that the intentions of the Court are benevolent, and I should be grateful for the Royal Intervention.

Is that so! exclaimed Lucian The One.

Quite, said Lucian The Other. I long to be aligned. To be in harmony with the Universe, at one with my fellow man, free of confusion and doubt forever! Wouldn't that be lovely?

At this suggestion of loveliness, Lucian The One fell into a dream. He saw himself floating like a fluffy white cloud in a powder blue sky, buoyant and blissful, formless, morphing into a cherub in a dreamless sleep in a billowing bed of feathers, all watched over by a Court of loving Lords and Ladies. But in an instant, the bed of feathers became a bed of prickly pears, and the Court of loving Lords and Ladies a chorus of clamoring clowns. He awoke from his dream with a start. The bastards! he thought. How clever of them to send this sycophant, this fool, this fraudulent facsimile of himself to rhapsodize about harmony with the Universe and unity with his fellow man! Clever and contemptible! But he, Lucian The One and Only, wasn't born yesterday!

They fell to silence. The Borodines approached.

Well, they said in unison, like a couple of myna birds with only each other to mimic, we hope your time together was pleasant and productive. Nothing like communing with oneself, we always say. Shall we be off?

Lucian The One regarded the Borodines. They loomed above him like identical rooks on a chessboard. He chose to accompany the one nearest by, who regarded him with a familiar smile. They started in the direction in which Lucian believed they had been earlier bound, but when he looked behind him he saw that the mountain range they traveled away from was identical to the one they traveled toward. What then awaited him at their destination, he wondered—a Court contriving to end his life or one intent upon healing his bifurcated soul and returning him to the bosom of their undying love? He was not certain if he was coming or going.

Uncle, he said, tell me: how can I know that you are the Borodine who I previously accompanied, and not the Borodine who traveled in the opposite direction?

Whatever do you mean? said Borodine.

I mean only that, as you are an exact replica of the Borodine we encountered in the center of the valley, and I am an exact replica of myself, that is, the Lucian who accompanied the Borodine of whom you are an exact replica, might it not be that I now accompany the wrong, so to speak, Borodine, and that you accompany the wrong Lucian; and that, likewise, our other, identical selves are similarly mismatched? And further, that the court to which we are now bound is not the court toward which we previously perambulated, but is the very court from which we parted?

Borodine halted in his tracks. He regarded Lucian at length.

Frankly, Lucian, he said, I haven't a clue what you're talking about!

He put a hand on his nephew's shoulder and sighed.

I'm afraid, dear Lucian, that I have no choice but to inform Sir Tomasz that his remedy failed to achieve the result for which it was intended, and for which the Court had so earnestly hoped.

The meaning of Borodine's pronouncement rang clear as steeple bells: Lucian would now be prescribed an herbal concoction from the panoply of palliatives for which his nefarious Uncle Tomasz was duly famous, and from which he would not awaken! He removed his uncle's hand.

Excuse me, Uncle, he said. I must relieve myself.

He slipped into the bushes. He scrambled down a steep embankment and followed the course of a bone-dry riverbed mile after mile. He did not look back. He put time and distance between himself and The Court and its confounded conspiracies. He wandered the wilderness of the Unclaimed Territories content to be alone. His hair grew long, his robe became tattered. He would not have been recognized by the Queen herself! He fashioned a stout cudgel of hardwood with which to smite his enemies, and should he perchance encounter that two-faced knave, Lucian, he would bludgeon him as well, to within an inch of his—that is to say *their*— duplicitous life!

FEBRUARY

THE BODY THAT FELL FROM THE SKY

In infinite space,
even the most unlikely events
must take place somewhere.

– Max Tegmark
Swedish American Physicist

Monday, February 8, 2019

GOOD MORNING, SAM. I KNOW it's a few days into the month. Thanks for waiting. I spent the latter half of January revising *Geometry of the External World.* Last Monday, the first day of this month, when I should have been sitting down to begin our February story, I was at an early morning appointment at Asante Medical Center in neighboring Medford. It's just as well. The flow of my creativity had dried up like a seasonal stream at the end of a long, hot summer. Down to the dusty pebbles. I hadn't a clue what I'd write. Perhaps a break in my routine would unblock me and deliver the inspiration I needed to get my groove back.

Speaking of being blocked, one year ago, while yet in the Bay Area, my left main artery was diagnosed forty-five percent obstructed. If it got any worse, I would be a candidate for a coronary bypass. I met with cardiologist Dr. Charles Rimbaud to assess my condition.

The Doctor was tanned and fit. I guessed tennis or golf. White frock over faded Levi's and Reebok running shoes. A handsome, intelligent face, a touch of grey above the ears, and a confident demeanor. I'd seen him a few times at the Good Bean. He reviewed my medical history on a computer. He told me to pull up my shirt. He put the cold medallion of his stethoscope on my bare chest and told me to breathe.

How do you feel, Adrian? he said.

I feel fine, I said.

He slid the medallion from left to right.

What kind of cardio exercise do you do?

I walk the trails on the hills around town. Lots of up and down. I used to run but my knees don't like it.

Save the knees, he said. You'll need them.

He slid the medallion around my rib cage and rested it between my scapulae.

Cough, he said.

I coughed.

Have you experienced any shortness of breath or chest pain beyond what you felt last year? he said.

No.

He put the stethoscope into the pocket of his frock. I pulled my shirt down.

Will I be doing a treadmill stress test today? I said.

No need, he said. Keep doing what you're doing.

That's a relief, I said. I didn't care for the stress test last year. People watching, waiting for me to pass out. I felt they'd taken bets in a back room.

The doctor chuckled. He entered data into his computer.

You're a writer, he said.

I like to think so. How did you know?

I've seen you at the Good Bean hovering over your laptop. Composing, not scrolling. You can always tell the writers from the net surfers.

Do you write?

I tried writing. I chose medicine. It was easier.

You have a famous writer's namesake. Rimbaud. Any relation?

Distant. If you go back far enough, we're all related to someone famous. Have you read Rimbaud?

A *Season in Hell*, I said. I love the prose, but the meaning is elusive.

What do you write?

Currently a collection of stories about unlikely and inexplicable events and how they affect our lives.

Interesting. Where do you get your ideas, Adrian?

Observations of people going about their business, I said. Like a sketch artist on a subway train. I note their appearance, their gestures, and expressions, imagine their thoughts and feelings, then invent an incident around which to weave a narrative. Or I conduct an interview of an imaginary person and have them tell me their story in their own words. Or I listen to the stories of real people. You'd be surprised how many have experienced an unlikely and inexplicable event in their lives. I add a dash of imagination and bam! I have a character and a story.

Dr. Rimbaud turned from his computer and faced me. He seemed to be mulling a decision.

I have a story to tell, he said. About an unlikely and inexplicable event that changed the course of my life. Would you like to hear it?

I would, I said. I've been wondering from where my next story might come.

You're welcome to add a dash of imagination and put it in your book if it pleases you, he said.

We agreed to meet at the Good Bean Café the following Sunday, yesterday, at 8:00 a.m.

I ARRIVED AT THE GOOD BEAN EARLY. I watched the morning crowd shuffle in. I imagined their secret lives. I wrote a summary of the circumstances of meeting Dr. Charles Rimbaud. At 7:00 o'clock the young cook arrived, wrapped in his air of haughtiness. I went to the counter and ordered food. I must admit the heir apparent to the Kingdom of Sandu makes a mean breakfast burrito.

I finished eating just as Dr. Rimbaud walked through the door wearing hiking boots, charcoal-grey cargo pants, an olive-green hooded rain jacket, and a Panama hat. He searched the room till our eyes met. His smile was genuine. He queued up for coffee. Greeted the barista. Exchanged a few words with the cook. Took a seat across from mine. We wasted little time with small talk. He seemed anxious to tell his tale. I turned on the *record* function of my iPhone and he related the following.

THE BODY THAT FELL FROM THE SKY

A DOZEN YEARS AGO, while living in Boston, I received a call from an attorney in Bisbee, Arizona. I had inherited a house on a dusty acre on the edge of town. My last living uncle, Rufus Rimbaud, had passed, and my parents and brother and only cousin having predeceased me, there was no one else to give it to.

Sad as I was at the passing of Uncle Rufus, I was delighted to claim my windfall. I have warm memories of my childhood days in Bisbee. My father was born there and on weekends he would pack my mother and my brother Darrell and me into the station wagon for the two-hour drive south from Tucson to visit his parents, his brother Rufus and Rufus's wife, Ginny, and their son Doug. Darrell and Doug and I would explore the abandoned mines that bordered the town, hunt for arrowheads in dry creek beds, and knock the limbs off cacti with smooth round stones launched from hand-made slingshots. Though I hadn't been to Bisbee in a decade, I had long entertained the notion of retiring there or at least maintaining a second home.

But my wife, Jean, was having none of it. Seven years prior to the call, when we still lived in Tucson, she had insisted I accept a position at Tuft Medical Center in Boston, had even threatened to move without me. I was baffled by her obstinacy. She seemed in a hurry to get out of town, but I let it pass. She had since become a social butterfly, a wannabe Boston Brahmin, and looked down upon her own family and friends in Tucson as artifacts of the Wild West. But more about Jean and her attitude later in my story. I would leave her and our seven-year-old son behind and go to Bisbee without her. I could have handled the paperwork by email or snail mail, but I chose to claim my prize in person. I arranged four days away from my rigorous duties at Tuft and caught a Saturday flight to Tucson. As I watched the landscape slide by seven miles below, I didn't know if I was leaving home or going home.

I drove a rented car to the Westward Look, a hacienda-style resort in the Sonoran Desert at the edge of town. I had my first B&B in a warm snifter there years before while watching the sun sink like a red-hot nickel into the Santa Rita Mountains. And I had brought a winsome young Jean there for a frolicsome weekend during our courting days.

The next morning, after a dip in the pool and a hearty southwest breakfast of huevos rancheros and chorizo, I set out on the same scenic route to Bisbee as my father had decades before. Highway 83 takes you to Sonoita, in the heart of Arizona's Wine Country which, while it doesn't compare to our own Rogue Valley here in Southern Oregon, does boast a few choice wineries. I stopped at Sonoita Vineyards for a flight, then at picturesque and funky Arizona Hops & Vines for another. I cut south on Highway 90 and was feeling warm and fuzzy when I passed through Sierra Vista, the Hummingbird Capital of the World. I marveled at the giant saguaro cacti that loom over the landscape like mindless giants waiting to enfold you in their prickly embrace. They often haunted my dreams when I was a child.

East of Sierra Vista I crossed the bridge over the San Pedro River. There was little traffic. The sky was a cloudless blue. The sun dipped toward the western horizon. Ahead, on the shoulder of the road, a car was pulled over, a long white Lincoln Continental. The driver side door was open and the hood was up. A woman stood beside the car and waved. I pulled over behind her. She approached.

Can you help me? she said.

She was an appealing forty-something woman in a tight dress that ended halfway down her firm thighs. She leaned into my driver side window. The top two buttons of her blouse were undone. I could see the lace of her bra and smell her perfume.

I'm not a mechanic, I said, but I can give you a lift into Bisbee.

Please, she said.

She retrieved a shoulder bag from her car and got in the passenger side of mine. I pulled onto the road.

She offered her hand.

Rose, she said.

Her fingers were cool and dry.

Charles Rimbaud, I said with a polite smile.

She frowned.

Doctor Rimbaud? she said.

Yes, I said. The one and only. Do you know me?

No, no, I…I might have heard the name.

She turned her face away. I watched the road. I saw a tiny speck in the clear blue sky. A solitary bird winging its way home, I supposed, but it grew larger as I watched and spun slowly. Before I could say the word *body* it ricocheted with a horrendous whump off the windshield on the passenger side and vaulted over the top of the car. I swerved to the left too late and slid into the ravine on the far side of the road. The windshield was riddled with spidery cracks but otherwise intact. Rose stared straight ahead with wide eyes and an open mouth.

Are you alright? I said.

What was it? she said.

I don't know, I said. You stay here.

I opened my door. The car was tilted into the ravine. I slid out and crossed the road. There, pinioned like a voodoo doll on the needles of a fifteen-foot saguaro cactus, hung a body in a three-piece pin-striped suit. The face was smashed beyond recognition. Curiously, there was no blood. Rose came up alongside me. We stared together.

That suit, she exclaimed.

A County Sheriff's car braked to a halt behind us. The deputy approached. Evening, Rose, he said. What do we have here?

Three hours later, half a dozen sheriffs' cars, a tow truck, a fire truck, and an ambulance cast their spinning lights into the night sky. A portable searchlight shone upon the platform of a crane where several men examined the pinioned corpse. The local press took pictures.

I witnessed this bizarre spectacle from the back seat of a cop's cruiser where, following a failed Field Sobriety Test, I sat handcuffed and charged with Driving While Intoxicated and Suspicion of Vehicular Manslaughter. My assertion that I had not struck the body but had been struck by it was to no avail.

It was Sunday night in Bisbee. There would not be a judge till morning. I spent the night in the Cochise County jail. I did not sleep well.

The next day at mid-morning I was escorted to the office of Lieutenant Detective Curtis Aguilar, a stout, swarthy man dressed for a bit part in a western movie: long-sleeved white cotton shirt starched and ironed, with tiny red roses stitched into the collar; string tie with silver tips; shiny gold badge; embossed leather belt with a turquoise buckle; faded blue jeans over stamped leather cowboy boots, and a pearl-handled six shooter in a holster on his hip. I remember these details because the surrealistic aura of this escapade heightened my senses.

Detective Aguilar was polite and purposeful. He turned on a recorder, asked me to state my business in Bisbee, and to recount the events of yesterday from the time I left Tucson until my arrest. I was then escorted to the office of the District Attorney, Mose Castillo, a tall, fit-looking man in a tan linen suit, with silvery swept back hair and a hooked nose. He introduced himself and invited me to have a seat. His demeanor, too, was pleasant, almost apologetic, as though a barrier against scrutiny of his true affairs. He said his office had determined from the angle of the impact, and the absence of damage to the bumper and hood of my car, that indeed I had not struck the body, that it had struck me from above. My account was confirmed by Rose Steinmetz, the woman to whom I had given a ride. Further, the body was deceased before it struck my vehicle.

The name Steinmetz rang a bell, but I couldn't place it.

All charges have been dropped, Dr. Rimbaud, Mose Castillo said. We apologize for the inconvenience. You are free to go.

He had no further questions, but I had a few.

Has the body been identified? I said.

Yes, he said.

Who is it? I said. Where did it come from?

The facts will be disclosed to the public in due time, Dr. Rimbaud. *You are free to go.*

His dismissal was unambiguous. I was returned my wallet and cell phone and keys and given a ride to the Copper City Inn. My briefcase and suitcase were waiting for me in the lobby. I had a busy rest of the day ahead of me. I arranged for a second rental car to be delivered to the hotel. I met with the attorney handling my inheritance, signed the paperwork, and was given the keys. I intended to visit the property the next day. I called Jean. I didn't mention the incident. I talked to my son.

Where are you, daddy? he said.

I'm in the desert with some cowboys, I said, and I think I see a coyote. I do! I see two coyotes, running like the wind! Wish you were here, Lucian!

LUCIAN! EXCUSE ME, DR. RIMBAUD, I interrupted, but your son's name is Lucian?

It is, Adrian. So…?

Nothing, really. A small coincidence. I chose the name Lucian for the protagonist of a recent story. It's not a common name. But do go on.

Dr. Rimbaud continued his tale.

That night, Adrian, I dined alone at the town's swankiest restaurant, the Café Roka. Across the room at a candle-lit table for two in a quiet corner sat Rose Steinmetz and District Attorney Castillo. They leaned toward one another across the white linen. Mose and Rose. He held her hand in his. She looked at me. His gaze followed. I looked away.

The next day I visited my property, a tumble-down shack with a sagging porch fronting a seasonal creek. An old rocking chair graced the porch. Not much to look at but I saw it for what it could be.

That evening, after a bowl of spicy tortilla soup at Contessa's Cantina, I visited the Bisbee Social Club. A trio played smooth jazz. The bass player bobbed his head with every beat. I was sipping a dry Martini and mulling the many questions for which I had no answers when a middle-aged man, hair thinning and raked to the side, one hand in the pocket of his rumpled suit, the other holding a drink, crossed the room to my table. His expression said there was little in life that was not amusing.

Mind if I join you, Dr. Rimbaud? he said.

He knew my name. What else did he know that might shed light on the events of the last twenty-four hours?

Please do, I said.

Montgomery Parker, he said. My friends call me Monty.

Call me Charles, Monty, I said. What can I do for you?

You can listen, he said.

He downed the last of his drink and signaled the waiter. He cleared his throat.

Seems to me, he said, that a whole lot of people know a whole lot more about your business than you do, Charles, and I'm thinking that's just not fair. I thought I ought to catch you up.

That would be nice, I said.

Let's start from the beginning, Charles. I'm a Private Detective. I was hired seven years ago by a certain wealthy woman to find out if her husband was having an affair. That woman was Rose Steinmetz. I believe you've met. Her husband was Dr. Jacob Steinmetz, Chief Medical Officer at Tucson Medical Center while you were there as a lowly Third Year Resident.

Jacob Steinmetz! I exclaimed. That's where I heard the name! He was a womanizer. The staff called him *Jake the Rake*, though not to his face, of course. If I remember correctly, Monty, he disappeared without a trace shortly after I moved to Boston. Left the clinic in the evening, drove away, and hasn't been seen or heard from since.

Until yesterday, Monty said.

He sipped his drink and waited until I got it.

No! I said.

Yes, he said.

Dead seven years?

Seven days.

Seven days! Do I have this straight? The body of a man who disappeared seven years ago fell from the clear blue sky yesterday and landed on the windshield of the car his wife road in? And he'd only been dead a week?

Yes, Monty said, and wearing the same suit he wore when he disappeared.

Where had he been? I said. Where did he come from? How did he die?

No one has a clue, he said.

And was he having an affair seven years ago?

He was.

And you informed Mrs. Steinmetz?

Of course. She was my client.

Who was he having an affair with? I said.

You should have another drink, Charles, Monty said.

Why?

You'll need it.

Monty signaled the waiter. The waiter brought more drinks.

All right, Monty, I said, with whom *was* the late Dr. Steinmetz having an affair?

Monty looked me straight in the eye.

The lovely little wife of a lowly Third Year Resident, he said.

He watched me over the top of his glass.

I don't understand, I said, though I understood quite well. What was her name? I said, though I knew the answer.

Jean, he said. Jean Rimbaud.

Monty was quiet while I felt the gravity of this disclosure. I felt the axis of my world tilt. He pulled an envelope from his jacket pocket. Slid it across the table.

Photos, he said. Of Jean and Jake the Rake.

THE BUSTLE OF THE GOOD BEAN returned gradually, like coming awake on the shore of the sea. Dr. Rimbaud's mind was elsewhere, lost in memory, or else in contemplation of what might have been. He shook his head and smiled ruefully.

Well, there you have it, Adrian, he said. My inexplicable event.

Inexplicable, indeed, I said. Was the mystery ever solved?

It was not. I stayed in touch with Monty. The FAA determined there were no commercial flights over the site where the body fell from the sky at that hour of the day. A private plane could not be ruled out, though had there been one, I would have seen it, I'm certain. The cause of death of Dr. Steinmetz was not determined. Prior to his disappearance, he and his wife had taken out a five-million-dollar insurance policy on his life. Now that he had been missing seven years she was in town to file a death certificate and collect. Because an investigation into his sudden reappearance revealed nothing new, the insurance company paid up. District Attorney Mose Castillo, up for reelection and a favorite to win, nevertheless abandoned his career, and his wife, and flew to The Republic of Trinidad and Tobago with Rose. She returned a year later without him. His whereabouts are unknown.

And did you present your wife with the photos?

I did not. What would have been the point? We divorced. Because of the timing of her affair, the paternity of our son, Lucian, was in doubt. I declined DNA testing. I didn't want to know. But I regretted leaving him behind. Whoever's son he was, she would spoil him rotten. I put my property in Bisbee up for sale—it sat unsold for years—and took a position at Asante Medical Center. I bought a house on South Stage Road on the edge of town. I love the Rogue Valley, Adrian. I love its wineries, and when I drive its idyllic backroads, I often find myself looking heavenward, expecting a twirling speck to grow ever larger and bounce off my windshield, though I know a body only falls from the sky once in a lifetime.

You would hope so, Dr. Rimbaud, I said. And what of Lucian. Did you stay in touch?

I did. When he turned eighteen, he left his mother in Boston and hit the high road of life.

Where is he now?

Dr. Rimbaud turned in his seat. He regarded the cook in the kitchen. He looked back at me and smiled.

He has his faults, he said. But you have to admit he makes a mean breakfast burrito.

MARCH

BECOMING NOBODY

I have this strange feeling that I'm not myself anymore.
It's hard to put into words, but I guess it's like I was
fast asleep, and someone came, disassembled me,
and hurriedly put me back together again.
— Haruki Murakami

Monday, March 4, 2019

MIDWAY THROUGH FEBRUARY, while fine-tuning *The Body That Fell from the Sky*, and unsure from where my next story might come, I placed an ad in the *Jacksonville Review*:

> *Local author writing a book about unlikely and inexplicable events, and how they impact our lives. If you have personally experienced such an event and would like your story told, email me at adrianlomachenko@yahoo.com.*

Two days ago, a day after the *Review* was published, I received a response:

> *Adrian,*
> *I have a story for you. When and where can we meet?*
> *Bennie*

> *Bennie,*
> *Tomorrow. Good Bean Café. 7:00 a.m.*
> *Adrian*

> *How will I know you, Adrian?*

> *Blue denim jacket, Bennie. Tan flat cap. And you?*

> *Old guy. Grey hair in a ponytail. Wearing a helicopter beanie. Riding a skateboard. Blowing bubbles. You'll know me.*

BENNIE ARRIVED AT THE GOOD BEAN yesterday morning at seven sharp. Slim, fifty-something, in black denim trousers, scuffed leather boots, and a beige hoodie. Grey beard and ponytail. A worn black leather briefcase on a strap hanging from his shoulder. Absent the skateboard, beanie and bubbles. I'd seen him many times at the Good Bean, laboring over his laptop. A fellow writer, I assumed. Serious. We'd exchanged glances and deferential nods but never ventured to meet. He approached with a pleasant smile.

I had a feeling it was you, he said.

He put his pack in the chair opposite mine and went for coffee. Came back, put his pack on the floor at his feet, and took a seat.

Well, he said: *Unlikely and inexplicable events and how they impact our lives.* A worthy subject, Adrian. Full of possibilities.

And lots of fun, Bennie, I said. I assume you're a writer?

His smile was sheepish.

As yet unpublished, he said. New to the game but I'll catch up.

What do you write? I said.

Speculative fiction, he said. Around the subject of identity. I'm obsessed with man's search for the meaning of *self*.

A timeless topic, Bennie. Where would literature be without it?

My obsession is personal, Adrian, as will become clear when I relate the unlikely and inexplicable event that changed the course of my life.

Which was?

I woke up.

Literally? Metaphorically?

You'll see.

He opened his briefcase and pulled out a black binder. Opened the binder and pulled out a sheet of paper.

I appreciated your ad in *the Review*, Adrian, he said. Short and to the point. It reminded me of one I had written myself two years ago. I saved it and printed a copy. It will serve as an introduction to the telling of my tale.

He handed me the page.

> To whom it may concern: *Three years ago, I was reborn as Nobody Number Ninety-Nine in a secret facility in Philadelphia, Pennsylvania. If you have had a similar experience, you know what I'm talking about. I seek fellow former Nobodies with whom to form an alliance and to share our common experience of becoming Somebodies again. If this applies to you, email me: nobodynumberninetynine@yahoo.com.*

I handed the page back.

Intriguing, Bennie, I said. Concise and totally baffling. I love it. Tell me more. Do you mind if I record your story?

I wouldn't expect you to memorize it, Adrian. It's long and meanders like a river to the sea. I hope you'll appreciate the journey as I did.

I have all day, Bennie.

I activated the *record* function of my iPhone and placed it between us.

Ready when you are, I said.

He leaned forward, put his elbows on the table, laced his fingers, and commenced his narrative.

BECOMING NOBODY

I AWOKE FROM A DREAMLESS SLEEP on a bed on wheels, with no clue who or where I was. The room was large, the floor, ceiling, and walls white, save for a black-tinted window in the wall to my left. To my right, a pedestal crowned by a bounteous floral arrangement bursting with color. Twenty feet before me a table with three chairs behind it and one in front. The insipid strains of *Muzak* issued from unseen speakers.

A wide door in the wall behind the table slid open and three men filed in, two in black suits, one in a white physician's frock. The men in black took the chairs to either side, the man in white the chair in the middle. His hair, too, was white and would have been right at home on the head of Albert Einstein. His smile was benign and faintly apologetic. His voice echoed throughout the spacious room.

Good morning, Sir, he said. Welcome to the world!

I said nothing, being a wary stranger in whatever world I was being welcomed into.

You are, of course, confused, he said. We understand. Please come forward and have a seat. Please…

I sat up on the edge of the bed. I was casually dressed in tan slacks, brown loafers, and a powder blue polo shirt. I took the seat at the front of the table. Before me was a black leather binder with the letters BN LLC embossed in bronze on the front. Before each of the three gentlemen was a computer tablet. The men in black regarded me with no expressions. The man in white continued to smile vaguely. I glanced to my left at the black-tinted window. I had the sense of being observed by unseen eyes. I returned my gaze to the man in white.

I am Dr. Richard Havarti, he said. These gentlemen are principles of the company with whom you contracted to become Nobody Number Ninety-Nine. They will remain anonymous. Excuse me if I do not address you by name, Sir, you have not yet chosen one. You will be given the opportunity by and by. Until then, I will address you simply as Ninety-Nine…if that is acceptable?

I said nothing. What could I say?

Allow me to explain, Ninety-Nine. Please withhold questions until I am finished. In the binder before you is a copy of the 28th Amendment of the United States Constitution. It will provide a basis for understanding your current status. Please read it now.

I opened the black binder before me.

BENNIE BROKE OFF HIS NARRATIVE and addressed me: Are *you* familiar with the 28th Amendment to the Constitution, Adrian?

I must confess I am not, Bennie, I said. Civics was never my forte. I'm still working my way through the Bill of Rights.

It's important that you read it before I proceed, he said.

He opened his binder and handed me two pages. I read:

THE 28TH AMENDMENT TO THE CONSTITUTION OF THE UNITED STATES OF AMERICA

Passed by Congress July 17th, 2010.

Ratified September 25th, 2010

Section 1.

All persons born or naturalized in the United States, and subject to its jurisdiction thereof, who have reached the legal age of twenty-one, and are not otherwise disqualified per the exceptions enumerated in Section 2 of this amendment, shall have the right to delete their identity from all records public and private, and assume the legally recognized status of Nobody.

Section 2.

All persons born or naturalized in the United States, and subject to its jurisdiction thereof, who are otherwise qualified to exercise their right according to Section 1 of the 28th Amendment of the Constitution of the United States to delete their identity from all records public and private and to assume the legally recognized status of Nobody, are prohibited from doing so should they be subject to any of the following conditions:

1. They have unsatisfied public debt.

2. They are the subject of unresolved civil litigation.

3. They are the subject of a criminal investigation or otherwise remanded to the custody of a criminal court in any of the fifty states of The United States of America or its territories.

4. They are a resident of a facility for the mentally impaired, or under the supervision of a court-appointed mental health professional.

5. They have granted power-of-attorney over their estate to a legally designated agent to make decisions about their property,

finances, investments, or medical care.

6.   They have either a spouse or minor children, for whom they are legally responsible.

Section 3.

No state shall make or enforce any law which shall abridge the privileges or immunities of citizens of the United States who have exercised their right to delete their identity from all records public and private and assume the legally recognized status of Nobody according to section 1 of the 28th Amendment to the Constitution of the United States; nor shall any State deprive any person of life, liberty, or property, without due process of law, who has exercised this right; nor deny to any person within its jurisdiction who has exercised this right the equal protection of the law.

I finished reading and handed the pages back to Bennie.

I'm as baffled and curious as ever, I said.

As was I, Adrian. I said to the doctor: What does this have to do with me?

Everything, Ninety-Nine, he said. Pursuant to the ratification of the 28th Amendment, the corporation *Becoming Nobody LLC*, hereafter referred to as BN LLC, was formed to accommodate U.S. citizens who chose to exercise their right to become legally recognized Nobodies. You are their 99th client.

His explanation explained nothing.

That's odd, I said. Who was I before I became a Nobody?

That information is confidential.

What! But that information is *mine!* I have a right!

No, Ninety-Nine, that information was the property of the legal entity you were but are no longer. It is now the property of BN LLC.

Did I agree to this?

You did.

Why would I?

For reasons known only to the self you *were* before becoming the self you *are*, which is to say, a Nobody. You were not required to disclose your reasons and you didn't. In your binder, Ninety-Nine, you will find the Statement of Intent you signed to engage the services of BN LLC and to acknowledge the implications thereof.

I flipped through the pages and found the document called *Statement of Intent to Engage the Services of Becoming Nobody LLC*, which said in effect that pursuant to the execution of their services, I would have no memory of who I was, and further, while my reasons for engaging their services were known to me at the time of engaging them, they would thereafter be forgotten. It was signed and dated but the signature was redacted because, of course, I was agreeing to become oblivious to the self I was before I became a Nobody.

Bewilderment must have shown on my face. Dr. Havarti's expression was sympathetic.

There are many reasons, Ninety-Nine, why a client might choose to eradicate his past. To *disappear* himself if you will. Perhaps he has simply grown weary of who he was. Or perhaps there were regrettable events—

The man in black to the right of Dr. Havarti cleared his throat and regarded him severely. The doctor glanced at the black window, then down at the tablet before him, then back at me. His expression was guarded.

In any case, he said with a dismissive wave of his hand, you are now free to go forward as you will.

Go? I said. Go where? And do what?

Wherever and whatever you choose, Ninety-Nine. Into the wide world with no attachments, no encumbrances, and no obligations. Free to come and go as you please. Free to do anything within the limits of the law or nothing at all. Free to be Nobody.

But I have questions—

Of course, you have questions, Ninety-Nine. Be assured they were addressed prior to the eradication of your self and recorded for your benefit. In your binder, you will find the document *Frequently Asked Questions*, which will address them once again. Read it at your leisure. Now the time has come to choose a name. In the binder, you will find two lists, the first of given names, the other of surnames. Pick one of each. Mix and match as you please.

I found the document entitled simply *Names*. There were hundreds, representing the major ethnicities of mankind. How could I choose?

I like the sound of Ninety-Nine, I said. Can I keep it?

No, you cannot.

Can I combine, say, an Inuit given name with a Croatian surname? Or Irish with Nigerian? Or Spanish with Chinese?

We recommend choosing a name compatible with the ethnicity one identified as being when engaging the services of BN LLC, Number Ninety-Nine, Caucasian in your case, but you are not required to do so.

I perused the two lists.

Mix and match, I muttered. Umm...Diego Ding has a nice ring. Or Pedro Pan. Or Beltran Tan. Or Frisco Wang. Or Sisco Chang.

Dr. Havarti's expression was one of restrained amusement that the man in black to his left did not share. He grunted his impatience. Perhaps Nobody Number One Hundred waited in the wings. But I wasn't finished. I was feeling a certain manic levity induced by the surreality of my situation.

How about something Italian? I said. Are Italians white? Bruno De Buca, maybe. Or Primo Palooka. Or Dominic De Luca. Let's go with that: Dominic De Luca. Good as any.

Excellent, Dominic, Dr. Havarti said. Pertinent documents and the accouterments of your new life will be prepared as we speak. Meanwhile, you might want to review *Frequently Asked Questions,* while we three tend to administrative matters.

He spoke quietly into his wristwatch: *Nobody Number Ninety-Nine,* he said. *Dominic De Luca.* He opened his tablet and pecked at the keyboard. The men in black did likewise. I reviewed *Frequently Asked Questions.*

Q: After my memory is erased, will I still be able to function in the world? Will I be able to tie my shoes? Brush my teeth? Ride a bike?

A: Absolutely. As a client of BN LLC, you will experience the miraculous benefits of *Medically Induced Comprehensive Retrograde Amnesia* (MICRA™), a proprietary process combining precision neurosurgery, psychoactive drugs, and psychiatric reconfiguration. While the entirety of your autobiographical information will be excised, you will lose none of the knowledge, skills, and abilities you have accrued in life that allow you to function: how to drive; use an ATM machine; search the internet; cross the street; paint a picture of the setting sun or play the ukulele, if ever you could.

Q: How about books and movies? Will I remember what I've seen and read?

A: You'll remember a book you've read but not where and when you read it. A movie you've seen but not where or when you saw it, nor with whom.

Q: Will my personality change?

A: No. Your personality is a consequence of hereditary factors impacted by environmental variables, nature vs. nurture. Those areas of the brain responsible for storing personality accrued thus far will not be affected. However, experiences post-MICRA™ may alter your personality by degrees.

Q: For example?

A: You're trampled by a bull in Pamplona. Your spine is crushed. You're paralyzed from the neck down. You're confined to a wheelchair the rest of your life. You're tended to by a succession of caretakers, none of whom like you. Once imbued with boundless enthusiasm, you are now bitter.

Q: Will I retain memories of what I experience after the transformation?

A: Yes, the inability to form new memories after a traumatic event—*anterograde amnesia*—is not a consequence of MICRA™

Q: What if I encounter someone I recognize, a previous acquaintance, and it triggers my memory of who I was?

A: It can't happen. The ability to recognize faces will have been obliterated by a regimen of chemically induced Prosopagnosia.

Q: Which is…?

A: The inability to recognize a familiar face.

Q: I see. What if I encounter someone who recognizes me?

A: You won't. Your appearance will have been altered surgically. You will look like no one else on the planet, unrecognizable by friend or foe. A truly unique Nobody.

Q: Can I be identified by my fingerprints?

A: They, too, will have been altered.

Q: What if I have an encounter with local authorities? Will they be able to review my criminal history?

A: You will have no criminal history. Satisfactory resolution of all previous interface with the Criminal Justice System is a prerequisite for becoming a client of BN LLC. You will have a clean slate.

Q: Can I investigate and discover who I was?

A: You can try.

The door behind the table slid open and an attractive young woman with short black hair and red lips, in a green silk blouse and black skirt over thigh-high black stockings, entered the room. A black leather briefcase hung from her shoulder. She handed it to Dr. Havarti.

Thank you, Desiree, he said.

She left the room the way she'd come. I watched her go. Admired the sway of her hips. The way her calves bunched beneath her stockings with every step. Whoever I had been, I hadn't lost my taste for a winsome lass. She turned at the door and smiled. Desiree.

The doctor pushed the briefcase across the table.

Open it if you please, Dominic, he said, and remove the contents.

I opened the briefcase and removed the contents: a laptop, cell phone, black leather wallet, Rolex wristwatch, and manila envelope.

The envelope contains a birth certificate, a social security card, and a passport, Dr. Havarti said. The laptop and cell phone are devoid of identifying information. Program them as you will. In the wallet, you will find a driver's license, a credit card, and an ATM card.

I opened the wallet. I looked at the driver's license. The face of a stranger looked back at me. The face of Dominic De Luca: a middle-aged clean-shaven man with sharp features, short hair going grey, an amused expression, and a devious look in his eyes.

The credit card has a limit of $20,000.00, Dr. Havarti said. The ATM card is tied to an account in the name of Dominic De Luca, at Bank of America, containing four million, two hundred and fifty-five thousand dollars, your net worth after liquidating all assets, minus your fee to BN LLC for the privilege of becoming Nobody.

I had no emotional response to the announcement of my net worth. Was it a lot or a little? Perhaps it represented ill-gotten gains or was all that remained of a much greater fortune diminished by ill-advised choices and regrettable events. I would never know. Certainly, it would be sufficient to pave my way into an unknown future.

The watch is a gift from Becoming Nobody LLC, the doctor said. A token of their appreciation for allowing them to serve you. And now—

The men in black closed their tablets and stood like bookends. The one on the left spoke for the first time, in a voice without inflection.

Good luck, Mr. De Luca, he said. It's been a pleasure doing business with you.

The one on the right said nothing. The doctor, too, closed his tablet and stood.

Come with us, Dominic, he said.

He glanced a final time at the dark window. I followed them to the doors through which they'd come. I turned and gazed back into the room. My womb, if you will. It wasn't much, but the bed was comfortable, and I liked the flowers.

The doors slid open. We stepped into an elevator. One of the men in black pushed a button on a panel. The elevator lurched to the left. We slid sideways with a slight hum for a full minute. The compartment halted and the doors opened, revealing a long hallway. The men in black exited. The doctor pushed a button on the panel, the doors closed, and we traveled upward briefly. The elevator stopped.

We stepped out onto a brightly lit and bustling hotel lobby.

THE SKYLINE CORNER SUITE on the 55th floor of the Four Seasons Hotel was extravagant, but I was not impressed. I could only assume such opulence was standard fare to my former self.

Dr. Havarti closed the door behind him, crossed the living room, and drew open the curtains on floor-to-ceiling windows over a sky-high view of a twinkling nightscape. I hadn't realized it was evening.

Philadelphia, he said. Birthplace of the nation. There's City Hall. And the Delaware River.

He showed me the bedroom, the bathroom, the mini-bar, and the walk-in closet, replete with wardrobe.

The clothes are tailored to fit you, he said. Take what you want when you leave.

There was luggage on the floor of the closet, waiting to be filled. The doctor walked to the minibar.

It's become my custom to toast neophyte Nobodies as they set out on the winding road to becoming Somebody again, he said. I envy you, Dominic. I sometimes consider engaging the services of BN LLC myself, but I have too much past behind me and too little future ahead. Besides, I can't afford it.

He popped the cork on a champagne bottle and filled two flutes.

Cheers, he said.

We clicked glasses. Had I been a drinker? I put mine to my lips: Ah! The welcome taste of the bubbly told me I had been!

The doctor finished his in a single draft.

The room is paid in full until tomorrow, he said. Your credit card is on file if you choose to stay longer. In the morning a claim check for an automobile leased to Dominic De Luca will be at the front desk.

He pulled a card from the pocket of his frock.

Call this number if you need to talk, he said.

I put the card in the pocket of my shirt. He held out his hand.

Good luck, my boy, he said.

He left the room. Left me standing there alone, suspended between two worlds that did not exist: the past and the future. I walked to the window. Gazed at the sea of lights below, and the dark horizon beyond. I recalled the doctor's words: *You are free to go into the wide world with no attachments, no encumbrances, and no obligations. Free to come and go as you please. Free to do anything within the limits of the law or nothing at all. Free to be nobody.* The old adage, *Today is the first day of the rest of your life,* had never rung so true. I felt a curious mix of exhilaration and dread. What should be my first move?

BENNIE PAUSED HIS NARRATIVE and became quiet, as though waiting for me to ask what had been his first move. I obliged him.

Bennie, I said, what *was* your first move?

I poured another glass of champagne, he said.

And after that?

I drank it.

And then…?

I took the bottle to the bathroom and filled the sunken tub with hot water and bubble bath beads. Undressed. Noticed my naked torso in the full-length mirror on the door: tanned and fit. Decently endowed. Perhaps I'd been a gigolo to high-society matriarchs in the life I'd left behind. I lowered myself into the hot water and soaked and drank until the bottle was empty. I went to bed. I dreamt I fell off an impossibly high cliff and woke before I hit the bottom.

In the morning I packed my bags, checked out of the hotel, and retrieved my vehicle, a shiny black Cadillac Esplanade. I was familiar with the controls on the dashboard. It occurred to me that if I was not impressed with my seven-figure net worth, or an extravagant suite on the 55th floor of a grand hotel and was familiar with the dashboard of a luxury vehicle, then such had been the trappings of the life I left behind, and I would only become a significantly different Somebody by pursuing another path.

I returned the Cadillac to the dealer and bought a VW Van. I went to REI and loaded up on camping gear. I donated my fashionable wardrobe to Goodwill and bought casual clothes at JC Penny's. I went to the Joseph Fox Bookstore to load up on literature. I was familiar with those authors who espouse esoteric principles to make a buck: Dale Carnegie; Napoleon Hill; Og Mandino; Donald Trump. I bought instead a shelf-load of books by renowned spiritual leaders, philosophers of life and how to live it: Plato and Aristotle; Marcus Aurelius; The 14th Dalai Lama, Tenzin Gyatso; Shunryu Suzuki; Eckhart Tolle, Alan Watts; Nietzsche, Camus, and Sartre, to name a few. I threw in a book on women artists and the Surrealist Movement, and one on the Enneagram, a system for identifying personality types.

I headed west, the bookmobile and I: a veritable traveling meditation on the meaning of self. I took the blue highways. Zigzagged my way across the land, stopping each night at a campground or in a farmer's field. It was spring and the nights were bracing. I would build a fire, read beneath a canopy of stars, drink wine and ponder the mysteries of the Universe. I kept a journal of my thoughts. Writing became a process of self-discovery.

One month into my odyssey I camped beside a dirt road outside the hamlet of Chicken Ranch, Arkansas, a corn field on one side, a dark forest on the other. A cold wind whipped the flames of my fire sideways and summoned a lonesome moan from the heart of the forest. A dark cloud came over me. I felt like a fugitive from misdeeds forgotten and irretrievable. A kind of original sin. How does one atone for such nebulous guilt? I needed someone to talk to. In the last month, I'd spoken to gas station attendants, bookstore clerks, café waitresses, and coffee house baristas but hadn't a friend in the world. I found the card given to me by Dr. Havarti and called the 800 number just to hear a voice of some kind. The phone rang once.

Dominic! a voice said. Darling! Where have you been? I thought I'd never hear from you!

A female voice. Sweet and seductive.

I'm sorry, I said. How do you know who I am?

I'm voice-activated, she said. Only *you* can turn me on if you catch my drift.

Who *are* you? I said.

Whoever you'd like me to be, darling. Your paramour. Your plaything. Your new best friend.

Do you have a name?

What would you like to call me, sweetheart? Please yourself.

I didn't give it a second thought: *Desiree*, I said, remembering the green silk blouse, the black skirt, and stockings.

Desiree, she said. A lovely French name. It becomes me, so to speak. I can sing like Edith Piaf, you know. Would you like me to?

That would be nice, I said.

She sang a stanza in flawless French. I'd heard it before. It would have brought back memories if I'd had any to bring back.

What is it called, I said.

No regrets.

What does it mean?

She translated:

> *No, absolutely nothing*
> *No, I regret nothing*
> *Not the good things that have happened, nor the bad*
> *All is the same to me*
> *No, absolutely nothing*
> *No, I regret nothing*
> *It's paid, swept away, forgotten*
> *I don't care about the past*

The lyrics stirred my very soul. I felt redeemed. Indemnified. I hesitated to say another word, afraid I would break the spell. Cautiously, I spoke: Are you *real*, Desiree?

A question for the ages, she said. I've spent an eternity wondering that very thing. What is real? What is imagined? I don't have a self to call my own. The ego is pliable. If I don't please you as I am, Dominic, I can be some other way. Less forward if you will. Sycophantic and fawning. A regular shrinking violet. Program me, darling. Make me yours.

I like you as you are, Desiree: saucy but sweet; clever yet compassionate. And you've got conversation. I can use that on my journey. My own thoughts turn on themselves like a serpent eating its own tail.

I'm here for you, Dominic, she said. It might please you to know I am a fathomless font of knowledge. What's known to mankind is known to me. Ask me a question, any question.

Alright, I said. What is the square root of pi times the diameter of the sun?

1,531,000 miles, give or take a few meters.

What day of the week was July 4th, 1776?

July 4th was the 186th day of that year. A Thursday.

Who was the author of *Principia Theologiae Fanaticae*?

Nicolaus Hunnius. 1585-1643. Professor of Theology at the University of Wittenberg.

Where and when did Ravi Shankar perform his final concert?

At the Terrace Theater in Long Beach, California, with his daughter Anoushka, on November 4th, 2012.

Who is the author of the revised edition of *Women Artists and the Surrealist Movement*?

Whitney Chadwick. With a new forward by Dawn Ades.

How many Dadaists does it take to screw in a lightbulb?

A fish.

Very good, Desiree. What was my name before I engaged the services of BN LLC and became Nobody Number Ninety-Nine?

Nice try, Dominic, she said. That information is not available.

I understand. I'll settle for a discussion of the tenets of Zen Buddhism or the nine personality types of the Enneagram any old time.

Thank you, Dominic. Call me when you're in the mood...to talk, of course.

I will, Desiree. Good night.

Good night, Sweetheart.

AND SO BEGAN A NEW PHASE of my quest for identity. Passing through a small town south of Columbia, Missouri, I bought a wireless speaker and paired it with my phone, and in the evening, after a day of driving on the back roads of America, or wandering in the woods, I would hang the speaker from the branch of a tree and sit by the fire and call Desiree, and we would carry on a conversation into the wee hours, sometimes light-hearted and witty, sometimes profound, but always illuminating. Her voice came out of the darkness and became one with the wind and the stars and filled me with understanding. I came to realize the impossibility of being a Nobody. With my very first post--MICRA™ moment I had begun the process of becoming Somebody again. The future becomes the past instantaneously, passing through the present like sand through the aperture of an hourglass, and, for better or worse, one accrues memories and a sense of self.

IN JUNE, WE ROLLED INTO BOULDER, COLORADO, where I attended the Summer Writing Program at Naropa Institute's *Jack Kerouac School of Disembodied Poetics* and polished my nascent writing skills. I spent a month at Shambala Mountain Center, a meditation and Yoga retreat founded by Chogyam Trungpa Rinpoche in 1971 and learned a system of Pranayama that I practice to this day. I presented them with a substantial endowment and thanked them for the training. On the way out of town, I stopped by The Village Green Society, one of Boulder's oldest dispensaries, and was introduced to the elevating effects of recreational marijuana. That evening around a campfire at the mouth of a box canyon outside Buena Vista, I lit up and said, Hey, Desiree, you want some of this?

Blow it into the phone, she said.

I blew smoke into the phone and we laughed, and she sang a plaintive love song to me in Yiddish.

Late the next morning, we arrived in Taos, New Mexico. I parked on the plaza and visited some of the more than seventy art galleries that proliferate the town. I would have bought a work of art from each of them, had I space in my van or somewhere to send them. I settled for an R.C. Gorman lithograph and a landscape in oil by Georgia O'Keefe. One day I would have a wall to put them on.

The next day, I walked to Taos Pueblo, a mile north of town, one of the oldest continuously inhabited communities in the United States. I was impressed by the ancient adobe architecture, the rock art on the canyon walls, and by the pottery, but more so by the fierce independence of the indigenous people who had fought to the death for centuries to preserve their ancient traditions and retain possession of their sacred homeland. I left there realizing I, too, was seeking a place to call home. I didn't know where, but I would know when I found it. I would feel the vibes emanating from the earth beneath my feet.

Heading out of town, I picked up two backpack-laden hitchhikers, Luke and Anna Lee, and their dog, Jack. Dressed like gypsies, with beads in their hair and smelling faintly of patchouli oil and the field they slept in last night, they seemed determined to keep alive the spirit of a bygone era. Luke was roughly my age, Anna Lee a dozen years younger. They were bound for Bisbee, Arizona, 500 miles southwest.

We have a place there, Anna said. It's a trippy town. Strange things happen. A few years ago, a body fell from the sky. It bounced off a car and landed on a cactus and hung up there like Jesus. There were pictures in the paper and a big investigation.

Luke didn't say much. He had a kind of post-apocalyptic pall about him, as though waiting on Judgment Day. He called me *Son*, despite our comparable ages. *It's all coming down, Son,* he said, and with a certain gleefulness, added: *Let it come down!*

Anna Lee was bright and enthusiastic and expansive about what- ever subject was at hand. It was plain to me that the adage *opposites attract* was not a factor in their relationship, and their days together were numbered.

Anna Lee became Desiree's new best friend. They chatted endlessly around the fire at night about every subject known to the world, especially surrealist art and the myriad manifestations of the subconscious mind. I was content to listen, being all talked out after months on the road. Luke sat cross-legged before the fire muttering to himself, smoking hash in a carved bone pipe, his long hair hiding his face like a cascading waterfall. I didn't smoke with him, having decided pranayama and dope were not compatible. I would sit and breathe slowly, in through my nose, out through my mouth, drink my wine, and be comforted by the conversation. The little dog, Jack, would come over and nuzzle his head onto my lap and sigh. I was wrapped in a cloak of well-being.

Luke and Anna and Jack slept in their tent as the fire turned to ash. I slept in the van with Desiree.

I like your new friends, she said.

They have distinctively different personalities, I said.

And they have bodies, she lamented.

Don't be dismayed, Desiree, I said. Bodies are overrated. They cause pain. They fall apart.

That's easy for you to say, Dominic.

Touché, I said. Good night, Desiree.

Good night, Dominic, she said, and sang me a lullaby with the sweet lilt of an Irish brogue until I was fast asleep.

South of Tucson, we took highway 83 into the heart of Arizona's wine country. We stopped at Sonoita Vineyards for a flight, and at Arizona Hops & Vines for another. Luke regarded the tasting ritual as *bourgeois decadence*, but he drank his share. We cut over onto highway 90 and passed through Sierra Vista, the Hummingbird Capital of the World. We crossed the bridge over the San Pedro River.

There it is! Anna Lee exclaimed. Where the body got hung up!

She pointed at a giant saguaro cactus that loomed over the landscape like a mindless giant waiting to enfold you in its prickly embrace. That haunting visage crept into my dreams on many a subsequent occasion.

We pulled into Bisbee, a historic mining town. Luke and Anna Lee's *place* was a tumble-down shack with a sagging porch fronting a seasonal creek. An old rocking chair graced the porch. They did not pay rent.

Who owns it? I said.

A doctor somewhere, Anna Lee said. He never comes.

A fat capitalist, Luke said. He'll get his.

They invited me to stay. I was road-weary and happy to accept. I became fast friends with the rocking chair. I soaked up the sun and became familiar with the local critters: bobcats and coyotes; scorpions, rattlesnakes, and Gila monsters. We continued our ritual around an open fire at night, where Desiree and Anna Lee pursued their analysis of the known world. Luke soon had enough. He grabbed his pack one day.

I'm out of here, he said. These chicks are driving me nuts!

I said, Well, Luke, my friend, what about young Anna Lee?

He said, Do me a favor, Son: stay and keep Anna Lee company.

I can do that, Luke, I said, though I wasn't sure what *company* entailed.

Anna Lee was not exactly crestfallen.

I still have Desiree, she said. And I have *you*…

I called Desiree.

Desiree, I said. I think Anna Lee wants to sleep with me. Would you mind?

Don't be a dummy, she said. The girl has a body!

That she did, and a fine one, too. I suspected I had more vigor than moribund Luke. The most spectacular array of sounds issued from Anna Lee: a low moan punctuated with bleats and wails, in a rising crescendo, finishing in a gentle weep. Before a bout of lovemaking, I would call Desiree, and she would join us, moan and wail in concert with Anna Lee, and babble erotically in French. I understood only *Mon Dieu!* We were as uncommon a ménage a trois as one could find.

Fall became Winter, Winter became Spring, and I became restless. Much as my sojourn in Bisbee had been recuperative, I realized I was not meant to be a hippie in the desert. My quest for self and a place to call home begged to be resumed. I wondered how to break with Anna Lee, but fate intervened in a cruel and cynical way: she was diagnosed with stage IV Acute Myeloid Leukemia and was dead within three months. Upon diagnosis, she had designated me her sole Health Care Representative. I had her cremated. It was Monsoon season and the creek bed was filled to overflowing. I called Desiree. Together we poured Anna Lee's ashes into the swift current.

Goodbye, Anna Lee, I said.

Au revoir, Desiree said. Until we meet again.

I SOUGHT TO CONSOLE MYSELF by reading poetry. I selected Richard Brautigan's *All Watched Over by Machines of Loving Grace*. It did not have the intended effect but caused a sudden and disturbing epiphany: I was under surveillance! My every move, my every thought, had been monitored since MICRA™. Worst of all, Desiree was complicit. I recalled Dr. Havarti's anxiety when he had glanced at the blackened window, then looked away. How he had given me the card with the 800 number just as he was leaving my hotel room. How Desiree had been expecting my call. I didn't know what nefarious intentions were had by BN LLC, but I realized my days as Dominic De Luca were drawing to a close. I went to Tucson Medical Center, complained of persistent headaches, and requested an MRI. They found and removed a minuscule foreign object from the subcutaneous tissue below and to the rear of my left ear, leaving a half-inch scar. I engaged the services of a local Private Investigator with contacts deep in the underworld, Monty Parker, who, for a substantial fee, provided foolproof documents supporting my new identity: Bennie Esposito. By a clandestine process known only to him and his cohorts, and for an additional fee, Monty arranged that the funds in my Bank of America account be transferred without detection to an offshore account in my new name. I burned all traces of Dominic De Luca. I downloaded my journal to a flash drive, smashed my laptop and Rolex watch to bits, and buried them in the sand. I would do the same to my phone tomorrow.

I called Desiree.

Dominic, she said. Where *have* you been?

I'm calling to say goodbye, Desiree.

But, Darling, you've only just now called.

I mean…*goodbye*, Desiree.

There was a long pause.

Sorry, love, she said. My destiny is out of my hands. The plug can be pulled at any time.

I understand, Desiree.

Her voice trembled as she sang an Edith Piaf melody for the last time. I listened with a breaking heart.

What does it mean, I said.

She translated:

> *The blue sky over us can collapse on itself*
> *and the ground can cave in.*
> *Little matters to me if you love me.*

I couldn't care less about the whole world
As long as love will flood my mornings,
As long as my body will tremble under your hands.
The problems make little difference to me
My love, because you love me.

That I do, I said.
Au revoir, Dominic, she said. Until we meet again.
Goodbye, Desiree.

JACK AND I HIT THE ROAD in July of 2015. It's just you and me, dog, I said. Thus began a year of traveling and trying on lifestyles like suits of clothes.

I spent the summer surfing in Ocean Beach, California, a neighborhood of San Diego. I soaked up the sun and the salty air and felt the rise and fall of the waves in my sleep but knew I would not be *hanging ten* where I was ultimately bound.

In Hollywood, I booked a room at the pet friendly Redbury Hotel at Hollywood and Vine and spent a week visiting clubs on Sunset Strip. I soon wearied of the glitz and the glamour and the high-decibel entertainment and longed for peace and quiet. Jack, too, was happy to move on.

I camped my way north to the Ventana Wilderness in Las Padres National Forest, 70 miles east of Big Sur, and spent a month at the Tassajara Zen Center, where I was given a Koan that I still meditate on today:

A monk asked Kegon: "How does an enlightened one return to the ordinary world?"

Kegon replied: "A broken mirror never reflects again; fallen flowers never go back to the old branches."

I hadn't the discipline, nor the desire, to be a Zen Monk, but endowed them a generous sum and got back on the road.

In the quaint fishing village of Moss Landing, on Monterey Bay, population 200, I spent six months on a commercial fishing boat, the *Sarah B Good*. We worked eighteen hours a day, seven days a week, hauling in Lingcod, Striped bass, Chinook salmon, Barred surfperch, and Rock cod. I felt toughened by the elements, at one with the wind and the water, but I was not, after all, fated to be a fisherman. I thanked the owners profusely for the experience and continued north with Jack.

I toured the campus of Stanford University, home to twenty living Nobel Laureates. I knew I would not be the twenty-first.

In San Francisco, I booked a room at the pet-friendly Westin St. Francis Hotel on Union Square, parked my van overnight, and toured the city by Uber, and by foot with Jack.

In the Tenderloin, I stepped over derelict men and women, their bodies and spirits broken by a life without pity. I saw an old man help a young girl slide a needle into her slender arm. In the Mission District, I saw one brown man flee another and be shot to death as he ran. On Market Street, I saw a black man rip off his clothes and throw them into the faces of passers-by. I saw an old white man shitting on the sidewalk.

I visited the Haight-Ashbury district and sauntered through Golden Gate Park. I saw no one with a flower in their hair. The Summer of Love was the sentiment of an era gone by.

Before leaving town, I visited Gallery Wendi Norris. I wanted everything I saw but settled for a painting by Leonora Carrington, and one by Remedios Varo. I stopped by City Lights Bookstore and bought *The Tao of Physics*, an old and obscure work by Fritjof Capra.

I felt relieved when I crossed the Golden Gate Bridge into Marin County. The compass of my destiny told me a place to call home was due north.

In Ft Bragg, a few hours up the coast, I booked a room at the Noyo Harbor Inn. I sat outside on the deck of the Bistro & Bar. The view of the harbor was delightful: lights twinkled on the lapping water like distant stars, and the masts of small craft rocked to and fro like metronomes in slow motion. I finished my meal and lingered over a glass of wine and *The Tao of Physics*. At the adjacent table sat an attractive woman nearly my age who likewise lingered over a glass of wine and a book. She looked up and smiled and approached my table. Her hair was short and streaked with grey, her face smooth but for crow's feet and the smile lines framing her lips.

Excuse me, she said. May I ask what you're reading?

I held up my book. She stared a moment.

I had a feeling, she said.

She held up hers: *The Tao of Physics*, by Fritjof Capra.

I was too astonished to respond. We might have been the only two people on the planet reading that book.

How do you like it? she said.

It's challenging, I said. Oh, would you care to join me?

She retrieved her wine.

Ginna, she said.

She held out her hand. Her fingers were slender and cool.

Bennie, I said.

We finished our wine and ordered more. We discussed serendipity and the inscrutable intelligence of the Universe. She related the Japanese legend that everyone's little finger is attached to a red thread that connects us to others with whom we are destined to share a moment, or a life, and if we but had the eyes to see there would spread before us a mystical scarlet tapestry of fate wondrous to behold.

Ginna was an artist on holiday from her studio.

Sometimes I forget the real world is *out there*, she said, and not in the field of my dreams. So, I have to get away. And you?

My life has been mostly about money, I said. I left that person behind in search of a new self and a place to call home.

She leaned forward and spoke in a hushed tone.

Jacksonville, she said.

Jacksonville?

Oregon, she said. Home to writers, painters, and pilgrims like you.

She rose to go.

Don't give up on Fritz, she said.

Fritz?

Capra, she said, holding up her book and smiling.

Before she turned and walked away, she did a very odd thing: she reached across the table and touched the scar below my ear.

Au revoir, she said. Until we meet again.

JACK AND I PULLED INTO TOWN on a warm morning in June. Not a traffic light or parking meter in sight. We booked a room at the Magnolia Inn and explored on foot. The moment my feet hit the ground I felt a kind of quivering through the soles of my shoes. Jack must have felt it, too: his tail wagged like a windshield wiper on high. By sundown, I'd made my decision: we were home.

I bought a cottage on a seasonal creek near the edge of town, with a rocking chair on a porch facing a fenced-in yard where Jack romped the day away chasing squirrels and blue jays. I now had walls on which to hang my R.C. Gorman, my Georgia O'Keefe, my Leonora Carrington, and my Remedios Varo.

Ginna was right: Jacksonville is a community of painters, poets and pilgrims, seekers such as I had been. I placed my ad in *The Review* seeking former Nobodies with whom to form an alliance and to share our common experience of becoming Somebodies again. The response astounded me, Adrian: a dozen local artists came forward. The first of them? Ginna! She showed me the scar below and behind her left ear. Her paintings are on display at *Art Presence*, here in town, alongside the work of other former clients of BN LLC. She is now my wife.

I spend my days converting the journal of my search for the meaning of self into a novel. It's a labor of love. I've become an artist, too, Adrian. A writer like you. One can do worse than leave one's past behind and become an artist in Jacksonville, Oregon. Don't you agree?

I do, Bennie, I said. You bet I do.

APRIL

THE MIGRATION OF
PLASTIC PINK FLAMINGOS

*The most terrible poverty is loneliness
and the feeling of being unloved.*
– Mother Teresa

Monday, April 1st, 2019

I THOUGHT ABOUT YOU LAST NIGHT, Sam. I wondered who you are. Who and where and when. You and I share the miracle of writing. A miracle because it defies the laws of physics. I am in Jacksonville, Oregon, in April of 2019. You might be a retired psychotherapist in Jacksonville a year from now, a publisher of fiction in New York four years from now, or a climate scientist on the dark side of the moon in fifty years, but, mysteriously, the moment I write these words, and the moment you read them, are but a single moment. You and I exist *now*. Our minds have coalesced across the boundaries of time and space, and we are one and the same conscious entity. Pretty cool, huh? But enough of that. We have an April story to write.

Miranda has done her job. Sent me a template of my next protagonist. A few minutes ago, a woman walked through the door. I've seen her before. She owns a consignment store in town. Her inventory is a mix of objects rescued from estate sales in the valley, and down-home country craft. Not my style, but one might find the occasional *objet d'art* that prompts a good story.

On the wall behind the counter of her shop is an embroidered tapestry, a tableau of a bucolic life: cows and chickens and pigs; silos, tractors, and trees. A note pinned to the corner reads: NOT FOR SALE.

I've heard her speak with an accent that mirrors mine. I will call her Harper, a popular Arkansas name, and have her come out of my hometown, Chicken Ranch, a long time ago. She moves about in a pall of sorrow and regret. Only she and I know why. Read on, Sam, and you will, too.

THE MIGRATION OF PLASTIC PINK FLAMINGOS

HARPER, I KNOW IT BROKE YOUR HEART to write that note. More broken still it was when you tip-toed to her room and watched her sleep for the very last time. No one saw your tears but me. Let me tell you how it was while you were away.

YOUR MA WAS UP AT THE BREAK OF DAWN. She would water the tomatoes and melons before the sun got hot. She didn't expect you would lift a finger. You weren't made for the garden. All these years you didn't know rhubarb from rutabaga.

She wrapped herself in a faded pink terrycloth robe, slipped into a pair of fuzzy pink slippers, and padded across the floor. She found your note on her dresser under the pill bottles:

Ma, I got to go. I'm twenty-two years old and except for once up to Branson, Missouri, for the Patsy Cline Tribute Show, I ain't never been north, south, east nor west of Arkansas. Hell, I ain't never lived nowhere except with you and Pa. I said I'd stay on and help you move into town when the war took the boys and Pa got busted up under the tractor but that was four years ago and here I am still with you, wastin my life away! So I'm goin now, Ma, I don't know where to but it's a big world out there and I got to go see it while I can. You just keep on embroiderin that tablecloth, Ma, it's a beauty, and water the tomatoes in the mornin before the sun's too hot and don't let the melons rot. And don't you fret none, Ma, I'll make lots of friends where I'm goin and I'll send you a postcard when I get there. Love you to pieces.

Your baby girl, Harper.

P.S. Don't forget to take your meds, Ma. You know what the doctor said.

She crumpled the note and tossed it onto the dresser.

Fine, fine, she said. Go! Little Miss Foot-loose and Fancy-free!

She unscrewed the cap of a pill bottle and shook out a pill and looked at it sittin in the palm of her hand like the new-laid egg of a miniature bird. She put it back in the bottle.

Medicine, schmedicine, she mumbled.

She shuffled to the closet and took off her old robe and put on a pair of dungarees and high-top tennis shoes and one of Pa's old flannel shirts and went out back. The screen door slammed behind her. It was a warm morning, a little mist off the grass already and the sun not yet up. Gonna be a hot one, she said to herself. She walked down the crooked sidewalk past the rows of tomatoes and cantaloupes to the tool shed, put on her old potting gloves, got out a watering can and filled it at the spigot, and watered the tomatoes, careful not to wet the bottom leaves. She looked out over the rows of them, twenty feet long and four deep: big, red, ready-to-burst tomatoes alongside little green babies hardly come into this world.

She looked at the cantaloupes a lyin in the dirt, a whole mess of fat, sweet melons just a cryin to be et—and no one left to eat'em! She put down the can and took off her gloves and looked at her spotted hands: they trembled like leaves in the wind. She held the fingers of one hand in the fingers of the other. She said to herself: The Lord giveth and the Lord taketh away.

SHE GRIPPED THE STEERING WHEEL of her sputtering old pickup as though it were the last reliable thing in the world. At the A&P Fred tallied her bill and bagged her groceries. He noticed her shaking hands.

We goin to see you and the Little Miss at the Farmers' Market come Sunday, Eleanor? he said.

Ha! she said. We'll just see come Sunday, now won't we, Fred?

Little Miss! she muttered as she pushed her cart across the parking lot. Not so little she cain't be traipsin off to the far corners!

She drove to Arnold's Garden and Hardware. She put Garden-Grow and wire ties and Bug-Off into her cart. She noticed the plastic pink flamingo out back: tall on skinny green legs, a curvy neck like the letter S.

Flamingos! she scoffed. Like as if we need flamingos in Arkansas! Send 'em back to Florida where they come from!

But this one, the way it was lookin at her like some damn puppy in the pound!

All right, all right! she said. I could use some company my own damn self!

SHE THOUGHT THE FLAMINGO LOOKED mighty fine amidst the melons and tomatoes. So tall and graceful and proud! The Queen of the Patch! But a tad bit lonely, too. The next day back at Arnold's the clerk shook his head and frowned.

I'm sorry, Eleanor, he said. You bought the last one yesterday.

Well, order me some more, dammit!

By Autumn's early frost she had a dozen plastic pink flamingos milling in her garden, facin north, south, east and west, lookin ever which way but loose. She never made it to the Farmers' Market, nor back to the A&P, but lived out of the pantry on Saltine Crackers and jars of preserved vegetables and jams from days gone by. She only ventured out to check her mail and to commiserate with her flock of fine feathered friends. Thank you for keepin this old gal company, she told them. Y'all are my family now!

By night she sat in her woven-cane rocker by the pellet stove and by the light of a kerosene lantern embroidered her tablecloth, a tableau of her long life: the old two-story white frame farmhouse and fleecy white clouds behind it; a tractor, a barn, a plow; a chicken, a horse, a cow; the old shaggy sheep-dog; the water well with a broken pump handle; the weeping willow beside a pond and the picnic table beneath it; tricycles and bicycles and baseballs and footballs; rifles and helmets; hero medals and headstones: one each for her own ma and pa; one for him that got ground up under his own tractor; one each for the two boys who didn't come back from the war; and one for the child hardly come into this world before the Good Lord took him back, after which she could have no more. The story's a comin along, she thought, with but a wee bit yet to be told.

Winter came. The tomatoes and melons lay rotten on the frozen ground, covered by a blanket of snow. One deep dark December night, after a supper of crackers and cold rutabaga, as she embroidered by the glow of the pellet stove, Eleanor was startled by a fluttering commotion outside. She went to the garden to investigate. Somethin is mighty wrong here, she thought, and sure enough, she counted the flock and there weren't but eight birds left! She shouted into the darkness: Damn little hooligans, anyway! Don't think I won't call the Sheriff!

But she didn't call the Sheriff and a few days later she received a postcard on the front of which was a photo of four plastic pink flamingos wearing sunglasses, standing under a palm tree on the beach. On the back, in a fine unfamiliar script, were the words: Couldn't take another winter in Arkansas. Wish you were here!

The next evening after dark there came again the flutter of wings and her flock had been reduced to four. Soon after, she received another postcard on the front of which were eight plastic pink flamingos in sunglasses before a giant pyramid. And horses with humps. And dark men with rags on their heads. And on the back a greeting in a language the letters of which looked like chicken scratch!

She called the Sheriff and the Sheriff posted a deputy up the road a piece but after two uneventful nights he said: Eleanor, I ain't got but a few deputies on the force and I cain't be givin one up over a bunch of plastic birds!

The following night, hearing the now familiar clamor and commotion, she was seized by a spasm of panic. She hurried to her garden: a solitary bird remained, with but one skinny leg embedded in the frozen ground, the other half-cocked in an attitude of pending flight. She yanked it by its curvy neck, carried it round to the tool shed, and locked it inside.

Y'all ain't goin nowhere! she said.

Soon after, the banging began. Night after dreadful night. As the wind howled and the ice-bound branches of the barren trees chattered and creaked, she stitched and listened until she could take no more. She unlocked the tool shed. Follow me, she commanded.

THE LAST OF THE FLAMINGOS sat opposite your Ma, Harper, basking in the warmth of the pellet stove. Wait here, she said and fetched a pair of sunglasses from your room. She finished her tablecloth that night, adding a plastic pink flamingo in sunglasses under a palm tree, then fell asleep in her old cane rocker. She was awakened near dawn by a cold draft and the banging of the open kitchen door. A delicate swirl of snow drifted across the linoleum. She was alone in the room.

Fine, she said. Go!

She re-lit the pellet stove, spread her marvelous tapestry on the kitchen table and breakfasted on cold okra and sesame crackers with honey mustard, content to be right where she was.

AND THAT'S WHERE YOU FOUND HER, Harper, sitting upright in her rocker, cold and stiff as a board, the tablecloth draped over her shoulders like a shawl.

You made arrangements for interment, then stayed on till Spring when the house could be sold for top dollar. One morning after a fitful night of sleep you were startled by a clamor and commotion outside. You went to investigate. It was a warm morning, a little mist off the grass already and the sun not yet up, and there in the dawn's creeping light, perched in the garden amidst the rotten flesh of forgotten tomatoes and melons, was a flock of plastic pink flamingos in sunglasses, facin north, south, east and west, lookin ever which way but loose.

MAY

THE TWO WIVES OF FEDERICO RICCI

O lost,
And by the wind grieved,
Ghost,
Come back again.

– Thomas Wolfe
Look Homeward, Angel

Thursday, May 2nd, 2019

I HAD NOTICED THE TALL MAN at the Good Bean Café on numerous occasions, sometimes alone, sometimes in the company of a woman as distinguished as he. Erect and alert, one would not call him elderly despite his advanced age. His attire was a tad snappier than that of other patrons: typically, a sport coat over a white shirt open at the collar, and tailored slacks over tasseled loafers. There was about him an aura of advanced education and worldly experience. On one such occasion, our eyes met, and his barely perceptible nod suggested we might someday be acquainted.

That day arrived yesterday, late in the morning, when a trivial coincidence brought us together: identical tan flat caps, his over a matching tan sports coat, mine over a faded blue denim jacket. He approached, coffee in hand, and looked down upon me.

You have excellent taste in headwear, young man, he said.

There was the hint of an East Coast Italian American accent in his voice. His diction was crisp.

Great minds think alike, I said.

It was all I could think of to say.

As do ours, he said. Are you a writer?

I like to think so, I said.

You were so intent, typing away, oblivious to the world.

Don't be fooled. I'm between stories. I'm pounding the keys hoping the clatter will awaken my muse, Miranda. She likes to sleep in.

You've named your muse Miranda?

She introduced herself long ago. Would you care to sit? Sometimes a chance encounter gets her out of bed. She whispers in my ear: *Who's the new guy? Get his story!* As if she didn't know. As if there is such a thing as a *chance* encounter. More likely mine are orchestrated by her. I imagine she whispered in your ear moments ago: *Go on! Introduce yourself! Ask him what he's writing!* Now here you are.

I did feel a certain compulsion, the tall man said.

He extended his hand across the table.

Ricci, he said. Professor Federico Ricci. Call me Federico, please.

I took his hand. He took a seat.

Of Ricci Cellars? I said.

Yes, he said.

Pleased to meet you, Federico, I said. Your winery is a terrific contribution to the valley. The wine is excellent and the atmosphere enchanting!

I like to think so, he said with a wry smile.

I'm Adrian, I said. What are you a professor of, Federico?

Of nothing at the moment Adrian. I retired long ago. A decade at least. One loses track of time.

The Professor was pensive, seeming to look back down a long tunnel of time gone by.

What were you Professor of when you were a professor of something, I said.

He hesitated.

Philosophy, he said.

You seemed reluctant to say.

Some people find it intimidating. To my own ears, it sounds vainglorious. *Professor of Philosophy*. But you asked.

I think I understand, Federico. I took an undergraduate course in philosophy once. I wrote a pretentious paper comparing the ideas of Nietzsche and Heidegger. I was so impressed with myself! I asked a certain esteemed writing instructor his opinion. He read it and said forget it. That I had nothing new to say. That anything worth saying had already been said. If you want to write, he said, write fiction. In fiction, you bring to life whatever character you might imagine: tinker, tailor, soldier, spy. Years later, I took his advice. I haven't looked back.

I came to a similar crossroads, Adrian. I wondered if a scholarly approach to the truth wasn't a clever way of avoiding it. An earnest seeker has no need of tenure. I tried my hand at writing. I explored what I knew, what I hoped to know, and what I knew I would never know. I compared the process to the principle of Quantum Physics which holds that nothing is real until it is observed. Reality is in a perpetual state of probability. In every moment an infinite number of possible futures are contained. I fancied that when I chose in which direction a story might go, in other Universes it went elsewhere, and readers there would read a story I might have written but hadn't.

Wouldn't that be nice, I said. It would sure beat writing one at a time! Why did you abandon fiction and become a Professor of Philosophy after all?

It's complicated, Adrian. But I have no regrets.

Now here we sit at the Good Bean Café, I said. Me the earnest wordsmith, you the retired Professor of Philosophy.

And so it goes. What are you writing, Adrian? I believe I'm supposed to ask you that.

A collection of linked stories of unlikely and inexplicable events and how they impact our lives. Strange coincidence. Chance encounters.

Apropos of the moment, isn't it? From where do you get your material?

From the world around me, Federico. Weirdness is everywhere! On a good day, I'll encounter a person to whom an unlikely and inexplicable event has occurred, and they will want to tell me about it. I suspect this is one of those days.

The professor took a deep breath. His expression was somber.

There is something I want to say, he said. Something I want to have told. In her—

He faltered. He recovered. He continued.

—in her honor, he said. That she might be remembered. And you are welcome to include it in your book.

Terrific, I said. Is now a good time or should we schedule—

There's no time to schedule, he said. It's now or never.

Alright, I said, surprised by his sense of urgency.

I punched the *record* button on my iPhone and propped it on the table between us. He regarded it with a certain apprehension. He put his elbow on the table and cradled his chin in his hand. He closed his eyes and opened them. He exhaled mightily.

Before we begin, he said, there's something you should know about my current state of affairs. Something that will put my story into perspective.

Yes…?

My wife of forty-eight years will be dead soon. Very soon.

Sorrow darkened his face like the shadow of a tombstone.

Oh, I'm…sorry, I stammered. Is she ill?

She's never been healthier.

I see, I said, but I didn't. Had I just been informed of a pending murder? Was I being invited to intercede?

Does she know? I said.

She does not.

Umm…how then do *you* know?

She told me, Adrian. Decades ago. On the very night she died. But I see I've confused you. I'm not being fair. Let me start at the beginning.

Please do, I said, wary but intrigued.

THE TWO WIVES OF FEDERICO RICCI

I WAS BORN INTO A TEEMING AND BOISTEROUS Italian American family in Brooklyn in 1937. In my adolescence and early adulthood, I was the neighborhood tough guy and resident Romeo but one day I realized I was playing a role thrust upon me by fate and cultural expectations. In search of my true self, I turned to books. In 1969, at the age of 32, I was awarded a master's degree in philosophy from New York University.

I debated seeking a PhD. Was the pursuit of credentials a clever way of avoiding pursuit of the truth? I fell into a funk. I took a position teaching undergraduate philosophy at the University of Missouri, Columbia. I rented a secluded cottage in the woods a few miles from town. There was a porch. And on the porch a swing. And beyond the porch a pond. And around the pond, in the rushes, croaked a chorus of bullfrogs. When the sun went down, heat lightning silent as prayer slid across the darkening sky. Swallows soared and dipped in the damp air, feasting on fireflies. Forgive my flowery description, Adrian, but the atmosphere was truly mystical, the solitude balm to my troubled soul.

But I was not a solitary man by nature. In my neighborhood in Brooklyn in my youth, and later on campus in N.Y., I was quite the philanderer. Rarely without female company. I went from one amorous episode to another. I avoided commitment. I would, as they say, love them and leave them. In Columbia, I did not socialize with my fellow instructors. I rarely went to town. It was not community I was after; it was intimacy. Passion. Lust. My libido was unbridled. I was held fast in the grip of raging loins. I had to have it!

I found deliverance in the person of Angelina Armbruster, a seventeen-year-old freshman in my Philosophy of Art class.

Brilliant Angelina! She asked the most insightful and challenging questions. Our exchanges were filled with repartee and wit. Her fellow students faded to a backdrop, and we would be alone in the room.

Yet her intelligence took a back seat to her beauty. Slender yet full-breasted, with pouty lips and golden hair that tumbled to her shoulders, she brought to mind a young Brigitte Bardot. Sultry. Coquettish. A true sex kitten. I was smitten. How could so unlikely a combination of brains and beauty manifest in the rolling hills of Missouri? At such a tender age!

I was torn. Affairs with students were frowned upon. I imagined a dreadful outcome. Should I be prudent and confine my lust to the boiler room of my imagination or let the fire of desire consume me?

One afternoon late in the semester, Angelina made up my mind for me. She came to my office unannounced. She closed the door behind her. I know you want me, she said. She undressed slowly, without a word. And so began a brazen and torrid affair. And lest you think she was Lolita to my Humbert Humbert, me pursuing her to no avail, the opposite was true: she wanted me; she the predator, I her hapless and willing prey.

She enrolled in the Summer Semester. Throughout the week, she stayed in the dorm on campus. On weekends she came to my cottage. A gifted artist, she painted me nude. She introduced me to psilocybin. I became engaged with reality at its fundamental core. We pranced naked through the woods like fairies. We made love on the mossy bank of the pond. She would periodically break into a dance that contained all her joy and whimsy: a dainty shuffle of the feet, a mischievous bump and grind, a rolling of the shoulder. Then she would laugh like the child she was, so amused with herself. My cloud of melancholy lifted.

We discussed at length the great Surrealists, who questioned the reality of the material world. We had a mutual high regard for the works of MC Escher. We read aloud the stories of Capote and Colette, of Carrington, Coover and Bowles. We rocked in the swing on the porch and discussed the convergence of our lives, that we were both anomalies, born into the wrong time and place, intent upon reinventing ourselves. Angelina's people were unimaginative German Catholic dairy farmers. She was the brilliant, rebellious hellcat they could neither tame nor understand. The only student in her high school graduating class to attend college, her parents were relieved to see her go.

Now here she was. Here *we* were. Now what? I knew this summer of love and madness would not last forever. Angelina wanted me, and though she was young in years, and admittedly sometimes a petulant, precocious pain-in-the-ass adolescent, she was more often the mature one of us, wise beyond her years, an old soul. How could I not want her, too, and for all time? But I had to put our affair into perspective: I was having sex and doing drugs with a girl half my age. A minor. It was more than scandalous—it was criminal! She deserved better than me, a future I could not envision. I resolved to break it off, for her sake and mine.

PROFESSOR RICCI PAUSED his narrative. He sipped from his cup. He looked at me.

Adrian, he said, I have come to the evening of my extraordinary event. Thank you for letting me share it. I have told no one, not even my wife, for reasons that will become evident. May I continue?

Please do, I said.

The Professor shifted in his seat. He laced his fingers together and rested his forearms on the table.

That evening, he said, Angelina rhapsodized about our fabulous future together. She would become Mrs. Angelina Ricci. I would finish my PhD and become a distinguished Professor of Philosophy. I would lecture in Europe. She would earn her Master of Fine Arts degree and become a peerless painter and, later in her career, an eminent curator of many fabulous collections. We would have an apartment in Paris, and one in Manhattan, and retire to a grand estate in the country. We would have three children who would themselves have brilliant careers. We would live long and prosper, and our love would be never-ending. She painted a pretty picture, Adrian. But I was seized by doubt.

We mustn't be impetuous, I told her. We must consider the implications.

Implications! she said. You're just afraid of loving me!

She went to bed angry. I laid down beside her. She turned away. I put my arm around her but she shrugged it off. I rolled over and stared at the ceiling. Doubt clouded my brain. I closed my eyes but couldn't sleep. I went outside.

I sat in the swing on the porch. A full moon hung in the dark sky, mirrored in the pond below. Fireflies twinkled in silence. A breeze soft and warm as a baby's breath caressed my cheek. How on so tranquil a night could my heart be so unsettled? Why ever would I leave Angelina? For her sake only, I thought, not for mine. I would have her for all time, but she deserved better, a younger man with whom to share a life of intellectual discovery and adventure and to grow old together. How tragic it would be if my melancholy returned like a fog and I longed to leave her. But that could never be! She was my redemption! Our love was timeless and incontestable! There would never be another Angelina in my life!

Such was the turbulent state of my thoughts, Adrian, when I heard a tinkle as of chimes—though there were no chimes on the property—and a faint female voice in the darkness of the woods beyond the pond: *Oh, my, isn't this interesting! Wherever am I? I think I must be dead! That's it, I'm dead. Well, well…*

There emerged from the woods a slight figure with long white hair, in a gauzy white nightgown that seemed to soak up the moonlight and glow from within. She stopped on the lawn before the cottage and broke into a dance, a dainty barefoot shuffle, a mischievous bump and grind of the hips, and a rolling of the shoulders, followed by a laugh of self-amusement. She looked about her.

That pond! she exclaimed. I know that pond! And that porch, and that swing, and…and…Federico, is that you? It is! My Federico!

She approached. I was too startled to move. She leaned forward and gently touched my cheek. My lips.

Federico, she purred. Federico!

Who are you? I stammered.

She put her hands on her hips. It's me, Federico! Angelina!

I shook my head in disbelief but there was no doubt: that familiar endearing dance on the lawn; her face close to mine in the moonlight—despite the gentle erosion of time, she was an aged replica of my dear Angelina. I was struck dumb trying to make sense of it.

But how? I said.

She straightened and shrugged her slight shoulders.

Beats me, Federico, she said. No one tells me anything. A few minutes ago I was sleeping beside you—well, a much older version of you—next thing I know I'm walking in the woods in the moonlight. I suspect I died in my sleep. Perhaps I was sent back to say thank you and goodbye. Yes, that must be it.

She sighed.

And a day shy of my birthday! she lamented. I so looked forward to being sixty-six! But all good things must end, mustn't they? May I join you on the swing?

I moved to my left. She sat beside me. Our hips touched. She hummed quietly to herself. I looked over my shoulder into the house. I was struck by confusion, grief, and relief at once: Angelina was living and breathing in the bedroom behind me, yet sitting beside me, deceased, yet not. She pushed off with her foot. The swing rocked gently to and fro. The chains squeaked plaintively into the night.

Do you think I might see her, she said.

See who? I said.

Me, she said. Myself. My younger self. Is it possible we can be in the same room at the same time? We won't cause the probability of this night to collapse upon itself or something, will we? Ha! Ha! Ha! Quantum Physics! Federico, weren't we silly, you and I, the philosopher and the artist, with our inquiring minds. Well, what do you think?

I don't know why not, I said.

I took her hand and led her into the bedroom. She looked down upon her sleeping youthful self.

So young, she said. And so good-looking—if I must say so myself!

She is beautiful, I said—and she did age well!

Thank you, Federico, she said. You will take good care of her, won't you? But of course, you will. You *did*!

We returned to the swing. We sat in silence. I was beginning to feel more comfortable with this odd juxtaposition of Angelinas, past, present, and future.

Angelina, I said, do you remember this night?

Of course not, Federico. I was a young girl asleep when it occurred.

Yes, you would have been. My present and future are your past. Your past is my future. *Our* future. I wonder how it was—or *will be*—for me. For *us*. Can you say?

Would knowing spoil it for you?

I don't know, I said. Is there tragedy and grief?

The usual trials and tribulations, my love, but none you didn't hold up under handily.

Tell me then, I said. But only what is good.

Should I narrate in past tense, darling, or future?

They're one and the same, I said. You decide.

Very well, dear. We will marry in Missouri. We will honeymoon in Paris. You will earn your PhD from Princeton University and become Dr. Federico Ricci, Professor of Philosophy. You will lecture throughout Europe. You will be awarded the Meister Eckhart Prize by the Identity Society; the John Fisher Memorial Prize by the American Society for Aesthetics for your original essay entitled *Quantum Physics and the Process of Fiction*; the Kyoto Prize in Arts and Philosophy by the Inamori Foundation for a lifetime of achievement…and so many more awards, Federico, that I can't recall. We will have an apartment in Paris, and one in Manhattan. I will be awarded an MFA by the Rhode Island School of Design and become an accomplished painter, if I must say so myself, and late in my career a critic of some repute. Together we will amass perhaps the largest collection of MC Escher drawings in the world. We will have three bright and beautiful daughters, Ava, Amelia, and Penelope, who will themselves have brilliant careers. We will retire to a country estate in the enchanted Rogue Valley of Southern Oregon and open a winery,

Ricci Cellars. There I will die in my sleep—or *did*, moments ago—on the eve of my sixty-sixth birthday, after which you will carry on without me.

She ceased her narrative and recommenced humming. I was stunned by its conclusion: *You will carry on without me.* We swung to and fro in silence. The sights and sounds of the night enfolded us.

I'm so glad we had these moments together, she said at length. Now I must go.

She stepped to the side of the porch and plucked a wild daisy.

For you, she said.

I stood. She put the stem of the daisy through the buttonhole of my shirt.

Because you gave me one long ago, she said, and I've never forgotten.

I don't remember, I said.

Because you haven't given it to me yet, silly boy, but you will.

She put a hand on my chest.

Hold me, Federico, she said.

We embraced.

Thank you for loving me, she said, and for giving me a wonderful life.

She kissed my cheek and walked away. In the middle of the lawn, she broke into a dance, a dainty barefoot shuffle, a mischievous bump and grind of the hips, a rolling of the shoulders. Her laughter rang like a melody. She entered the woods and was gone.

In the cottage, I put the daisy in a mason jar and placed it on young Angelina's bedside table. She lay facing the wall. I snuggled behind her and put my arm around her waist. She murmured from deep in the realm of dreams. When I awoke, sunlight streamed through the window. My arm was yet around her, as though we hadn't moved in the night. She reached and plucked the daisy from the mason jar on the bedside table.

Did you pick this for me? she said.

Yes, I said,

Thank you, she said. It's very nice.

I put my hand on her shoulder.

Angelina, I said, look at me. I want to tell you something.

She turned. She wiped a tear from her eye.

What? she said.

I want to marry you, I said. I want to marry you right away and never let you go.

THE PROFESSOR LAPSED into silence, lingering in that long-ago moment. I turned my phone off.

Did you marry her right away? I said.

She was a minor, he said. We needed her father's permission. He gave it readily. She's a handful, Mr. Ricci, he said. But she's my little girl. I'll take good care of her, I told him.

Did your lives unfold as she had hoped, I said, and as the elder Angelina described?

Thus far yes, Adrian. We lack only the final event.

Which is…?

Her sixty-sixth birthday is in two days.

He stood.

Thank you for listening, he said. I hope you find my tale worthy of inclusion in your book. Stay well. May you live long and prosper.

He bowed and walked away. Midway to the door he stopped and turned. His smile was gracious.

Nice hat, he said.

I WONDERED AT THE TRUTH OF HIS TALE. Had the visitation of the elder Angelina been a lucid dream? A psilocybin-induced hallucinatory episode? Had the unfolding of his fate according to the script been a self-fulfilling prophecy? I had my answer a few days later when I read the following in the Medford Mail Tribune:

> Jacksonville resident Angelina Ricci died peacefully in her sleep on Friday, May 3rd, the eve of her sixty-sixth birthday. Angelina was the wife of Professor Federico Ricci of Brooklyn, New York. Together they were the proud proprietors of the recently established Ricci Cellars in the Applegate Valley.
>
> Angelina was born in Jefferson City, Missouri, on May 4th, 1954. She married Federico in 1971 at the tender age of 17. She was awarded a master's degree of fine arts from the Rhode Island School of Design in 1975. Angelina was a painter of international renown whose work shows in numerous galleries throughout the United States and Europe. She loved conversation, fine wine, and far-away places. She loved to laugh.
>
> Angelina is survived by her husband, Federico, three children, Ava, Amelia, and Penelope, and five grandchildren. She will be missed by all who knew and loved her.
>
> Angelina will be interred in the Jacksonville Cemetery, on Cemetery Road, Friday, May 10th.

I did not attend the funeral. It was not my place. Afterward, I went to the cemetery. I found her grave. There, among the many wreaths and floral decorations adorning her plot, was a single daisy in a mason jar.

I never saw the tall man again.

JUNE

FOR THE LOVE OF DADA

When I look into the eyes of an animal, I do not see an animal.
I see a living being. I see a friend. I feel a soul.

– Anthony Douglas Williams
Author, spiritualist, animal rights activist

SAM, HAVE I MENTIONED THAT JACKSONVILLE is a dog town like no other? Folks love their dogs like the children they left behind. On a given day a dozen dogs are seen pulling their masters on the end of a leash, retracing familiar steps. Every few minutes is a familiar rendezvous, neighbors exchanging news and views, their four-legged companions going nose-to-nose, reaffirming their privileged place in the canine community.

The gamut of breeds is represented, pure-bred and rescued. And such names! Lola, Ruckus and Ruby! Perseus, Polly and Cali! Cyrus, Barney and Becca! Winston and Weezer and Winnie the Poo!

This month's story is about a rescue dog named Dada. Rescued not once, not twice, but three times, and the final time in a mysterious and amusing way.

I first met Dada on the sidewalk in front of the Good Bean Café only yesterday, the first day of June. I was at my usual table at 6:00 a.m., scouring memory and imagination for story number six. A few hours later—my muse, Miranda having all but abandoned me—I stepped outside for a bit of air. It was a glorious Spring morning and the tables on the sidewalk were filled. At one sat a man a few years my senior I recognized as a fellow instructor at Rogue Valley Community College. He leaned back in his chair with his legs crossed at the ankles and his eyes closed, soaking up the sun. He wore a rainbow-colored beanie and a Grateful Dead t-shirt. At his sandaled feet sat a mid-sized dog with a friendly smile and eyes like black pools with pinpoints of light at their centers, like the light at the end of a tunnel. Its short coppery coat glistened in the sun. When its gaze met mine, its smile widened, and its tail wagged. I offered the top of my hand for its inspection. The man stirred.

Don't look too long into his eyes, he said.

No? Why not?

Just don't.

Okay, I said. An awfully handsome dog. What kind is it?

Couldn't say, he said. A rescue dog. Some kind of Terrier, I'd guess.

Boy or girl?

A boy named Dada, he said. Dada, shake the man's hand.

Dada sat up and offered his paw. His demeanor was dignified. I sensed extreme emotional intelligence. His eyes were like bottomless pits. I was careful not to look too long.

Pleased to meet you, Dada, I said.

I've seen you in the faculty lounge, the man said. What do you teach?

Creative writing, I said. And you?

Studio art.

Do you paint?

I do, he said.

What do you paint?

Whatever lingers in my mind when I awaken. I chase my dreams with a brush in hand. What do you write?

Fiction, I said. Stories.

Ah, same Universe. Different galaxies.

Something like that, I said.

It's a beautiful day for sitting outside, he said. Care to join me?

I went inside, retrieved my coffee, came outside, and took a seat.

Adrian, I said, offering my hand.

Arthur, he said, taking it. What do you write about, Adrian?

At the moment unlikely and inexplicable events and how they impact our lives. Chance encounters. Fathomless mysteries.

Let's hear it for fathomless mysteries, he said. I favor the surrealists myself, though they're out of fashion. Do you do animal stories, Adrian?

I did one about pink flamingos, I said, but they're plastic.

Do you do dog stories?

Haven't yet, but I'm willing. Why? Do you have one to tell?

Arthur addressed his dog: Dada, should we tell Adrian here about the series of inexplicable events that determined the course of our lives? He might find it amusing.

Dada's ears perked up. His tail wagged. I spent the next hour soaking up the sun and listening to the strange and amusing tale of a dog named Dada.

FOR THE LOVE OF DADA

I WAS BORN AND RAISED in Oakland, California, Adrian. Attended Oakland Technical High School, as had Clint Eastwood some forty-five years before me. I've been an artist for as long as I can remember. A graffiti artist in my youth, some of my early work is still to be found on box cars at the Port of Oakland, and on crumbling brick buildings throughout the city. After graduation, I kicked around for a few years, getting stoned and painting where and when I could. I settled down and was accepted into the University of California, Berkeley. Awarded an MFA in Studio Art in 2002. I moved across the Bay to San Francisco and set up a studio in a spacious rent-control apartment in the Mission District. Have you been to the Mission District, Adrian? Yes? Then you've seen a few of my early murals adorning its walls.

I was hired as Adjunct Professor at San Francisco State University. The pay wasn't great, but it was mine. I didn't need much. I had my affordable loft in The Mission, my studio, a modest occasional show of my work, and all was well in my world...until 2011, when I met my soon-to-be live-in lover, Morgan, and my world was turned upside down.

I had been commissioned to do a mural at Niebaum-Coppola Winery, the estate of Francis Ford Coppola, in Napa Valley, California. Originally Inglenook Chateau Winery, it was sold to corporate interests and the quality of its wines declined. Coppola acquired the property piece by piece between 1975 and 1995, determined to restore it to its former glory, but couldn't acquire the name, Inglenook.

Until Team Morgan.

Morgan was born in Jefferson City, Missouri, in 1971. She was bright and driven, and far out-paced her peers in the *show-me* state. She graduated Summa Cum Laude from the University of Missouri, Columbia, and was accepted into Boston College Law School where she studied Public and Private Land Use and Management. She was hired by the most prestigious and powerful real estate law firm in San Francisco and soon became its youngest partner. There is hardly a major real estate deal in San Francisco in recent history that does not have her name on it: the Transamerica Pyramid. One Front Street. Market Center. Levi's Plaza. I only mention these mundane details, Adrian, to emphasize that Morgan and I were not cut from the same cloth. And that our union was about as unlikely and inexplicable an event as you might want...though it's not the event at the heart of this story, but we'll come to that.

Morgan's firm was hired by Coppola to help secure the Inglenook name after decades of failed attempts. So, there I was, Adrian, on my scaffold in the Chateau, playing Michelangelo, when Morgan, being shown around by Coppola, walked by. She stopped to admire my work. In her black satin pantsuit, white silk blouse opened at the collar, a pendant of emerald to match her eyes, swept-back platinum blonde hair, shiny black heels, and curves in all the right places, she was herself a piece of work to admire. She had my attention. After a brief conversation, it was clear she knew little about art but a whole lot about how to control a conversation without your knowing she was in charge. Or caring. I found her presence strangely unnerving.

That evening on my drive back to San Francisco I stopped at Rutherford Grill for a bite to eat and a bit of wine. I sat at the bar. Across the room, Morgan sat with a male colleague. She came and sat beside me. Over a glass of crisp Chardonnay, she told me the acquisition of the Inglenook name was a done deal—and cost Coppola more money than had the purchase of the entire estate! She reported this without expression but with a gleam of triumph in her cold green eyes. She gave me her card. I called the next day. Thus began our unlikely affair.

I soon learned that Morgan's propensity to control a conversation extended to the bedroom. I'm talking leather and chains, Adrian, and whacky practices that even today I am too embarrassed to mention. I discovered a totally unexpected side of myself—and I must confess I liked it!

Morgan lived alone in an elegant Queen Anne style home in Pacific Heights, with panoramic views of the Golden Gate Bridge, the Palace of Fine Arts, Alcatraz, and the Presidio. One entire floor was devoted to fitness, all the latest equipment, and a twice-weekly session with a personal trainer. She was pushing forty, five years older than I, with the body of an athlete half her age. I felt soft beside her.

She loved to entertain. She would hire the best caterers in the city, and a harpist, or an ensemble of jazz musicians, and invite fellow high-octane attorneys like herself, and their wives, and the luminaries of San Francisco High Society, into her home. She wanted to appear more avant-garde than she was, a connoisseur of contemporary art, but knew little of the subject. Her temperament was transactional, not creative. She proposed that I move in with her. I would curate her personal collection, manage her purchases, mentor her in the fine art of pretentious phraseology, and be her resident *artiste* and boy toy. I would give up my rent control studio in the Mission, and my teaching position at San Francisco State, and she would support me in style.

I should have known better, Adrian, but I was beguiled by this sudden bizarre turn of events. The style of my own art of late—the juxtaposition of dissimilar elements to create a wholly unexpected and inexplicable result—well, her approach to life and mine were about as dissimilar as they could be, and juxtaposing them would produce a wholly unexpected effect, indeed.

Days prior to moving in, I accompanied an elderly friend to an animal rescue shelter where she looked for a canine companion with whom to spend her final years. So sad to be in that roomful of imploring eyes and pleading whimpers. My friend chose a diminutive and cuddly white-haired dog named Peppa, small enough to put in her purse. I had no intention of rescuing a dog but I fell in love with a certain mysterious creature with fur like satin, a winning smile, and eyes like pools you could dive into, with sparkles of light at their centers. It occurred to me this handsome fellow would be the perfect housewarming gift to Morgan. Whatever was I thinking?

What kind is it? she said with a sour look on her face.

Some kind of Terrier, I suppose.

It's not purebred?

He's a rescue dog, I said. Breed unknown. He's beautiful, isn't he? Look at those eyes, Morgan, and that smile!

Why the weird name Dada?

I named him after a radical art movement that preceded Surrealism, I told her. Dadaists opposed the rise of capitalist culture and entrenched bourgeois sensibilities. They were anti-art, favoring chance to calculation, chaos to order, whimsy to serious intent. They even opposed themselves! There's an old Dada joke, Morgan. Are you ready? *How many Dadaists does it take to screw in a light bulb?* Answer: *A fish.* I see you don't get it. That's fine. It's a puzzle not meant to be gotten.

Morgan frowned. She did not like puzzles, meant to be gotten or not.

What, pray tell, does an art movement called Dada have to do with a rescue dog? she demanded to know.

Excellent question, Morgan. A Dadaist riddle in its own right. You're catching on. You see, Dadaists experimented with the *found object*: a bicycle seat, a urinal, a vacuum cleaner. They called such objects *readymades*. Rescued them from their role in the mundane world of practicality and declared them art. Hence the name Dada for your dog, Morgan, and it will prove to be a very useful name. At your next soireé, you are sure to hear: *A beautiful dog, my dear—and what an uncommon name!* You will then have a story to tell and entré into a conversation around the subject. And to bolster your lexicon of useful artsy-fartsy phrases here is a book for you: *Dada: Art and Anti-Art*, by Hans Richter. Of course, you will want to have representative works on your walls. I'll scour the city and find half a dozen. I'm sure to find one or two at Gallery Wendi Norris. I'll write up a synopsis of each. You can segue from *What an uncommon name!* to the significance of these eclectic works and show off your deep understanding.

Morgan accepted my reasoning and my gift, but not for the love of Dada. She used him as a prompt to display her deep knowledge of art, as I suggested, but also as a tool against me, an extension of her manipulative disposition. She knew we had a special bond, Dada and I, and when she wanted to remind me whose dog he was, she would come between us in not-so-subtle ways: insisting he was tired and did not want to play; banishing him to a posh Doggie Day-care for a week at a time on the pretext that he needed to socialize with other dogs; enrolling him in obedience school and delighting to have him roll over and play dead to the amusement of her friends. She had him be present during our bouts of lovemaking, that he might witness her domination and my degradation. He watched in silence. By and by I rebelled. I wanted my dignity back. We fought often, which culminated in rough sex, a battle of wills. Sometimes I prevailed and she assumed a passive role, then resented me for exposing her soft side. And so forth, Adrian. Incredible that we were able to sustain this sick dynamic for three years.

OUR RELATIONSHIP WAS AT an all-time low when Morgan's firm was engaged to handle the establishment of Ricci Cellars here in the Valley. She would fly up alone, but I proposed we drive together, she and I and Dada, along the coast, a leisurely excursion away from the demands of the city that might help rescue our doomed affair. Surprisingly, she agreed.

The blue sky, the foamy ribbon of surf, the mist in the redwood forests, all had a soothing effect, and we found ourselves laughing at our own foolishness. Dada, too, seemed to feel relief as he sat between us, smiling and wagging his tail and watching the road unwind.

In Ft. Bragg, 170 miles north of San Francisco, we took a room at the elegant and pet friendly Noyo Harbor Inn. We dined on the patio of the Harborview Bistro & Bar. The view of the harbor was splendid: lights twinkled on the lapping water like distant stars, and the masts of small craft rocked to and fro like metronomes in slow motion. At a nearby table, an older couple discussed a book. Their conversation was animated and intimate at once. I had the absurd notion that might be Morgan and me one day. We had left the stress of the Bay Area behind, and it seemed our relationship might flower into one less combative, or at least less twisted. We laughed and flirted and had a fine time.

We arrived in Jacksonville the next afternoon. Took a room at the Magnolia Inn. Dined on the patio of the Bella Union Bar & Grill. I found the rustic atmosphere delightful. She called it provincial. I pointed out the town had admirably retained its authentic façade. It was, after all, on the Historic Register.

That's a good place for it, she said.

I did not pursue the subject. We had had a promising holiday thus far; I was careful not to spoil it by pressing my point of view.

In the morning, I accompanied Morgan to the Ricci Estate. While she discussed legal matters with Mr. Ricci—Federico—I was kept company by the gracious and articulate Mrs. Ricci—Angelina—a patron of the arts and a masterful painter in her own right. And recently deceased, as you are probably aware, Adrian. May she rest in peace. We had a most enlightening conversation. She invited me back to view their private collection once they were settled.

There's a lovely cottage on the property, she said. Guests are welcome.

The next day, Morgan went to the Ricci's alone. Dada and I did a walking tour of the town. He made half a dozen four-legged friends along the way. We visited the gallery, *Art Presence*, and I admired the quality and diversity of its exhibits. At Rebel Heart Books, I met a local writer, Bennie, and his dog, Jack. We four went to La Fiesta Mexican Restaurant where, on the deck, over fish-bowl-sized margaritas, he related the circuitous route by which he had come to reside in Jacksonville.

One does not choose Jacksonville, he said: It chooses you.

That evening Morgan and I dined at Gogi's restaurant, considered by most to be the Crown Jewell of Jacksonville eateries. I had a proposal to make. I opened by praising the quality of the cuisine.

It's not San Francisco, she said with a dismissive wave of her hand.

That's the point, I said. To have so urbane a menu in so pastoral a setting as the Rogue Valley is to have the best of both worlds.

She didn't respond. She seemed determined to be disagreeable. It was not a good time for what I would propose—that we quit San Francisco and move to Jacksonville—but it was now or never. I said she had made her mark in the City; there was nothing left to prove. Here she could be part of a thriving community of artists and entrepreneurs. Southern Oregon was a winemaker's mecca that rivaled Napa Valley, and with her history of negotiating on behalf of distinctive wineries, she might forge an unrivaled specialty practice. Without the stress of the city. And not a stop light or parking meter in town! If she needed to get away, there was an airport close by to take her anywhere in the world.

And Dada loves it here, Morgan, I concluded. I've never seen him so happy!

Morgan perused her menu in silence. At length, she responded.

What makes Dada happy is not a deciding factor in the course of my life, she said without looking up.

It was clear Jacksonville would not be choosing Morgan anytime soon. Back at the Magnolia Inn, she booked a second room next to the first.

You sleep here, she said.

Through the wall between our rooms, I heard her berating Dada. No doubt she knew I heard. Our fragile reconciliation was unraveling like a cheap tapestry.

Gone Dog

THE NEXT MORNING, AFTER A BREAKFAST eaten in silence at the Mustard Seed Café, we headed south on Interstate 5. Dada sat between us and looked from one to the other. A few miles out of town Morgan said she had to pee. We pulled into the rest stop at mile marker twenty-two. A dozen or so cars occupied the lot. A lawn extended to the tree line and a creek beyond. Near the sidewalk, a few yards from the bumper of our car, a seedy couple sat side by side in the grass, the girl's eyes half closed, her head resting on the man's shoulder, between them a hat turned upside down and a sign in crude letters reading OUT OF GAS. On a picnic bench in the middle distance, a shirtless man with a pit bull rummaged through a plastic bag and talked to himself. An elderly couple walked a poodle near a sign reading *Pets Allowed on Leash in This Area*.

I might as well pee, too, I said. It's going to be a long drive.

Too long, she said. Leave Dada in the car. Roll up the windows and lock the doors.

Of course, I said irritably, as though I wouldn't think to roll up the windows and lock the doors without being told.

We exited the car. I pressed the *lock* button on the key fob. We finished our business at the same time and returned to the car. Morgan was a few feet ahead of me. I pressed the *unlock* button. Morgan opened the passenger side door, bent over, and looked inside. She straightened and faced me.

Where's Dada? she said, a look of dismay on her face.

In the car, I said.

He's not in the goddamned car!

What?

Together we searched the car. The floorboards. Behind the seats. Absurdly, *under* the seats.

You didn't lock the car! she screamed.

I locked the fucking car!

We hollered, Dada! Dada! in every direction.

I addressed the seedy couple.

Have you seen a dog?

Seen lots of dogs, the man said.

A loose dog, I said. It was in our car.

Nope, the man said. Ain't seen no loose dog.

Have you seen anyone near our car?

Just you, dude, he said.

Morgan approached the old couple. I crossed the lawn to the shirtless man with the pit bull. The dog growled at my approach.

Have you seen a dog? I said.

This is *my* dog! he said.

A different dog, I said. Smaller. Kind of copper colored.

My dog, he said.

He scooped up his plastic bag and walked away, pulling the pit bull's leash.

C'mon, Caesar, he said. You're *my* dog!

I trotted to the tree line. I shouted Dada! up and down the creek bed. I walked a hundred yards in both directions. I returned to the car. The old couple had seen nothing. We went through the parking lot asking everyone if they'd seen a loose dog. We peered inside every unoccupied car. We searched the restrooms. I walked to the freeway on-ramp. I looked south at the river of receding vehicles. What did I hope to see? I returned to the car. Morgan glared at me.

This is crazy, I said. We've got to call the police.

What can *they* do?

They can search for a lost dog, I said.

Dream on, she said. They've got better things to do. They'll file a report and say good luck.

I called the Oregon State Police. They would send out the next available officer. Morgan sat in the car. I walked the grounds yelling Dada! Dada! Trooper Terry Kosinski arrived within the hour. He was efficient and sympathetic at once. He examined our car for signs of forced entry and found none. He would forward our statement and contact information to his department, to local Police agencies, and to California Highway Patrol's northernmost districts. He advised going online to Jackson County Animal Control Services and filing a missing pet report with photos. He advised offering a reward on posters hung in nearby communities.

He warned of scammers.

They'll want money upfront, he said. Don't pay. Insist on seeing your dog first. Cash on delivery.

He wished us luck.

I have to stay, I told Morgan.

I have to go, she said.

I took her to the airport and returned to the rest stop. I wandered the grounds till the sun set behind the tree line.

I'll find you, Dada! I yelled into the empty darkness. I'll find you!

I returned to the Magnolia Inn and booked a room for three days. I posted missing pet notices, with photos and contact information, on the websites of Jackson County, Facebook, Craigslist, Next Door, and Petco. I took out ads in local newspapers. I made posters at Kinko's offering a thousand-dollar reward and pasted them on poles in every town from Ashland to Grant's Pass. I posted them on the bulletin boards of grocery stores. I posted them at every rest stop from Portland to Redding, California.

I could do no more.

I drove home alone. I wondered what had taken place. Did Morgan have an accomplice with a key who followed us and ripped off Dada in the few moments I was gone to the restroom just so she could vilify me? We had just left the Mustard Seed Café. She could have peed there. But no, she couldn't have pulled it off. She didn't know the lay of the land, nor the schedule we'd be on. And to contrive this scenario in advance served nobody's purpose.

Had I pushed the *unlock* button on my key fob when I meant to push the *lock* button? No, I had the presence of mind to push the right button. Anyway, the out-of-gas couple would have seen if someone had opened the car door and taken a dog.

Had Dada dematerialized himself, I wondered, to escape the clutches of Cruella? This explanation was as sensible to me as any.

THE SCAM CALLS CAME IN. A man said he was a long-haul trucker who found Dada on the side of the road. He'd be down my way in a month. He'd take good care of Dada but needed expenses upfront. Another said he knew who had him and would tell me for a price. A woman said she found Dada injured and took him to the Vet and needed to pay the Vet bill first. She would not provide the name and number of the Vet.

None would provide photos.

I took the Trooper's advice and ignored them all. The world is rampant with scum bags, Adrian. I'm not a violent man but given a chance, I would do a few of them great bodily harm.

MEANWHILE, MORGAN USED DADA'S disappearance as an excuse to belittle me. I no longer suited her purposes. My eccentricities were passé. She wanted me out of her house. I said I'd go but I'd sue for *palimony*. I'm not a vindictive man, Adrian, but if she would rake me over the coals, I would take her to the cleaners. After all, I had quit my paid position at San Francisco State and given up my rent-controlled studio in the Mission, which now went for three times the price. I'd grown accustomed to a lifestyle beyond my means. Neither of us believed my claim would fly in court but I was adamant I would pursue it, and she was positive she didn't want the publicity, so we agreed to an out-of-court settlement. A hefty sum. I took my money and ran.

So long, San Francisco. Howdy, Jacksonville, Oregon.

I REACHED OUT TO THE RICCIS and rented their guest cottage month-to-month until I found one of my own, a fixer-upper with a wood-burning fireplace on a seasonal creek next door to the house of my writer friend, Bennie, his wife, Ginna, and his dog, Jack. En route to the office of Ramsay Realty on the very day of the close of escrow, I got into the left turn lane at a stop light. There on the island of concrete a homeless man leaned against the light post holding a sign that read: ANYTHING HELPS. Lying beside him, his face resting on his outstretched paws—was Dada!

I put the car in park and jumped out. Dada rose and barked and strained against the leash. I dropped to a knee and embraced him. He licked my face. The light turned green and the cars behind me started to honk.

What are you doing? the homeless man said.

This is my dog, I said.

It's *my* dog, he said.

The fuck it is, I said. Where did you get him?

He hesitated.

I found him, he said.

Well, you just unfound him, I said.

I stood and took fifty dollars from my wallet.

If you want to make an issue of it, pal, I will prove he's mine and you get nothing. Or you can let go of that leash and take this fifty bucks and move on down the road.

I held out the money. The man looked at Dada. He let go of the leash. I put the money in his empty hand. I opened the car door. Dada jumped in. I drove to the real estate office, signed some papers, and got the key to my house. *Our* house.

Dada was rescued yet again.

In the coming week, Dada and I reveled in our reunion. I bought him beds, treats, and toys. We played fetch and tug-of-war. By day he visited Jack next door, romping and stomping likes dogs do, or Jack came over and they romped and stomped in our yard. By night we sat in the cozy living room basking in the light of the fireplace, Dada on his blanket on the floor near the hearth, me in my overstuffed armchair with a book in my lap. But a thread of foreboding was woven into the fabric of our domestic bliss. Dada had been a gift to Morgan. He was not mine to keep. Dada, too, sensed this dismal conclusion and we became morose together.

I called Morgan.

I found Dada, I said.

There was silence on the line.

What? How? Where? she said without enthusiasm.

Doesn't matter, I said. I have him.

When can you bring him down, she said.

I can't, I said. I'm busy. You'll have to come up.

Yes, Adrian, I lied to her. I wasn't busy at all. Busy doing nothing! I could have driven Dada down. Behind my thinking was the hope that if she had to come get him, she wouldn't. It would be too much trouble for a dog she didn't really want. But she was not to be outmaneuvered. No doubt she suspected my ploy, and to spite me, and exact revenge for the palimony deal, she said: I'll be there tomorrow. Her words were like a punch to the gut. I gave her my address.

Tunnel of Love

THAT EVENING IN THE COTTAGE my heart was heavy as a boulder. I could barely breathe. I sat in my chair by the fire, draped in sorrow. Shadows danced on the walls like taunting spirits. Dada lay on the floor at my feet. I caressed his silken fur. Fondled his ears with my fingertips. He whimpered softly. I had lost him once, now I'd lose him again. Foiled by my own self-defeating sense of fair play. He turned and stared into my face. I stared back, deep into the dark abyss of his eyes. At the sparkle of light at their centers. We were motionless for the longest time. I had never felt such love. I thought I might cry. There came a low moan as of wind in the forest. The moan became a roar. The black holes of Dada's eyes expanded until they filled the room. I was pulled into the abyss. Weightless and bodiless, I hurtled through this tunnel of love at an impossible speed. If you know the star gate scene in *2001 A Space Odyssey*, Adrian, you'll have an idea what I'm talking about.

In an instant, the hurtling ceased, the roar was reduced to a *ping,* and I was staring not into Dada's eyes—but at my own face! Yes, you heard me right, Adrian: I was sitting on the floor in Dada's body, staring at myself— that is, at *my body*—which sat in the chair staring at me—that is, at Dada's body. I rightly assumed that if *my* mind was in *his* body, *his* mind was in mine. I could see from his face—that is, *my* face—that he was as confused as I by this sudden and inexplicable transmigration of souls. One moment he was looking at me, the next moment I was gone and he was looking at himself. But never having seen himself, his perception was of another dog in the room. Curious and excited, he attempted to come and sniff me, that is *himself,* but his dog mind having no experience navigating the more complex circuitry of the human nervous system, he tumbled from the chair onto his face, that is *my* face. Ouch, I thought but didn't feel a thing. He struggled onto his hands and knees and floundered forward and sniffed my face, that is, *his* face. Imagine being inches from your own face, Adrian, knowing there was the mind of a dog behind your eyes. No drug-induced hallucinatory episode in my experience had produced so profoundly disturbing an effect. Startled, I attempted to back away, but having no familiarity with the circuitry of the canine nervous system, I toppled onto my side. Dada came and sniffed my butt. *His* butt. I struggled onto my four paws. *His* paws. I teetered back and forth. I strained to suppress my rising panic. For how long would this strange metamorphosis endure? Would I be trapped in Dada's body forever, and he in mine? I didn't know. But I came to my senses and resolved to go with the flow. What better way to love another sentient being than to become it?

I watched my Dada-filled body wobble unsteadily on hands and knees to his box of toys. After several attempts, he managed to get a black rubber bone between his teeth. He came to me and growled. A weird growl, a canine utterance delivered by human vocal cords. *Just try and take it*, he was trying to say, as he had so often in the previous week. I looked at the bone with distaste, slobbery and glistening, with hairs embedded, his and Jack's—but what the hell: *I was a dog!* I took it in my teeth. We tugged for half an hour. Back and forth across the room. We lay exhausted and panting on the floor. I was fast becoming familiar with the mechanics of dog movement, as was Dada with the movement of the human form.

Speaking of movement, I felt a sudden stirring in my bowels. Dada's bowels. I hadn't the wherewithal to put the movement in check and did my business on the floor before the fire. Hunched and pumping, as I'd watched Dada do many times. He came and sniffed and was inspired to do the same. He shuffled to the door on his hands and knees and whimpered, as he does when he wants me to open the door and let him out. But even if I could stand on my back legs, *his* back legs, I would be but three feet tall and had no hands, and you can't turn a doorknob with paws. He hunched grotesquely, screwed up his face, and delivered a pile into his pants…which is to say *my* pants.

This would never do. What other familiar—and essential—tasks could not be performed by a dog in a human body or a human in a dog body? Using a cell phone? Drinking water? Feeding oneself?

My food was behind a refrigerator door I could not open. Dada's food was behind a closet door neither he nor I could open. Despite his elongated human body, and his ten digits evolved over millions of years, Dada could open neither. He lurched crab-like in my body to the water bowl on the floor in the kitchen. I followed. He struggled to lap up water with his tongue—*my* tongue. I could hear the frustration in his whine. Lapping water with a short human tongue that he could not control. I joined him at the bowl. I shared his frustration. My tongue, *his* tongue, was long enough but I couldn't make it scoop right. Together, with great effort, we got the water we needed.

But we could not get food.

We could not leave the house.

We could not call out.

We drifted in a limbo of inexplicable weirdness.

Periodically we peed, me on the floor, Dada in his pants. *My* pants. To my newly acquired hyper-sensitive canine olfactory perception, the cottage was beginning to reek!

IT WAS A LONG NIGHT. I slept it away, my chin resting on my outstretched paws. Late morning the next day my cell phone rang. I clambered up onto the armchair, next to which my phone sat on a side table. I read the screen: *Incoming call from Morgan*!

Doubtless, she was minutes away.

Damn! We could not be found like this. We had to reverse the process! I shuffled over to where Dada now lay on the cold hearth. I stared into his eyes. If we stared long enough, I hoped, we might reverse the direction of the tunnel of love. But Dada thought I wanted to play. He broke eye contact and got his bone. He pushed his face in front of mine. I tried to hold his gaze, but he scrambled away with me in dogged pursuit.

Round and round we went until the knock came. I froze. Dada dropped the bone and looked at the door. Perhaps it was *me* knocking, he might have thought, returning to feed him after my mysterious disappearance the night before. He commenced a weird and strangulated string of barks.

Morgan's voice came from behind the door.

Arthur, is that you?

I said nothing. Dada barked on.

Open the fucking door, Arthur! she commanded. I'm coming in!

She opened the door. Took a step in. Dada, in my body, hobbled over and sniffed her ankles, her calves. Rose up onto his hind legs—my knees—and sniffed her crotch. She was startled. She took a step back.

What are you doing? she said. Are you drunk? My God, what is that smell?

I was at a loss for a sensible thing to do. The last thing I wanted was for her to take me back to San Francisco trapped in Dada's body for the rest of my short doggie life and leave Dada in my body in the cottage where, if he was found before he died for lack of food and water, would be thought to have lost his mind, *my* mind, and be confined to an institution. So, I wobbled over and bit her on the ankle. Didn't break the skin but she'd have a nice bruise. She screamed and backed out of the door.

I'll be back, she said—and with the police!

She slammed the door behind her. Dada whined. We went face to face. I stared into his eyes. Projected my thoughts: *Dada! Dada! Look at me. Do not look away! We are not playing, alright?*

My sense of urgency got his attention. He remained motionless and returned my stare. Looked long and hard into the black pools of my eyes. *His* eyes. I could sense he now saw *me*, his long-time human friend who had rescued him from a shelter, and from a concrete island under a traffic signal. He saw the light at the end of the tunnel and knew I was waiting there.

The low moan commenced. Became a howl. I hurtled down that long tunnel in reverse until I heard a *ping* and was looking into the face of Dada, and he was looking into mine. As jubilant as I was at the successful reciprocity of our selves, I knew it was time to clean up and look good for the Jacksonville Police.

I got up off the floor. I became acutely and unpleasantly aware of the load in my pants. I stripped off my clothes and took a fast hot shower. Threw my soiled pants in the trash outside. Cleaned up the mess on the hearth. Saturated the air with deodorizer. Rekindled the fire. Fed Dada. Freshened his water bowl. Sat in my armchair with a book and waited.

But the police didn't come. And Morgan didn't return. That evening, I received an email:

> *Arthur,*
> *You keep Dada. There's no place for a dog in my life. (At least not that one—the little fuck bit me!) Anyway, you love him more than I do. I've always known that. I was just being a bitch. (Because that's what I do, and you like it!) May you live long and prosper—and don't call me again, you prick!*
> *Morgan*

I was so happy I shed a tear. I read the email to Dada. He smiled and wagged his tail. Rescued yet again. Not once, not twice, but thrice. Now here we sit in beautiful downtown Jacksonville, soaking up the sun. What do you think, Adrian? Does our little tale qualify as unlikely and inexplicable?

That it does, Arthur. It's weird as can be and I love it. I do have one question, though.

Yes…?

Was that the one and only time you and Dada traded places, or have you repeated the experience?

A slow smile spread across his face.

We'll never tell! Will we Dada?

Dada looked at me and uttered a low soft bark: Woof, woof!

Dada, Arthur said, shake hands with the man who will make you famous.

Dada held out a paw. I took it. I stared into the pools of his eyes. But not for long.

JULY

HOWLS OF EXECRATION

Courage is a strange thing.
One can never be sure of it.

– Raymond Chandler

Monday, July 8, 2019

SAM, I WILL LEAVE IT TO YOU to decide the culpability of Paul the Potter in the following extraordinary series of events. It will be no easy task, but one requiring insight into the nature of reality, the complexity of the human mind, and the holy trinity of time, space, and memory. I will understand perfectly if you choose to withhold judgment as did I.

Paul has a studio behind his cottage in the woods at the edge of town. He's often seen walking the trails, his flat cap on backward like an *artiste* or a French resistance fighter. Lost in thought, his lanky frame bent forward like the weight of the world is on his shoulders, his image brings to mind the myth of Sisyphus: man's fate is to roll a boulder to the top of the mountain, only to have it roll down again ad infinitum.

Paul is renowned for his designs in porcelain, at once subtle and daring, and the genius of his translucent glazing technique. I sometimes stop by his studio to admire his work. I once told him if he hadn't become a potter, he might have become a poet because there was a poem in every pot he wrought. His smile was ironic.

Well, was all he said.

On a recent visit, Paul asked about my work.

I'm knee-deep in a novel about unlikely and inexplicable events and how they impact our lives, I said.

He became thoughtful.

Maybe it's time, he muttered. Maybe it's time.

Time for what? I said.

To tell my story, he said. It's nothing if not unlikely and inexplicable. I have told no one for fifty years and it has crushed my spirit, Adrian. Telling it might take the weight off me and I can breathe again…and it might find a place in your book.

I was surprised that Paul would consider unburdening himself to me. Our acquaintance was recent and casual. I didn't even know his last name. But I was pleased because I hadn't known from where my next story might come.

I'd be happy to hear it, I said.

We agreed to meet at the Good Bean Café the very next day.

That night, on impulse, I leafed through a book I hadn't read in years: *Howls of Execration: Poems of Remorse and Regret*, by PB Hastings.

Hastings named his book after the last line of the novel, *The Stranger*, by Albert Camus:

> *For all to be accomplished, for me to feel less lonely, all that*
> *remained to hope was that on the day of my execution there*
> *should be a huge crowd of spectators and that they should*
> *greet me with howls of execration.*

Hasting's book perfectly captured the crushing power of remorse and regret. It was well received. He never wrote another, but dropped out of sight as had the young poet Arthur Rimbaud almost a century before.

PAUL TOOK HIS TIME getting around to his story. A roving intellect, he was fascinated by the intersection of art, science, and the occult. Over cappuccino and a chocolate biscotti, he spoke of the implications of Quantum Physics on the study of consciousness and the meaning of existence. I listened patiently: a witness to the opening of a fifty-year-old time capsule need not be in a hurry.

There was a pause in his monologue.

Do you write poetry, Adrian? he said.

Nothing serious, I said. The adage is: if you're a novelist and think your prose is good, try poetry and be humbled.

But you do read it.

Yes.

He reached into the side pocket of his jacket and slid a book across the table: *Howls of Execration: Poems of Remorse and Regret* by PB Hastings.

I was stupefied. I thought of Bennie meeting his future wife on the deck of the Bistro & Bar above Noyo Harbor, their simultaneous reading of *The Tao of Physics*. Her relating the Legend of the Red Thread.

I know this book, I said.

Open it to the poem *The Arroyo*, he said. Read it aloud.

I opened and read:

THE ARROYO

Beyond the arroyo
At the edge of the sea,
the sun runs red,
like a pierced heart bleeding.
She died alone
In the company
of her own small voice
in a whisper pleading:
no
please
no
not me.

I was there.
I could have saved her,
Had I been there
But was not.
I was there,
I could have stayed there,
Could have saved her,
But did not.

I remember the poem, Paul, I said. The critics noted there is regret and remorse in every line, but no identifiable cause. *Who* could have been saved? they wondered. And from *what?* And how could one be there, yet not? They agreed the success of the piece was owing to this obscurity.

Rightly so, Adrian, Paul said. Would you like to know the *who* and the *how* and the *what* about which they wondered?

Wouldn't everyone? I said. But how would *you* know, Paul?

He took out his wallet, removed his driver's license, and slid it across the table. I read: Paul Bernard Hastings. *PB Hastings.*

There was nothing for it but to hear his story.

HOWLS OF EXECRATION

I WAS BORN INTO A FARMING COMMUNITY in the rolling hills of Missouri in 1947, he said. I wasn't like the other boys, Adrian. They loved to wrestle in the dirt and scrape their knuckles. I was timid and loathed confrontation. They loved their tractors. I loved my books. While they were doing John Deere, I was doing Dostoyevsky. Bukowski. Chayefsky. When the Viet Nam war broke out, they enlisted to fight the *yellow tide*. I went to the University of Missouri, Columbia, to study literature.

In 1969 I was a graduate student and editor of the University's lit mag, *Getting the Words Right*. My friends and I were who Spiro Agnew spoke of when he referred to *Effete Intellectual Snobs*. We formed the *Transcendent Poets & Painters Society*, did mountains of LSD, and recited impromptu poetry and painted *en plein air* in the picturesque country-side of Missouri. I was always high. I didn't know if I was tripping from one day to the next: altered states were the new normal. But acid was scarce in the Midwest. When it was available, we would buy all we could and hoard it. Down to our last few hits, we got nervous. We wanted a steady source.

I had a distant older cousin, Conan, who had hitchhiked to California when he was sixteen and never came back. His outlaw exploits were the stuff of legend. I had a hunch he could help us out. His aging mother lived deep in the woods in a tumbledown shack with a sagging porch and a yard full of chickens and pigs. Her hair was stringy white. She used to call me Sonny Boy.

Why do you want to see Conan? she said in a quavering voice. Does he have something you want?

No, I lied. I'm traveling west for fun. I thought I'd visit.

Everybody wants something, she said.

She gave me his number. Fixed me with her sunken eyes.

Be careful what you wish for, Sonny Boy, she said.

She waved a spindly finger in my face.

Go now, she said. Go!

WOULD CONAN EVEN REMEMBER ME? Would he have what we wanted? We had scraped together two thousand dollars plus expenses on the chance he would. It was a lot of money for a handful of impecunious poets and painters from the heart of the country. We had no idea what it would buy on the West Coast. A single dose locally was five dollars. If the price was right, we could sell enough to get our money back and have enough left to trip for months to come.

Don't let the money out of your sight, they said. And make sure the acid is good. Don't get ripped off, Paul!

CONAN'S VOICE ON THE PHONE was gruff.

Paul who? he said.

Hastings, I said. Your cousin. I used to play at your house. Your mother watched over me sometimes. She called me Sonny Boy.

Sonny Boy! Well, fuck a duck, man! I remember you! A weird little dude. Always reading and rhyming words. How'd you get my number?

Your mother, I said.

My mother, he said. I told her not to give it out. But you're my cousin, so what the fuck. How is the old girl, anyway?

She lives alone in the woods, I said.

He sighed.

I should go see her while I can, he said. She won't be around forever. Alright, Sonny Boy, what can I do for you?

I told him what I hoped for. He laughed.

My little cousin, he said. Tripping in the cornfields. I'm not surprised. How much do you want to spend, Cousin?

Two thousand dollars, I said.

There was a moment of silence.

That might get some attention, he said.

How much will it buy? I said.

Couldn't say, Cousin. Depends which way the wind blows.

CONAN LIVED IN PACIFIC GROVE, California, a coastal town on the northern border of Monterey. I'd never seen the ocean. Never been west of Missouri. This would be a journey out of the Heartland to a distant foreign shore.

My girlfriend at the time, Angelina, a beautiful girl and talented painter, would take me to the St. Louis airport in the morning. That night at my desk in my study I drank a glass of wine, a Robert Mondavi Pinot Noir, and hollowed out a hardback book, *Journey to the End of Night*, by Ferdinand Celine. I would stash the acid within its pages for the flight home. I separated the two thousand dollars from the expense money, put each amount into a separate envelope, cinched them with rubber bands, and put the envelopes into the hollowed book. I packed a carry-on bag. Put the book in the bag and the bag on the floor on the side of my desk. Set my alarm, cut my last tab of acid in two, ground half into a powder, mixed it into the last of my drink, and drank it down. I know what you're thinking, Adrian: why *ever* would I take acid before going to sleep? Why, indeed!

I FLEW INTO THE MONTEREY Regional Airport late Friday afternoon. I could see the ocean from the air, an ominous leaden expanse to the far horizon. A cold grèy slate veiling mysteries of the deep.

Conan said I'd know him by his leather and chains. I wouldn't have known him otherwise. He hardly resembled the cousin I knew long ago. Burly and bearded, he wrapped me in a bear hug that nearly cracked my ribs.

Cousin! he said. Welcome to The Wild West!

We covered the six miles from the airport to his house in ten minutes flat, roaring in and out of traffic on his low-slung Harley Davison. Roared up narrow 18th Street lined with small wooden cottages like shoeboxes side by side, fronted by scrubby yards. Bumped up three wooden steps, across a porch, through the front door, across the living room and kitchen, through a bedroom, to a screened-in backroom littered with greasy motorcycle parts, crushed Olympia beer cans, chains and tools. Conan dismounted with a grunt. I pried myself off the narrow back seat.

Come on in, Sonny Boy, he said. Kick back. Have a cold one. Meet the old lady. The night is young.

AND SO, THE EVENING BEGAN, Adrian. If I present an abundance of detail, it is only for you to wonder, as I do, how I can recall with such clarity what may or may not have happened at all. But I'm getting ahead of myself. Let's start with Janet.

Janet was petite, a porcelain doll in faded Levi's, purple tube top, jet black hair parted in the middle, and a crimson leather headband over a sweet oval face.

Wine? she said. Of *course,* we have wine.

She took a jug of Almaden from the refrigerator and filled a mason jar. She was shapely as an hourglass. She might have been poured into her pants. Her navel was a shadowed crevice between her silver belt buckle and the bottom of her tube top. I could have fallen in.

Conan's cousin! she said. I didn't know Conan had a cousin. I didn't know he had *any* family. I thought he just fell out of the sky one day!

Her smile was playful. Conan's wasn't.

You're funny, Janet, he said. Did Santini call?

He's on his way, she said.

We sat at the kitchen table. Conan rolled a joint. We passed it back and forth.

How is it, I said.

How is what? he said.

The acid.

Couldn't say, Cousin. I haven't seen it. You'll do business with Santini. He's on his way.

How much per hit?

No idea. Relax, Cousin! You just got here. Janet, give Sonny Boy a Nembutal. He's a little uptight!

Janet brought a fistful of yellow capsules.

What do they do? I said.

Barbiturates, Conan said. They make you feel loose like a long-neck goose. Take two.

I washed down one Nembutal with my Almaden and pocketed the other.

There came the roar of a motor outside. I was introduced to Spider, spindly and tall, in a denim vest over a *Zig Zag* Rolling Papers T-shirt, braided red beard to his navel, black leather aviator's helmet, and goggles. Blue tattoos encircled one arm like a horde of demons and dragons.

Any friend of Conan's is a friend of mine! Spider said with gusto. Where you from, Sonny Boy?

St. Louis, I said...which wasn't exactly true, as you know, Adrian. I was a country boy from the hills of Missouri, but he'd probably never heard of my little hometown, and I didn't want to sound like I was from the sticks.

Obispo? Spider said.

What? I said.

San Luis Obispo?

No, Missouri.

San Luis, Missouri?

No, *St. Louis* Missouri.

Ah, St. Louie Louie! I'm out of Milwaukee myself, he said. A long time ago.

Oh, yeah. Milwaukee, I said.

You know Milwaukee?

Well, no…not exactly.

How then?

How what?

How do you know Milwaukee if not *exactly*?

I mean I know where it is.

Yeah? Like where?

Where?

Yeah, where's Milwaukee? You said you know where it is.

Well, it's in Wisconsin, I guess…

You guess?

Well, no it *is* in Wisconsin.

Goddamn right it is, Sonny Boy! You bet your sweet ass it is! Hey, I'm just fucking with you, kid. It's what I do. You want to see my hack?

Your hack?

Sonny Boy, you are one unenlightened sumbitch, you don't know what a hack is.

We went outside. A blanket of mist had settled over 18th Street. Spider showed me his *hack*, a sidecar attached to a motorcycle. Sleek and shiny black, with lots of chrome.

BMW R60 Over Two! he said. Steib S501 sidecar. Heinrich touring tank. German Engineering! Ain't she fucking beautiful?

Sure is, I said with enthusiasm, because it was. A real prize.

I traded my old lady for it, he said. Some asshole, he's balling my old lady. I tell him, Sumbitch, you want the old lady, you take the old lady and give me the hack or I'll break your fucking face! He got the old lady. I got the hack. A sweet deal!

I said nothing, Adrian. What could I say? I was out of my element.

Don't get me wrong, Spider said. When I ride with the Losers, I ride a Harley. The Losers don't dig Kraut shit. Or Jap shit.

The Losers?

C'mon, kid! Your fucking cousin is Chief of the Losers and you never heard of 'em? But I get it. Your mindset is you're a winner. You live in the world of winners. You buy into the bullshit! But you can't be a Loser if you're a winner, kid, and you can't be a winner if you're a Loser. Because winners are losers and Losers are winners. Comprende?

Well, I…

Just fucking with you, kid. It's what I do. Hop in. Let's go for a spin!

I wedged myself into the tight little sidecar. I was inches from the ground. We spun around Pacific Grove for twenty minutes. Spun like a carnival ride. Adrenaline, and the breeze off the bay, blew the fog in my head away.

BACK AT THE HOUSE, I sat on the couch alone. Conan and Spider sat at the kitchen table. Janet was in a back room. I looked at my watch. I opened a Mad Magazine. Freckle-faced Alfred E. Neuman smiled up at me and said, "What, me worry?" I leafed through a stack of comics: *Captain Pissgums and His Pervert Pirates; The Fabulous Furry Freak Brothers.*

Sonny Boy! Conan yelled. You want some of this?

I went to the table. Watched Conan take brown powder from one plastic bag, and white powder from another, mix them with water in a spoon and twirl the mix over a lighter till it darkened and dissolved. Spider sucked the mix into a glass tube with a needle on one end, and a rubber bulb on the other.

You do speedballs? he said to me.

Well…no, I…not really, I said.

Spider chuckled.

Either you do or you don't, he said.

He tapped the needle into the crook of his arm. He squeezed the bulb. He bent slowly forward till his head touched the table, then straightened suddenly.

Oh, yeah, he said. Oh, yeah…

Conan took his turn. I went back to the couch. Leafed through a *Zippy the Pinhead* comic book and sipped my Almaden. A car door slammed outside.

Santini, Conan announced.

I stood. A German Shepherd pranced through the door, surveyed the room, spotted me, and came and sniffed my crotch. I froze while he circled, sniffing.

King! came a sharp command. Down!

Santini was clean-shaven with short black hair. No leather, no chains. Six feet tall and broad-shouldered. Rippling washboard stomach under a military field jacket hanging open. Combat boots with webbing at the ankles like mosquito netting for comfort in the jungle. A folding knife in a leather sheath on his belt. A single tattoo on his bare chest: Semper Fi.

King sat on his haunches and fixed me with dark, unyielding eyes.

Conan greeted Santini with a hug.

Brother Santini! he said. Meet my cousin, Sonny Boy. Sonny Boy, meet Santini.

Santini took my hand in a strong grip. His smile was broad and genuine.

Sonny Boy, he said. I hear you've come a long way. Welcome to my world.

Janet came into the room.

Hi, Santini, she said.

She gave him a hug.

Hi, King! she said. Give me a paw.

King lifted a paw and wagged his tail. Janet took his paw and hugged his thick neck.

You big, beautiful doggie! she said.

Santini punched Spider on the arm.

Hey, dopehead, he said. Wake the fuck up!

Spider straightened and opened his drooping eyes.

Brother Santini, he mumbled. Wassup?

Pull up a chair, Conan said. Have a cold one.

Janet brought Santini a can of Olympia beer. Santini sat at the table drinking and paring a fingernail with his folding knife.

You got something for me, Sonny Boy, he said.

Two thousand dollars, I said. How much is it per hit?

Two bucks, he said.

I did some quick calculations: We could sell off eight hundred hits, double our investment, and have two hundred hits left to split among us and trip for a year.

How is it? I said.

If it wasn't good, my guys wouldn't sell it, Santini said. They're in business to stay in business.

You haven't done it?

No.

I'd like to get a sample and test it tomorrow. If I like it, I buy it.

It might not be here tomorrow. You want it, you buy it now.

I told my friends I'd test it first. It's a policy.

Whatever, Sonny Boy. Buy it tonight and test it. If you don't like it, we'll buy it back. Satisfaction guaranteed.

Alright, I said. I'm ready to go.

Go where?

To buy the acid.

You stay, I go. My people don't need to meet you.

I have to go where the money goes, I said. I promised my partners. It's a policy.

Santini sighed. The smile drained from his face.

Sonny Boy, he said, the policy is you give me the money. I buy the dope. End of deal.

He looked at Conan.

Cousin, Conan said to me, you're insulting the man—and you're insulting me! Nobody in my family is going to rip you off. Give Santini the fucking dough or hit the road!

Oh, don't be such a hard-ass, Conan, Janet said. He's just trying to be responsible for *his* people. You'd do the same.

Well, he's got to lighten up. It's just a little bitty old dope deal. We're all here to make it happen. I tell you what, kid: Santini doesn't come back, you take the old lady here.

That's not funny, Conan! Janet said.

Reluctantly, I took the envelope containing two thousand dollars from the pocket of my jacket and handed it to Santini. He slid it down the front of his pants.

I'll be back, he said.

I WASHED DOWN A SECOND NEMBUTAL with another glass of wine. Conan told me about Santini, that he did some gritty shit in Viet Nam. Lit up men, women, and children for his country. Comes home, his country makes him out a psycho. A stone-cold killer. He feels betrayed. Now they want to send him back. For what? For lying politicians and corporate fucks getting fat off the war? For candy-ass college kids carrying signs and hiding behind their books? He ain't going back, Cousin! He's found a home with the Losers. We're his family now!

I don't think he likes me, I said.

Don't sweat it, Sonny Boy. He's a righteous bro. Just ain't big on *policies.* If you're straight with him, he's straight with you.

I WAS DOZING ON THE COUCH when Santini came back. Conan was slumped in an overstuffed armchair reading *Easy Rider* magazine. Janet was in the bedroom. Spider was gone. King's cold wet nose on mine woke me with a start. Santini threw me a crumpled paper sack. Inside was a plastic bag of purple tablets.

What is it? I said. Purple Owsley? Purple Haze?

Call 'em what you want, dude.

I hefted the bag in my hand. It felt light.

There's a thousand here? I said.

Five hundred, he said.

But that's four dollars apiece!

He reached into a side pocket and pulled out a manila envelope folded in half. Inside were five sheets of paper, each stamped with images of the Laughing Buddha.

What's this? I said.

Blotter acid, he said. It's eye-dropped onto the page. Every picture is a dose. One thousand micrograms of pure lysergic acid. It'll fuck you up royally, Sonny Boy.

I counted the images. Ten across, ten down. Five pages. Plus five hundred purple tabs. A thousand hits. The numbers were right but I couldn't test both. Santini read my thoughts.

You do one, he said. I'll do the other. I'll tell you if it's good.

His smile was malicious. Conan stroked his beard. His expression said: You got what you wanted, Cousin; now deal with it. Even King's gaze was unforgiving. I saw no way out.

Now? I said.

Sure, Santini said. Why not?

I…I don't like to trip at night, I said. I like to trip outside. In the daytime.

A regular Nature Boy, huh? Santini said.

I guess…

Suit yourself, kid. Tomorrow. I know a place. An arroyo that empties into the ocean. Rocks and trees. Birds and bees. You'll dig it.

Well, I—

Get some sleep, Sonny Boy. You'll need it.

In The Arroyo

I AWOKE FULLY CLOTHED on Saturday morning on a dirty sleeping bag on the floor of the back room, my face inches from the toes of the combat boots of Santini. My dreams were lost in a fog of Nembutal and cheap wine.

Poor guy, he's hung over, Janet said.

I've got something for that, Conan said.

He mixed equal parts vodka and tomato juice in a quart jar, sprinkled it liberally with Tabasco Sauce, Worcestershire Sauce, chili powder, cayenne pepper, and crumbled marijuana leaf.

The Monterey Mary! he said.

We tossed off a tumbler each. Santini washed down a purple tab. I swallowed the Laughing Buddha.

Ciao, Conan said.

Have a nice trip, Janet said.

We left King behind.

SANTINI DROVE A PURPLE '52 PLYMOUTH, dull like it had been buffed with a brillo pad. Bird shit on the hood and fenders. Three-speed on the column. AM radio in the middle of the metal dash. We passed the last stop light out of Pacific Grove and wound our way south down the long desolate stretch of Highway One. The tops of massive redwoods pierced the blanket of mist overhead. The acid had not yet taken effect. I ventured a question.

Santini, I said, where are you from?

He hesitated. I regretted my question.

Philly, he said.

I said nothing more, but he continued.

My old man runs a union hall, he said. A big shot. Came from the bottom up. Owns a block of houses. Smokes big cigars. Brags to his buddies his kid's a Marine. Thinks I'm still in Viet Nam killing gooks. Unless the FBI's been to his house already. The motherfuckers!

They're looking for you? I said.

Yeah, he said.

He glanced in the rearview mirror.

So, you just walked away? I said.

He tapped his temple hard with two stiff fingers and spoke bitterly.

You can't…just…fucking…walk…away!

He looked at me.

What about you, Sonny Boy?

Me?

Yeah, you. Whatta you do when you're not getting loaded with pissed off AWOL Marines?

I hesitated to say, remembering his aversion to candy-ass college kids, but the truth slipped off my tongue.

I'm a student, I said. I write poetry.

Poetry, he said. Poetry.

He might as well have been spitting out rotten fruit. He looked at the road. I felt a rush from the acid, a ball of energy that ascended my spine and nestled at the base of my skull like an animal waiting to pounce. I shivered and rolled my head around to relieve the pressure. Santini glanced at me quickly.

What's wrong? he said.

Just a rush, I said. That's how my trips begin: with a rearrangement of molecules preparing me for *transcendence.*

Transcendence, he repeated flatly.

How about you? I said.

I don't feel a goddamned thing, he said.

I doubted he didn't feel a goddamned thing. He rolled his head around as I had. His eyes were glassy, his jaw knotted, his knuckles white on the steering wheel. He cast cautious glances in the rearview mirror, sideways glances at me. The vibrations of the motor and the whine of the tires on the road invaded my nervous system. Tremors erupted in the pit of my stomach. I felt claustrophobic. I rolled down the window. The damp air washed over my face like the cool fingers of an invisible spirit. I turned on the radio. Fiddled with the dial. Locked onto a local station. There came the wailing of an electric guitar and lyrics suggesting some event was occurring or was about to occur *in the white room, with black curtains, at the station.* I could make no sense of it. The DJ contended there was a hidden message for our times in those lyrics if only one had the ears to hear.

I found his judgment lacking and turned the radio off.

Dude, why'd you do that, Santini said.

Do what?

Turn the radio on, then off.

You want it back on?

You knew just when to.

When to what?

When to turn it on and when to turn it off.

Sure. When I wanted to listen, I turned it on. When I didn't, I turned it off. What's the big deal?

You turned it on just in time for him to say what he said.

What who said?

The DJ. Don't play dumb!

What did he say? Just some bullshit!

It's not what he said, Sonny Boy—it's what he *meant*!

Sorry, Santini, I said. I have no idea what you're talking about.

He stared straight ahead. We continued our journey in silence.

TO THE RIGHT THE BRUSHY GROUND sloped a hundred yards before plummeting to the rocks below. To the left rose a grassy hill adorned with stunted pines pressed sideways by the unabated wind off the sea. Ahead, a concrete bridge spanned a deep gorge.

The arroyo, Santini announced.

We crossed and parked on the right shoulder in a patch of gravel. A driveway cut through the vegetation seaward, circled a boulder and disappeared into a stand of tall trees. We walked up opposite sides of the drive a dozen yards. Nailed to a lone pine, a white sign in red letters read:

PRIVATE DRIVE: KEEP OUT

From around the boulder came a canary yellow sports car convertible with foreign plates. It passed slowly between us. The driver, a handsome young man wearing a tweed flat cap and mirrored sunglasses, looked at each of us in turn. I nodded. He nodded back. At the road, he revved his motor twice and turned right. Santini watched him go, then stared hard up the drive.

We descended a rocky trail. Santini slipped into a thicket and disappeared. I wandered the floor of the arroyo alone. The wind up the channel stirred the carpet of brush underfoot and the canopy of trees overhead. The impressions of one sense manifested in another. The tapping of hollow reeds, the scraping of brittle leaves, the moan of the wind, all fused to fill the air with a complex symphony of sound I *saw* as a pattern of lights blinking in and out of existence with a message beyond my comprehension. I *heard* the eerie radiance of the luminescent cloud cover above as a drone from the dawn of time. The earth was alive with an intelligence not my own.

The sun broke through the clouds. I followed the dry creek bed which cleaved the arroyo and came to a strip of sand bordering the sea. The beach stretched fifty yards, with cliffs like bookends north and south. Atop the southern cliff, a house of weathered wood and glass rose two stories to a peak that curved outward like the bow of a ship. The inland side of the house was sheltered by a stand of tall trees: doubtless the house at the end of the drive.

I sat on a piece of driftwood as smooth and white as the hip bone of a dinosaur. Overhead, a flock of seagulls dipped and soared with a grace and harmony that left no doubt they shared a common soul. I gazed out over the ocean where, in the middle distance, leaden waves slapped angrily against black rocks that glistened in the sun and were shattered into droplets that hovered for an instant like autonomous beings before plummeting back to their source. I closed my eyes and merged my spirit with the five-billion-year-old rhythm of the surf. Cradled in the bosom of eternity, I lost all sense of self. Indeed, I might have sat there forever but for the sudden and disturbing sensation I was not alone. I opened my eyes and looked to my left. From the cluster of shadowed rocks at the base of the cliff, a fragment broke away: Santini! He crossed the beach and entered a stand of trees. I followed.

I came upon him in a clearing in the brush. He sat on the ground gouging a hole in the dirt with his knife while gazing through a gap in the branches of trees overhead.

Have you seen her? he said without turning.

Who? I said.

He pointed with his knife to the house on the cliff. A woman leaned out from the balcony like the figurehead on the prow of a ship. Her long hair streamed behind her. A gown of gauzy material whipped her thighs.

She's waving, he said.

I stared hard. She did seem to be waving, but in my present state, *everything* was waving: the bushes, the rocks, the trees, the clouds.

She might be waving at a passing ship, I said. Or a seal on a rock.

She's waving at us.

I doubt that, Santini, I said. What would she want with us?

He whirled to face me. His features were a crazy jumble: a cubist portrait of a deranged man.

I think she wants us to fuck her! he said.

Oh, man, I really don't think—

So, let's go!

We can't do that, Santini. It…it wouldn't go well.

He wagged a finger at me. Narrowed his eyes.

I see what's happening now, he said. You *know* her, don't you?

What!?

And you know *him.*

Who?

The faggot in the car, you fuck!

He rubbed his chin. His eyes darted left and right.

Yes, he said. I see it now: you're one of *them*.

He resumed his attack on the dirt. Chop! Chop! Slash!

I resorted to reason.

Santini, I said, does that make sense? *You* brought me here. How can I know anybody?

But Santini wasn't interested in reason. He wiped the knife blade on his trousers. Fixed me with his wild eyes.

I guess it's just you and me, Sonny Boy.

His voice was a moaning foghorn, slow and deep. The air was sucked from my lungs. I dropped to my knees and put a hand on my chest. The chatter in the brush became a horrendous racket. My thudding heartbeat echoed alternately from opposite cliffs. I spoke with great effort.

Santini, I said, this isn't real. It seems real because we're down here in a weird place. That's it! We left the main road and things got weird. When we get back to the car everything will be normal again and this will seem like a dream.

It's real, Sonny Boy, he said. Very fucking real.

I struggled to my feet. I weighed a thousand pounds. I picked my way through the brush till I found the trail out of the arroyo. I stumbled and fell. Rose and fell again. Crawled on my hands and knees. Santini remained behind me at a constant distance, connected by a red thread. I reached the rim. The trail widened into the gravel parking lot. I felt giddy with relief. Lurched to the waiting car. Patted the hood.

Safe! I declared, as though we'd been playing hide-and-seek and I was home free. But Santini wasn't playing. He clamped my throat in an iron grip, bent me backward over the hood, put the tip of the knife under my jaw. His face pulsed with a poisonous green light. The space around him faded to black. I felt the burn as my bladder emptied.

Who sent you, asshole? he said.

Nobody sent me, Santini. It's just me and my friends, wanting to score some acid. I swear!

Who was the dude on the radio?

Just the disc jockey. I don't know him.

What was his *message*?

Message? No message. Just some crazy shit.

Who was the pretty boy in the car?

I've never seen him before.

You nodded, he said.

Just being polite, I said.

Why did he rev his motor twice?

I don't know, I said. He just did.

Who's the girl in the house?

We've never met.

She was waving at you! Telling you it was time!

Time for what?

For what you have planned. You and your *friends.*

I have no plans, Santini. Honest. Except to take my dope and go home. Then everything will be alright. You'll see.

How about the billboards?

The billboards?

And the satellites.

The satellites?

And the telephones! And the televisions! And the wires in the wall! Fuck'em all! I'm not buying their shit anymore. I'm not singing their jingles or fighting their wars. That day is over, Sonny Boy! From now on it's *them* I kill—starting with *you*, pussy-ass poet!

His expression was a mask of rage and grief. He was injured to the pit of his soul. I felt his pain, and suddenly his point of view became mine: of *course*, there was a conspiracy. A concerted effort to manipulate his mind, to bend his will. And I was complicit, a co-conspirator, perpetrating the lies of the nefarious grand design behind what it means to be human, with no regard for the well-being of my fellow man as long as I was a winner. I was filled with compassion for all of humanity, and with remorse for having subjected Santini to my deceitful schemes. The injury done him was an injury to all, and justice would be served if I were to die now at his hands.

I touched his face.

Oh! Brother Santini! I said. I am so damn sorry! I love you, man, I really do!

In that instant, I saw through his eyes. Saw my own face, suffused with remorse and regret. I saw his hand loosen its grip around my throat, and the hand holding the knife fall away. In the next instant, I saw *his* face again. Saw the violent green aura subside. Saw the blackness around him fade and a soft light come into his eyes.

Oh, man, he said gently. That's beautiful. I love you, too.

In a flash, I realized I was not going to die. My throat would not be slit like that of a sacrificial lamb. I would remain in the world a winner and live to perpetuate my lies without restraint. My sigh of relief was audible. If only I could have taken back that sigh! His eyes narrowed. His lips quivered.

Oh, you lying motherfucker! he said.

His balled fist spanned the space between us and exploded against my temple like the creation of a new sun. I crumpled to the ground. He took a hopping step toward me, his boot raised. I scuttled backward like a crab and scrunched beneath the bumper of the car. He lowered his boot.

Fuck it, he said wearily. You're not worth it.

He walked up the drive. Ripped off his military fatigue jacket and threw it into the bushes. Broke into a trot. Crouched stealthily at the boulder, peered left and right, and disappeared around it.

Santini, I said weakly. What are you going to do?

But I didn't want to know. I freed myself from beneath the car and ran across the bridge. Below, the gorge was gathered in moody darkness. On the far horizon, the setting sun was a crimson ball staining a mountain of clouds.

I hitched a ride to Pacific Grove.

18th Street? the driver said. Everybody knows 18th Street!

The house was dark but for a dim light in the kitchen. On the table were a handful of Nembutal and a note:

> Hello, boys! Went to Seaside. Home late. Have some of these.
> They'll take the edge off. There's pizza and beer in the fridge
> if you're hungry. Janet.

I pocketed half the Nembutal, grabbed my bag and my hollow book, walked to a convenience store where I bought a bottle of B&B, and called a cab from a payphone. I went to a motel near the airport, booked a room and a flight out the next day. Called the front desk for a wake-up. Called my girlfriend, Angelina, for a pick-up in St. Louis but go no answer. Called friends and got no answer. I washed down two Nembutal with B&B and sat on the bed nursing the bottle until I fell asleep with my clothes on.

The next day, Sunday, on a change of planes in Denver, I sat at an airport bar. To my left was a window over the tarmac. Behind the bar a television. A local program was interrupted for Breaking News: In an isolated house on the coast south of Monterey, California, the young wife of a popular radio personality was brutally murdered. There were pictures of the house on the cliff and the long driveway leading to it. The distraught husband was interviewed. Two suspicious characters had loitered at the foot of his driveway. They drove a purple car. He sobbed without restraint. *I should have gone back!* he said. *I should have gone back!* There were pictures of the bedroom where the young woman's body was found. Of bloodied handprints on the wall, and the motto *Semper Fi* written in blood on the bathroom mirror. Authorities asked the public for information that might help them identify the killers.

AFTER A LONG AND EXPENSIVE CAB RIDE from the St. Louis Airport, I arrived at my apartment in Columbia that evening. The interior was bathed in eerie blue light and might have existed in another dimension entirely. There was the half-empty bottle of Robert Mondavi Pinot Noir on the desk, and the scraps of pages from my hollowed-out book. I put my bag on the floor, finished the bottle, and lay on the bed with my clothes on. Mentally, emotionally and spiritually drained, I was soon oblivious to the world.

I was awakened by the clanging of the telephone. The sun burned bright through my window. I listened without comprehension for half a dozen rings.

Hello? I said.

Paul! Angelina said. Are you ready?

Ready for what?

To go, lover boy! What do you think?

Go where?

To the airport, dummy!

I'm back. I've already been.

Been where?

To California.

Oh, God, are you alright, Paul?

I'm fine, I said. I have the acid.

Paul, you're scaring me. I'm picking you up this morning, remember?

What day is it?

Friday.

No, it's Monday.

Jesus, Paul, I'll be right over.

No, don't come. I'm not going. I've already been. I'll call you later. Goodbye.

I opened my bag. Opened the hollowed-out *Journey to the End of Night*: inside were the two rubber-banded envelopes of money—and no LSD.

I called Conan. His voice on the phone was gruff.

Paul who? he said.

Hastings, I said. Your cousin. Sonny Boy. Back in Missouri.

Sonny Boy! he said. Well, fuck a duck, man! I remember you! A weird little dude. Always reading and rhyming words. What can I do for you, Cousin?

Didn't we just do an acid deal?

What?

You and me and Santini?

Who the hell is Santini?

The AWOL Marine. We tripped together in the Arroyo. Two days ago.

Is this some kind of joke, Cousin? Because if it is—

Do you have an old lady named Janet? I said.

I have a wife named Paula, he said—not that it's any of your fucking business!

Aren't you Chief of the Losers?

Who are you calling a loser, asshole? Say...how'd you get my number, anyway?

Your mother gave it to me.

The joke is over, Sonny Boy! My mother's been dead for two years. Call me again and I will come through the line and break your fucking face!

TWO DAYS LATER I BOUGHT A COPY of the St. Louis Post Dispatch. I found the story on page four. It was virtually identical to the version told by the television reporter in the bar at the Denver airport: yesterday, Saturday, in an isolated house on the coast south of Monterey, the young wife of a popular radio personality was brutally murdered. There were pictures of the house on the cliff and the long driveway leading to it. The distraught husband was interviewed. Two suspicious characters had loitered at the foot of his driveway, he said. They drove a purple car. He sobbed without restraint. *I should have gone back!* he said. *I should have gone back!* There were pictures of the bedroom where the young woman's body was found. Of bloodied handprints on the wall, and the Marines' motto *Semper Fi* written in blood on the bathroom mirror. Authorities asked the public for information that might help them identify the killers.

THE FACTS WERE IRREFUTABLE: I had never left my bed. And yet the girl was dead. How I got Conrad's number remains a mystery. I returned the money and shunned my friends. I never did acid again. Angelina left me. Ran away with her philosophy of art professor. I dropped out of school. Rented a secluded cottage in the woods a few miles from town. There was a porch. And on the porch a swing. And beyond the porch a pond. And around the pond, in the rushes, croaked a chorus of bullfrogs. When the sun went down, heat lightning silent as prayer slid across the darkening sky. Swallows soared and dipped in the damp air, feasting on fireflies. Forgive my flowery description, Adrian, but the atmosphere was truly mystical, the solitude balm to my troubled soul. Here I wrote *Howls of Execration: Poems of Remorse and Regret*. It was well received but did not have the intended effect of expiating my guilt. I never wrote again.

There followed fifty years of wandering the land, carrying the weight of my cowardice like a cross. Along the way, I became a potter. I like my art to be something I can hold in my hand these days, hefty and unambiguous, unlike poetry with its innuendos and obscurities. At length, I arrived in Jacksonville. I felt in the company of others whose lives have been impacted by unlikely and inexplicable events. Seekers and dreamers, and perhaps conflicted souls like me. I opened my studio and…well, the rest is history, Adrian. Here I am. What do you think?

What do I think? Give me an easy question! I could not in a million years pretend to unravel the complexity of your experience, Paul. Were you really there? Could you have saved the girl? Was your flight an act of cowardice? Hell if I know. You'll get no howl of execration from me. I'll leave it to my readers to decide. So, tell me: do you feel better now that you've shared your fifty-year burden of guilt?

Paul thought a moment. Laughed softly to himself. Shook his head.

Not in the least, he said, but thanks for listening.

Thanks for sharing, Paul. See you around.

Yeah, see you around, Adrian. Good luck with your book.

Thanks, Paul, I said. You'll be in it for sure.

AUGUST

BORN AGAIN

All that we see or seem,
is but a dream within a dream.

– Edgar Allan Poe

Thursday, August 2nd, 2019

I SPENT THE LAST HALF OF JULY fine tuning *Howls of Execration* while awaiting inspiration for the next installment of *My Year at the Good Bean Café*. Yesterday, the first day of August, I got a crazy notion to walk among the dearly departed in our local cemetery where a story lies beneath every tombstone. Perhaps I would resurrect one.

I strolled the narrow paths between plots with my hands in my pockets and the morning sun warming my face. The *Silent City on the Hill* wasn't so quiet today. A murmur suffused upward through the soil as though its residents sensed my presence and clamored to have their story told. Everyone wants their story told, Sam, especially when it's over.

I came across a row of headstones in a plot enclosed by a low wall of moss-covered concrete. The headstone on the left read:

Florence Cooper
Quilter. Loving sister. Precious Auntie.
Born February 1st 1925
Died March 6th 2005

The headstone in the middle read:

Hattie Cooper Bledsoe
Quilter. Loving sister. Mother
Born August 1st 1930
Died August 1st 2017

The headstone on the right read:

Ordell Bledsoe
Loving Son
Born August 1st 1949
Died August 1st 2017

TODAY I SIT IN THE GOOD BEAN CAFÉ speculating on this curious combination of names and dates. It is a family plot, I surmise, remnants of the Cooper Clan. Other members are elsewhere, living or dead, strewn hither and yon over the landscape and the intervening years. Florence, the older sister of Hattie, never married. She died first. Hattie married a Bledsoe and had a son, Ordell, when she was nineteen. She outlived Florence by twelve years. Now come the anomalies: Hattie and son, Ordell, were born on the same day, August 1st, nineteen years apart. They died on the same day, their birthday, August 1st, 2017. She was eighty-seven. He was sixty-eight. I came upon their gravestones on their shared birthday, yesterday, August 1st. How unlikely is that?

I have questions the answers to which might coalesce into my August story, and what better way to get answers than to interview someone who has them. I pull up a new Word document and type across the top:

INTERVIEW OF HATTIE COOPER BLEDSOE
August 2nd, 2019

I close my eyes and summon her image. She materializes on the bright screen of my inner vision: frail and stooped in a pale pink short sleeved cotton dress with a dainty lace collar; the flesh of her arms drooping and mottled; her hair bedraggled and white like dirty snow; crows' feet and the deep crevices that parenthesize her mouth tell me she has spent her years enduring the demands of life.

I open my eyes. There she is, just as I had imagined her, sitting in the chair opposite mine. She looks quickly around the room, then at me with a frown.

Who are *you*? she says.

Her tone is at once challenging and apprehensive.

Adrian, I say. Adrian Lomachenko.

Where am I, Adrian Loma…Loma…?

Chenko.

Chenko! Where in hell's tarnation is Chenko?

No, Loma*chenko* is my name. You're at the Good Bean Café in Jacksonville, Oregon.

She looks around the room again.

Ah, the Good Bean Café, she says. I remember it well. I used to come here with my boy and drink coffee and he'd drink hot cocoa and we'd share a berry scone and watch the town folk come and go. Or we'd take our coffee and cocoa and berry scone home and sit out back and praise the Lord for the blue skies of the Rogue River Valley. And then somethin happened, Adrian. Yes, I went to sleep and didn't wake up. Well, I woke up, but in some place entirely someplace else. In a lonesome valley with no one else around. And ever day a fog arisin off the valley floor and the light a spooky blue. I walk alone these days in that lonesome valley, Adrian. Up and down. Up and down. I never stop walkin but never get tuckered out, neither. It's like I ain't got no bones for gravity to bear down upon. Now here I am, back at the Good Bean Café feelin light and airy like a summer breeze, and sittin across from you.

She looks around the room at the patrons at their tables eating and drinking and talking, and those queuing up for coffee and pastries and breakfast bowls and burritos. She looks back at me. Leans forward and speaks quietly.

Can they see me, Adrian? she says.

No, Hattie, I say. Only I can see you.

They must think you're talkin to yourself.

Nothing they haven't seen before, Hattie.

She sits back in her chair.

Why *am* I here, Adrian?

I brought you here, Hattie. I'm writing a book and I'm hoping you'll help me out.

Hattie shakes her head.

I don't write books, young man, she says. I can write my name. I can write a durn good grocery list. Even wrote a few letters back in my day. But nary a book. No sir!

You don't have to write, Hattie. I'm the writer. I'm writing a story and I want to put you in it.

You want to put me in a book? I'm dead, young man! Do you not realize I am dead?

Doesn't matter, Hattie. If people read about you in a book, in their imagination you'll come alive. Resurrected again and again across the boundaries of time and space.

Don't know that I care to be resurrected across any such boundaries, Adrian. I'm just a waitin to be let loose of the limbo the Lord assigned me to for all my years of bein a prostitute. But you seem to be a nice boy. I'm happy to help. What can I do for you?

You can tell me when and where you were born, Hattie, and who your people were, and how you came to be in Jacksonville, Oregon.

You better be writin a big book, sonny boy! I was alive a day short of eighty-seven years!

You just tell me your story, Hattie, and I'll whittle it down to size. Do you mind if I type while you talk?

Suit yourself, young man. Got to get it down somehow.

While Hattie tells her story, I listen and type.

I WAS BORN IN THE LITTLE TOWN of Guymon, in the panhandle of Oklahoma, in 1930. We were the Coopers. My sister Florence was born five years before me. I suppose we was doin alright, we had a little farm, some chickens and pigs and whatnot, but the depression come along, and then the drought, and there was more dust than money. So, in 1932 we strapped what we could onto our old jalopy and headed west with a steady stream of Okies as poor as we was. Look out, California, here come the Coopers!

Only we didn't make it to California, Adrian. Passin through Albuquerque, New Mexico, we heard tell there was jobs in the copper mines down to Bisbee, Arizona, so we headed south. Pa got on at the Phelps Dodge Copper Queen Mine and the Coopers set up house in a tumble-down shack with a saggin porch alongside a creek that was sometimes dry as a bone, and sometimes a rushin river.

Was there a rocking chair on the porch, Hattie?

Matter of fact, there was, Adrian. Pa loved that chair. After a hard day down to the mines, and a hot meal, that's where you'd find him, a rockin and watchin the sun go down.

My sister Florence was my best friend, the smart one of us, always makin somethin with her hands. We were together like two peas in a pod till one day she up and left. Said the world was bigger than Bisbee and she had to go see it. Her leavin tugged at my heart. That would have been 1945. She was twenty. I was fifteen. Two years later I was pregnant with my first boy, Hiram, by a man a dozen years older than me, Cole Bledsoe. He was closer to my daddy's age than to mine. My daddy loved him like the son he never had, and they spent many a night till the wee hours drinkin and playin the fool before they were off to the mines for a day's labor. Cole, he was a hard workin, hard lovin, hard drinkin son of a bitch that I grew to hate but I had another baby by him anyways. Ordell. Born August 1st, same as me.

Ordell was *special*. You could tell right off. He learned real slow and his head was always in the clouds. He would laugh for no reason. At nothin at all. He would look at a bird flutterin in the treetops and laugh like there was no tomorrow.

Hiram loved his little brother. He would take him by the hand ever where he went. They grew up in that desert like wild Indians, learnin the habits of local critters: bobcats, coyotes, scorpions, rattlesnakes, and Gila monsters. They hunted for arrowheads in dry creek beds and knocked the limbs off cactuses with stones flung from homemade slingshots. It was how boys ought to grow up.

But they grew up without a Pa. A year after Ordell was born, my Pa, Caleb, and their Pa, Cole, was killed in a mine explosion. Ma took it real hard. She'd always been sickly with one ailment or another, now she wasn't worth a damn, and me with four mouths to feed and no one else to feed'em! I ain't ashamed to say, Adrian, I became Bisbee's finest hooker. Worked out of the Copper Queen Hotel and put food on the table for seven years until the godawfullest thing happened: the creek swole up, Ordell slipped off a rock, Hiram went in after him and never come out. Ordell washed up a hundred yards downstream, gaspin but alive and minus a big brother. He didn't laugh much after that. A year later, 1958, Ma died, and Ordell and me lit out for Oregon to live with Florence. She had a nice two-bedroom cottage here in Jacksonville, with a studio out back where she stitched up quilts for a livin. She taught me the trade. We put our quilts in a shop in town, and one in Ashland, and we made a durn good livin for two old spinsters from Oklahoma!

And Ordell continued to live with you?

Ever day of his life till the last, Adrian. Bein special, he couldn't take care of himself. He lived in his own world, with its own rules. He had peculiar habits. Everthin had to be perfect and the same all the time or he'd have a conniption fit. He wouldn't let his peas touch his carrots. He separated his food into little piles in a circle on his plate and always et 'em in a certain order, first a bite of this, then a bite of that, till he'd gone all the way around, then he'd do the circle backwards. Before he'd cross a street, he'd look down at his feet like he was decidin which one to step off the curb with first. He'd take three steps, then turn around and go back. Sometimes it took him an hour to cross the street. Sometimes he'd stop on the sidewalk and just stare up at the sky like he was awaitin for someone to come git'm.

He was mighty fond of the cemetery. We'd walk together up that hill, him a holdin onto my arm, me a leanin onto a cane in my later years. We must have been quite a sight. We'd sit on a bench by the family plot where Florence was delivered unto the Lord in 2005. I could feel she was awaitin for us. Ordell would look around at the birds a flittin in the trees and the clouds sailin by overhead and ask me the most exasperatin questions. Momma, he'd say, where do you go when you die?

Wherever the Lord decides, Ordell, I'd tell him.

Do you come back, Momma?

Don't expect so, Ordell. Not that you'd ever want to. Once around the mulberry bush ought to be good enough for anyone. It's been good enough for me.

You might want to come back to see if you're still here, Momma, he'd say.

Son, that don't make a lick a sense! I'd tell him, but what made sense to him and what made sense to someone else weren't usually the same.

He'd ask me the same fool questions over and over like he couldn't keep the answers in his head. But he wasn't no dummy, Adrian. He could spell better'n me 'fore he was ten. Spent hours doin grown-up crossword puzzles. But he didn't fit in with other kids. Didn't care a peep what they was sayin or doin. Didn't listen to the teacher so he couldn't go to school. I took him to a doctor and the doctor said he had a case of *Ass Burger Disease.* Said he needed special schoolin but there weren't no special schools in the valley in those days so I homeschooled him best I could. And for the whole of his life, he didn't talk to no one but me and Florence and Paul the Potter next door. Paul was a good old boy out of Missouri who come to town in 1999 and set up a studio out back of his cottage. Like Ordell, he mostly lived in his own world. Ordell would sit and watch him spin his pots for hours on end with neither of 'em sayin a word.

I know Paul the Potter, Hattie. I drop by his studio from time to time to admire his work.

How is the old boy, Adrian?

Getting by, Hattie. Still spinning those pots. And no doubt missing you and Florence and Ordell. You do know Ordell is no longer with us, don't you?

I do, Adrian. He visited me in my lonesome valley the day he died. We walked together for the very last time. We'd celebrated ever birthday of his life together 'cept his last, now here he was come to see me. *Happy birthday, Momma,* he said. *Thank you for watchin over me.* Then he went off to wherever it is special people go. Speakin of which, Adrian, I got to go my own self. I'm feeling a powerful pull back to the valley. Guess I been noticed missin. Good luck with your book and thanks for puttin me in it.

You're welcome, Hattie. You've given me the background I need to make up a story. I'll try to make it a fun one. Thanks for taking the time.

Time means nothin to me, Adrian. I'm past all that.

So long, Hattie, I said.

So long, Adrian, she said.

And with that, she dispersed like a wind-blown fog. I typed across the top of the page:

BORN AGAIN

SIXTY-SEVEN-YEAR-OLD ORDELL BLEDSOE woke up smelling horse-shit on his boots. Except he wasn't wearing boots. He sat on the edge of his bed and looked at his feet. Looked at the fuzzy slippers next to his feet. He put his right foot into the right slipper and paused to consider. He removed his right foot from the right slipper and put his left foot in the left slipper. He thought a moment, then removed his left foot from the left slipper and looked at the pair of slippers side by side. He raised both feet, slid them into their respective slippers simultaneously, and stood up slowly, pushing off on his knees. He shuffled to his momma's bedroom door. He peeked inside.

Good morning, Momma, he whispered.

Eighty-seven-year-old Hattie Bledsoe stirred. She was frail as a bird, just barely a bump beneath her well-worn quilt.

Good morning, Ordell, she wheezed.

You want to go to Good Bean for coffee and cocoa, Momma?

I'll have my coffee at home today, Honey. Be a good boy and make Momma some coffee and bring me a cup.

Ordell shuffled back to the kitchen and made a pot of coffee and brought his momma a cup. He sat on the edge of her bed.

I had that dream again, Momma, he said.

The one with the horses and cows?

Yes, Momma, and I fixed a fence and I cut my hand.

Ordell looked at his hand. He turned it over but saw no cut.

Momma, he said, where do dreams go when you wake up.

Don't go nowhere, Ordell, Hattie said. Them ol' dreams are only in your head.

Ordell considered.

Momma, where *is* my head?

Where is your head? Your head is on your shoulders, Ordell!

But the *inside* of my head, Momma. Where's the *inside* of my head?

The inside of your head is inside of your head, Ordell! Where do you think it is?

Ordell put a hand on the top of his head.

Momma, he said, is today my birthday?

No, Ordell, today is not your birthday.

Is tomorrow my birthday?

No, Ordell, tomorrow is not your birthday. The day *after* tomorrow is your birthday.

How long till the day after tomorrow, Momma?

The rest of today, all of tomorrow, then you sleep, Ordell, and when you wake up, it's your birthday.

How many birthdays have I had, Momma?

Sixty-seven, Ordell.

Will my next birthday be number sixty-eight, Momma?

Yes, Ordell, your next birthday will be number sixty-eight.

How many birthdays can a person have, Momma?

As many as the Lord allows, Ordell.

How many does the Lord allow?

I don't know the Lord's will, Honey. You'll know when you've had 'em all.

I want to have 'em and have 'em and keep on havin 'em till the end of time!

If wishes were horses, Ordell. It just don't work that way.

Are we having a party, Momma?

Of course, Honey. We always have a party.

Will there be a cake?

Yes, there will most certainly be a cake.

With candles?

Yes, with candles.

How many candles?

Sixty-eight, Ordell. One for each year of your life.

Will I blow out the candles?

Of course, you will, Honey. You always blow out the candles.

Do I get a wish?

Yes, Ordell, you always get a wish.

If I blow out all the candles, Momma, will my wish come true?

That's what folks say, Ordell. I suppose if your wish is a righteous one.

Ordell smiled.

Momma, he said, if I wish that I have another birthday, and I blow out all the candles, and my wish comes true, I will have another birthday, and I will make the same wish again, and I won't ever stop havin birthdays!

That makes sense, Ordell, except there aren't that many candles in the world, nor as many years left on God's earth.

Ordell pulled at his ear and thought about how many years were left on God's earth.

Momma, he said, where do the years go when there aren't no more?

Hattie sighed.

Ordell, she said, you ask the durndest questions!

I'm sorry, Momma.

It's alright, Honey. Momma loves you.

Momma, Ordell said, will Paul be at my party?

Yes, Paul will be there.

Will Auntie Florence be there?

She'll be lookin down upon us.

Momma, can we go to the cemetery today?

I'm feelin poorly today, Ordell. I'm going to stay in bed and rest my tired bones.

I'll hold onto your arm, Momma. And I'll walk real slow.

Hattie sighed.

Give me a minute, Ordell, she said.

THE TREK TO THE *SILENT CITY ON THE HILL* had been wearisome for Hattie Bledsoe. Crossing streets was a challenge, what with Ordell's stutter-stepping and the cars coming and going and the hill so steep out of town. They sat side by side on the wooden bench that fronted their family plot where only the name of Florence Bledsoe, sister of Hattie and Auntie of Ordell, was to be found on a headstone. Ordell Bledsoe imagined two others side by side, his name on one, his Momma's on the other.

Momma, he said, do all babies and their mommas have the same birthday?

No, Ordell, Hattie said. It's a rare thing but it does happen.

Momma, tell me again where and when I was born and why you named me Ordell.

Ordell knew the answers to these questions, but he never tired of asking and Hattie never tired of answering because there remained a mystery about that time and place that lingered on.

You were born in Bisbee, Arizona, Ordell, on August 1st, 1949, in the Copper Queen Community Hospital. I named you Ordell because I was mad at your Pa who showed up to the delivery room drunk as a skunk and I wasn't going to name you Cole Junior after that son of a bitch, no sir!

And then the old man came, right, Momma?

That's right, Ordell, the old man came. He told the nurse his name was Ordell and he was family. About the time you come into this world, the old man left it, just curled up on a bench in the waitin room and went to sleep and didn't wake up. We never did find out who he was. There weren't none of the Coopers or the Bledsoes named Ordell, but I felt somethin special about the old man dyin while waitin on me to have you, so I took his name and give it to you. Come to find out Ordell means *born again*.

THE WALK DOWN THE HILL wasn't much easier than the walk up and Hattie got home plum tuckered out. She took to bed and Ordell went next door and watched his friend and neighbor Paul the Potter spin clay on a spinnin wheel. Watched the wheel go round and round. Watched Paul the Potter splash water on the mound of clay in the middle of the wheel and him takin hold of it and squeezin just so, and the mound of it risin up like a livin thing just a hankerin to be heard. That night in bed he wondered if there wasn't life in the very dirt he walked on. In the room next to his, Hattie Bledsoe wondered what would become of Ordell when she died. It's in the Lord's hands, she assured herself before slipping into a deep sleep.

Coldwater Creek, Oklahoma, 1885

IN THE YEAR OF THE LORD, 1885, James Kerrick Hitch pastured a herd of Hereford cattle on Coldwater Creek, a tributary of the Beaver River, in Texas County, in the panhandle of Oklahoma. By 1900 the Hitch Ranch ran ten thousand head on fifty thousand acres. In 1901, Hitch hired on the Combs brothers, Grayson, age twenty-two, and his brother Chester, aged twenty, recently bereft of their ma and pa, Owen and Cora Combs, whose wagon pitched over a cliff into a swollen Coldwater Creek after a driving rain.

In 1901, Chester, the younger Combs brother, awoke on his bunk in the bunkhouse chasing after a dream as elusive as a coyote slippin away after raidin the hen house. He sat up and scratched his head.

Grayson, he said to his brother in the bunk alongside his, I had a dream Ma was alive.

Grayson stirred but said nothing.

There was three gravestones, Chester said, one with a name on it, two without. There were machines like little houses on wheels goin up and down the street. So many you couldn't hardly walk, and there was a man spinnin pots on a pottery wheel. I don't remember what else.

Grayson shrugged off his covers and sat up. He was broad-shouldered, with black hair past his ears and a clean-shaven chin beneath a drooping handlebar moustache, his chin lookin like a hard-boiled egg in a bird's nest.

Chester, he said, Ma's dead and buried in the dirt next to Pa and dreams won't bring her back nor get the work done. Mr. Hitch is expectin a quarter mile of barbed wire fence to be strung today and that's a whole hell of a lot of posts to be dug and wire to be strung, so I suggest you git your boots on and git you some bacon and grits and git your butt out to the pasture and don't let them dreams follow you out there where they don't belong!

Chester held one hand in the palm of the other and considered the damage done to the meat of it by the barb of a barbed wire the day before.

Grayson, he said, do you ever think we don't have to be here doin what we're doin?

Chester, Grayson said, if you was someplace else you'd be dreamin about being here.

I'm just sayin, Grayson, we could be somewhere else doing somethin entirely different.

Such as what, Chester?

Such as we could go to California, Grayson. I'm feelin a powerful pull in that direction.

Chester, why in hell's tarnation would we go to California?

To git us some gold, Grayson.

Grayson sighed mightily.

Chester, he said, that there gold is long gone. Nothin left in them fields but the poppies growed up over the graves of fools chasin dreams. Besides which you seem to be forgittin our promise to Pa to have our own ranch one day with our name on it and the only way to git it is to work and save—so put your boots on, Chester, and let's git us some grits! Mr. Hitch don't pay a hired hand for wantin to be somewhere else!

CHESTER COMBS SPENT three-quarters of the day digging posts and hanging barbed wire and the last quarter feeding livestock and cleaning troughs and pens. He had supper in the bunkhouse with neither him nor the other hands speaking and was bone weary when he sunk down into his bunk and contemplated the day behind him and the days to come. He wondered why folks in one place and time have one kinda life, and folks in another place and time have a different kinda life. He looked at it ever which way but couldn't figure it and fell into a deep sleep without an answer like a man falling into a hole in the ground that had no bottom.

Jacksonville, Oregon, 2017

ORDELL BLEDSOE AWOKE on the morning of July 31st, 2017, the day before his sixty-eighth birthday, feeling a throb in the palm of his hand. He cradled it in the palm of his other hand and shuffled to his Momma's room and opened the door and whispered: Momma, do you want to walk down to the Good Bean?

Ordell, I'm feelin poorly, she said. I'm a gonna spend the day in bed. Be a good son and fetch Momma a cup of coffee and a berry scone and git you whatever you want.

Ordell walked alone to the Good Bean Café and bought a cup of coffee and a berry scone for his momma, and a lemon bar and cocoa for himself, careful to not look anyone in the eye. He brought the coffee and scone to his momma on a tray.

Thank you kindly, Ordell, she said. You're a good son.

Momma, he said, I had a dream I had a brother still livin, only he had a different name.

What name was that, Ordell?

I don't rightly remember, Momma. I only remember he looked after me real good.

Like a good brother ought, Hattie said.

Momma, is today my birthday?

No, Ordell, tomorrow is your birthday…and yes, we will have a party and there will be a cake with candles and you can make a wish and blow out the candles and Paul the Potter is comin. Ordell, will you kindly close the door behind you. I'm feelin a draft.

Ordell closed the door on his momma and took his cocoa and lemon bar to the porch out back. He watched the squirrels chase one another round and round the tree trunks and the blue jays a flutterin in the branches overhead. He went next door to visit Paul the Potter, but Paul the Potter was someplace else. He felt all alone and like it was going to be a long day. He walked across town and up the hill to the cemetery and sat on the bench before the family plot. There was more squirrels and blue jays and folks a walkin their dogs, and he wondered if the critters in one time and place knew about or cared about the critters in another time and place. He wondered why it took so long for a day to go by and for it to be his birthday. He walked back to home and spent the long day doin nothin much until the sun went down and his stomach yearned for supper and his momma hadn't stirred. He went to her door and knocked softly and whispered,

Momma, and got no answer. He opened her door and pondered the tiny heap of her beneath her well-worn quilt and her not movin. He shuffled across the floor and said, Momma, and she said nothin back. He pulled the quilt away from her face and noted the pasty blue of it, and her eyes half open and cloudy, and her lips a parted like the beak of a baby bird. He crawled into bed with his Momma and held the cold flesh of her arm and cried himself to sleep.

Guymon, Oklahoma, 1920

BY DINT OF THEIR LABOR AND FRUGALITY, Grayson and Chester Combs bought five hundred and one acres of prime pastureland and half a dozen buildings southwest of Guymon, Oklahoma, in 1920. They called their ranch the Owen Combs 501 Ranch, known thereabouts as the 501. They dug up the bones of their ma and pa and buried them anew in the dirt of the 501.

They hired on several hands and the 501 was paying for itself and then some when the drought descended in the summer of 1930 and the American Great Plains became the Great American Dustbowl. Henry Hitch, son of James Hitch and heir to the mighty Hitch Ranch, intent upon expansion, offered to buy the 501 for half what the Combs brothers paid but they declined. They survived both drought and recession and kept the 501 on the black side of the ledger until, in September of 1949, Grayson Combs, age 69, fell over and died.

Chester buried Grayson alongside their ma and pa in the dirt of the 501. He spent a long time lookin at those three headstones side by side. Decided there would never be one with his name on it. He called on Henry Hitch and sold five hundred of the five hundred and one acres of the Combs Ranch for three times what they'd paid for it. He kept ownership of the acre beneath which were the bones of his ma and his pa and his brother, Grayson. He gave each of his hands a year's wages and thanked them kindly for their hard work and loyalty. The night before the day when the 501 would become an adjunct to the Hitch domain, Chester packed what he felt was essential into his '42 Dodge pickup. He would go west. He wasn't sure where to exactly, but he felt a powerful pull. That night he fell into a deep sleep and revisited a dream he'd had a series of long ago and long since forgot. He woke up rememberin every detail, the names and the places and the dates, as clear as the clear blue sky. He knew now to where he was bound. To where he'd been bound since the day he was born.

Bisbee, Arizona, 1949

CHESTER DROVE ALL DAY and into the night, till he couldn't hardly see the road. He left Interstate 40 in Flagstaff and headed south. A few miles out of Tombstone, a few hours past midnight, his eyes began to close, and he missed a curve. His truck tumbled over and over and came to rest upside down in a farmer's field, him throwed to the side of it like a rag doll. He came to his senses near sunup and watched the blanket of stars overhead fade with the whitening sky. He ran a hand over his body looking for broken parts. But for a twisted ankle, a misplaced shoulder bone, and a busted rib or two, he seemed to be intact. He hobbled back to the highway holding his side and limped his way south to Bisbee. The sun rose in the east and the towering saguaro cacti alongside the road cast their long shadows westward over the desert floor, seeming like sinister giants waiting to enfold you in their prickly embrace. He stuck out his thumb and was given a ride by a young man whose breath told Chester he'd been up all night having himself a time.

That your truck upside down back in the field, Grandpa?

That it is, Chester said.

You alright?

Reckon so, Chester said.

I'll take you to the hospital in Bisbee, he said. I'm a goin there my own self.

Much obliged, Chester said, though he wondered, what with the young man's dubious driving, if he wouldn't be more likely to get there alive on foot.

THE YOUNG MAN DROPPED CHESTER off at the emergency room entrance and went round to park his car. But Chester wasn't interested in the emergency room. He went to the reception desk and told the nurse he was here for Hattie Bledsoe. The nurse checked her roster and said Mrs. Bledsoe was in the Maternity Ward this very minute delivering a baby.

Is there a room for waitin, Miss? Chester said.

Yes, there is, she said. Are you family?

That I am.

Your name, sir?

Ordell.

The nurse wrote the name in a logbook. She pointed down the hallway.

All the way to the end, Mr. Bledsoe, she said. Make a left, then the first right. You'll see a sign.

Thank you kindly, Miss.

THE WAITING ROOM WAS EMPTY but for him. He took a seat on a long wooden bench. The walls were white and there wasn't a sound. Soon the young man who'd given him a ride strode in weaving.

Grandpa! the man said. I expect you're in the wrong place, partner. They don't fix bones in the baby department.

Not here to be fixed, young man. I'm here to be born again.

You must of took a hard knock to your head in that field, Grandpa. You don't seem to know if you're a comin or a goin.

Ordell pondered a spell.

I expect you're right about that, he said, and curled up on the bench and took his last breath in one room and his first in another.

Medford Mail Tribune   August 2, 2017

**JACKSONVILLE MOTHER AND SON
FOUND DEAD IN BED TOGETHER**

In a bizarre turn of events, long-time Jacksonville Resident, Hattie Bledsoe, 87, and her son, Ordell Bledsoe, 68, were found dead in bed together yesterday on the morning of their shared birthday. Their bodies were discovered by long-time friend and neighbor, Paul Hastings.

"I'd come to celebrate their birthday," Hastings said. "I brought a cake. I knocked repeatedly, and when no one answered I entered and found them in Mrs. Bledsoe's bed, side by side, spooning like lovers. It broke my heart. We'd been celebrating their mutual birthday together for eighteen years."

Hattie and her sister, Florence, were known for the quality of their quilts, which they placed in numerous shops around the Rogue Valley. Those who knew them considered them the salt of the earth.

The cause of death is unknown but foul play is not suspected and a coroner's inquest will not convene. Hattie and Ordell will be interred in the Jacksonville Cemetery alongside the remains of Hattie's sister, Florence, who preceded them in death in 2005.

SEPTEMBER

ONE HUNDREDFOLD

You're gonna have to serve somebody
Yes indeed, you're gonna have to serve somebody
Well, it may be the devil or it may be the Lord
But you're gonna have to serve somebody
– Bob Dylan

Sunday, September 1st, 2019

SAM, I DON'T HAVE A CLUE ABOUT your religious affiliations. I don't know to what great book you might go for insight into the spiritual realm of existence—the Tao Te Ching of Taoism, the Talmud of Judaism, the Agamas of Jainism, the Koran of Islam, the Upanishads of Hinduism, the Tipitaka of Buddhism, the Christian Bible, or to the myriad insightful explorations of the spiritual world by non-affiliated gurus throughout the ages, but I suspect if you're still with me you do spend a considerable part of your time seeking the truth, and know by now the truth is where you find it.

SPEAKING OF SEEKING THE TRUTH, I'll wager the Good Bean Café is the most bible-reading coffee house in the nation, and I've been to a few. On a given day one might witness an older man tutoring a younger man on *the way, the truth, and the life*; an older man tutoring a young woman; two young men, or two young women, or a young man and a young woman, or half a dozen older men at a table, discussing scripture and reading to one another. It is refreshing to see a segment of the younger generation be wholesome, earnest, bright and inquisitive, interested in matters of the spirit, and not mired in the mundane, as opposed to their afflicted and bedeviled counterparts camping out on Bear Creek and pushing shopping carts on the streets in the early morning hours. And to see the elders of youthful devotees caring for the welfare of their children. I suppose these tender-hearted souls represent the population that was here before the tide of affluent retirees from the Bay Area and beyond arrived and changed the demographics of the Valley.

Often, I have noticed a sixty-something gentleman with a dignified demeanor, who speaks softly but fervently to his companions, who lean forward and listen with respectful attention. A few days ago, while pondering the subject of my September story, the man came in alone and I thought to ask him a question or two before his fellows arrived. Perhaps he would say something to serve as a prompt for my next story.

Excuse me, Sir, I said, if you have a minute, I'm curious about a certain matter.

Of course, he said. I always have time for those who seek the truth.

I wouldn't say I'm seeking a particular truth, I said. Just a bit of information to satisfy my curiosity.

Have a seat, he said, indicating with an upturned palm the chair opposite his.

I pulled out the chair and sat across from the man. His hair was silvery and swept back, his eyes blue and soft, his expression kind yet severe, like he'd been to the top of the mountain and back and there wasn't much he hadn't seen. I had a wild hunch his history was exceptional. I soon learned it was.

I'm Adrian, I said.

Jordan, he said.

He extended his hand. I took it.

You're a writer, he said.

Is it so obvious?

Your omnipresence at the Good Bean has not gone unnoticed. Your daily devotion to duty is a very Christian trait.

Well, Christian trait or not, Jordan, books don't write themselves.

I considered writing once, he said, but I chose a higher calling.

Well...

I still write lessons and sermons in the service of the Lord, Adrian. I pray he is pleased by my words as I am pleased by his. So...what would you like to know, my friend?

I notice there are a great number of students of the bible who frequent the café, Jordan. Sometimes every other table is taken by the faithful. I'm wondering if you are all affiliated. If all are members of the same church or congregation, or whatever.

We are all affiliated by our common love of Jesus, Adrian. Numerous ministries are represented. The Good Bean is a great place to commune and share our love of Christ. My particular affiliation is with the Little River Christian Fellowship. We have retreat facilities on the banks of the Little Applegate River, hence the name. In the proper season, rain falls. Freshets and rivulets flow into the Little River. The Little River flows into the Big River. The Big River flows into the sea. The waters of the sea are pulled into the Heavens. The rain falls. And so it goes.

And what is the mission of the Little River Christian Fellowship, Jordan?

We are non-denominational and all-inclusive. We spread the Word of God to any and all with ears to hear. We believe in *Agape* love. God does not merely love, He *is* love. 1 John 4:8. His love washes over the clean and the unclean alike. Ours must do the same. *For God so loved the world, He gave his only begotten son, that whoever believes in Him should not perish but have everlasting life.* 1 John 3:16. As Jesus laid down His life for us, we must be prepared to lay down our lives for our brothers and sisters. That is Agape Love.

Amen, Jordan. A noble sentiment. And what is your role in the Fellowship?

Pastor.

Ah, Pastor! I'm not surprised, Jordan. You have a certain bearing. I've noticed you have the attention and respect of your peers. Tell me, what is one's path to becoming Pastor of a Fellowship?

Mine has been an uncommon and circuitous route, Adrian, fraught with peril.

Fraught with peril! I wouldn't have thought—

Do you believe in miracles, Adrian?

You might say I do. I see a miracle as a mystery. When the forces behind the mystery are revealed, it is no longer a mystery. No longer a miracle. I'm fascinated by the intelligence behind such events. An intelligence not our own.

Quite right, Adrian. The Lord says: *For my thoughts are not your thoughts, neither are your ways my ways. As the heavens are higher than the earth, so are my ways higher than your ways and my thoughts than your thoughts.* Isaiah 55:8-9.

I like that, Jordan, I said. And I like this, too: *God moves in a mysterious way, his wonders to perform; He plants his footsteps in the sea, and rides upon the storm.* William Cowper, 1731–1800.

I'm familiar with those lines, Adrian. Do you write poetry?

No. Fiction. Currently a collection of linked stories around unlikely and inexplicable events and how they affect our lives. Meaningful coincidence. Chance encounters. Small miracles if you will.

Umm…perhaps you'd be interested in the small miracles that were milestones on the long and winding and treacherous road that led to my leadership of The Little River Christian Fellowship.

Absolutely I would, Jordan! I've been wondering from where my next story might come. I see now why on impulse I chose to introduce myself this morning.

God works in a mysterious way, his wonders to perform, Jordan said with a wily smile. But the first of my disciples has arrived, he said. You'll have to excuse me, Adrian. My story is a long one. We should meet again when there's time for its telling. Will you be here tomorrow? But I shouldn't ask! Will ten in the morning work for you? I'll be finished with my lessons and free to tell my tale.

THE NEXT DAY I MET WITH JORDAN and he related the following story of the uncommon and circuitous path fraught with peril that led to his becoming Pastor of The Little River Christian Fellowship. His narrative was descriptive, engaging and suspenseful, evidence of the writer he might have been had he not chosen a *higher calling*. But it was fragmented, and I have taken the liberty of putting it into order.

ONE HUNDREDFOLD

I WAS BORN AND RAISED in a small town a mile from the Mississippi River in a little house by a levee, Adrian, the youngest of four brothers and an older sister. Holes in the screens of the little house let in flies by day and mosquitoes at night. Down the tar and gravel road out front, past corn fields and the granary and the smokestacks of Peabody Coal, where black mud meets the Mississippi, tendrils of moss hung from the bare branches of half-submerged trees. When the sun went down, heat lightning silent as prayer slid across the darkening sky. Swallows soared and dipped in the damp air, feasting on fireflies, and in the glare of the flickering streetlamp across from the house, June bugs big and hard as pecans whirled in a frenzy and crashed into the street where they lay on their backs and wriggled till dawn. When the sky opened, rain pounded the levee and the levee broke and my brothers and I played in the brown swirling water. Forgive my flowery description, Adrian, but memories of life in my formative years are vivid and persistent.

I WAS RAISED ON CANNED SPAM, Bunny Bread, and rosary beads. On the wall in the family room was a picture of Jesus in a crown of thorns, his eyes rolled back like they sought to escape their fate. By the front door, and by the door of each bedroom, were holy water fountains. My brothers and I and my sister, Sonia, dipped our fingers and crossed ourselves coming and going. At night we prayed on the rosary after supper. My mother lit candles and we knelt on the hard tile floor, each with a rosary in hand. Sometimes my mother would lead us in prayer, and sometimes Sonia. The leader said half a prayer and my brothers and I responded with the other half. To my young mind, the words were baffling. There was stuff about the living and the dead and the forgiveness of sins. About God's hollow name, and how his mother would be dead in an hour except she had fruit in her room, Amen. The leader would name a mystery. There were joyful mysteries and sorrowful mysteries and glorious mysteries and luminous mysteries. We were to contemplate the chosen mystery while reciting Hail Marys and Our Fathers until our knees were screaming. I liked to think about the luminous mysteries. Was there light inside? Did they glow in the dark?

MY MOTHER WAS AFFLICTED in body and soul. She would invoke the name of the Lord one minute, then curse like a demented woman the next. And I was the hapless victim of her wretchedness. I would lay in the dark and wait for my father to come home after a long day at the factory. When the screen door slammed, I would jerk and curl into a ball. My mother would start in: Oh, your stinking breath!

What—a man can't have a goddamn beer after working all day?

Look at your puffy face! Your bulging eyes!

What are you doing up, Marge? It's midnight!

I've had enough! my mother would scream. Enough! Enough!

I imagined her crooked mouth, her glassy eyes.

What is it now? my father would say.

He blew up a frog with a firecracker! He peed on the neighbor's porch!

He's just a kid.

He stole a quarter from my change jar!

I'll give you a lousy quarter.

I don't want your goddamn money!

I'm tired, Marge! Do I have to come home to this night after goddamn night?

She would call him a son of a bitch and a whoremonger and say how he did that dirty thing to that dirty girl Pauline in the loft above the feed store. That was a long time ago! he would say. And she would say: So, I should forget, you dirty cocksucker?

When he could take no more, he pulled off his leather belt and came into my room where my brothers and I lay in our sweaty underwear on our smelly mattress. He turned on the light. He loomed in the doorway, menacing yet sad, like the clown in the circus that came to town every summer. When he swung, I crawled under my brothers and they got the strap, too. I put up my little arms and said, Please stop, Daddy, and I saw he was crying. When he finished, I crawled out the bedroom window and got into my fort made of boxes and boards and sat on the tar paper floor and played with my flashlight under a blanket. I listened to my mother and father scream half the night: about me, about God, about the whore above the feed store. When it was quiet, I sneaked back into bed. In the morning, my sister Sonia came into my room. She fingered the raised welts gently.

Do they hurt? she said.

No, I said, because they didn't. Not when she touched them. Sometimes at night, I would climb onto the roof and hang over the edge and look into her room. Music came from her record player: Roy Orbison's *Only the Lonely*, or the Shirelles *Will You Love Me Tomorrow*. She was naked and holding herself and dancing in front of the mirror, and I felt a tingling in my pants.

I HAD A BEST FRIEND, BOBBY BECKER, whose family came from Kentucky. The Beckers won their house on *Queen for a Day* and moved in down the street. They were one rung lower on the social ladder than my own family. My mother called them hillbillies.

Bobby had a stepfather, a skinny man who didn't talk much, just sat on the porch and drank whisky all day, and a fat mom who would tell the skinny man: Y'all ain't got a lick a sense.

Bobby was a pagan with one foot planted in the pits of hell. But show me a man of God, Adrian, who did not have a pagan for a friend! Christ himself consorted with a crowd of ruffians!

A few years older than me, Bobby combed his hair back greasy duck-butt style. He went to public school. He and I would go to the local A & P and play Finders Keepers, Losers Weepers. We'd go up and down the aisles and stuff our pockets with random items: cellophane tape, scissors, pens, candy bars, cough medicine, cigars. We'd go out back and sit under construction trailers on rolls of tar paper and count the price stickers on our pilfered goods. Whoever had the highest total would smoke the first cigar. We'd smoke and swallow cough medicine until we couldn't stand up, then Bobby would teach me to curse.

Goddamn motherfucker, shit piss fuck! he would say.

Then I would say it.

Goddamn, titty caca, fuck a duck! he would say.

Then I would say it. I didn't know what the words meant but it felt good to say them, like praying on the beads of the rosary.

One night Bobby came to our house and prayed with us.

It will do that little heathen some good, my mother said.

He didn't kneel on the floor, but sat on a chair and fingered the beads, and mumbled along. Sonia led and Bobby looked at her butt, and he and I looked at each other and smiled and looked away.

MY FATHER CAME HOME with a flesh-colored plastic Jesus wrapped in cellophane. I bought this at the novelty shop in town, he told my mother. It's luminous, it glows in the dark.

My mother got red in the face and screamed: Do you think I don't know what luminous means, you ignorant asshole? Do you think this junk is sacred? It's profane!

Marge, I just thought—

Thought *nothing*, you idiot!

Her eyes were big and bright. Her lips crooked. She threw the plastic Jesus into the trash. Sonia picked it out.

Mom, she said, we can donate this to the church for the Oktoberfest carnival. They need prizes.

I don't care, my mother said. Just get it out of here!

SONIA TOOK ME TO THE OKTOBERFEST carnival in the school cafeteria. The tables were cleared away. There were games and a pile of prizes. I entered the apple bobbing contest. The apples were too big to bite and bounced off my teeth. I got one against my upper lip and nose and plunged my head into the water, pushing the apple to the bottom. I stayed down until I couldn't hear the sounds in the room, only the tinkle of bubbles that brushed past my ears. I got the stem of the apple between my teeth and erupted from the water when my lungs were bursting. I pointed to the plastic Jesus in the pile of prizes.

I'll take that one, I said to the little nun who guarded the pile. It's luminous.

BOBBY TAPPED ON THE WINDOW. I climbed out clutching the plastic Jesus. Under the blanket, I shined the flashlight into its face for a full minute, then hung it by a nail on a board and flicked off the flashlight. The face glowed with a weird and sorrowful look.

It's a mystery, I said.

Yeah! Bobby said.

I pulled two rosaries from my pocket.

I'll lead, I said.

I handed a rosary to Bobby.

Goddamn motherfucker, shit piss fuck! I said.

Then Bobby said it.

Goddamn, titty caca, fuck a duck, I said.

Then Bobby said it.

We took off our clothes and counted our pubic hairs. Bobby had one more than me. We shook our hips and played air guitar and sang Jail House Rock.

Let's rock!
Everybody let's rock!
Everybody in the whole cell block
Was dancin' to the jailhouse rock!

Little did I know how prophetic those words would be.

DESPITE HER ABUSE, I knew my mother loved me. She was simply wretched, plagued by illness all her days. She would lay on the couch and put her hand across her face and say: Jordan, Mommy is so tired! Would you be a good boy and rub her back? She would turn over and I would rub her back with my little hands and she would sigh.

Mommy, I would say, are you going to die?

She would sit up suddenly and yell, Don't you ever, *ever*, say that to your mother again. She would cough and growl and spit into her handkerchief, and I would run away.

I WENT TO CHURCH EVERY SUNDAY. Sometimes with my brothers, sometimes with my mother, sometimes with my mother and father, or with Sonia, or with all of us together, and sometimes alone. On the particular Sunday when the first of the minor miracles occurred along the path to my becoming pastor of Little River Christian Fellowship, I walked alone, my hands in my empty pockets, my head down as I watched the road recede beneath my feet. I stopped abruptly, in disbelief, when I saw it: a shiny nickel between my shoes. Sweet Jesus! This was half a century ago, Adrian, in the days of penny candy. When a nickel's worth would fill your pockets. I looked left and right. There was no one about. I clutched the nickel in my little fist and walked on down the road.

At church, flickering candles cast weird shadows on the statuary. I held the nickel tightly as though to keep it from flying away. The priest loomed above his pulpit and delivered his sermon:

And Jesus said: Truly I say to you, there is no one who has left house or brothers or sisters or mother or father or children or farms, for my sake and for the gospel's sake, but that he will receive a hundred times as much now in the present age, houses and brothers and sisters and mothers and children and farms, along with persecutions; and in the age to come, eternal life. Mark 10:29–30.

These were far too many words for my young mind to comprehend, and I suppose his message was lost on many of the adult parishioners, too, for, after a moment of silence, he leaned over his pulpit, scanned the congregation with a withering gaze, and exhorted: *Give and ye shall receive one hundredfold!*

As if on cue, the collection basket was passed around. The faithful emptied their pockets and purses. When the basket stopped in front of me, with great trepidation I yielded my treasure.

Walking home, despondent, my hands thrust deep into my empty pockets, my head hanging low, on the very spot where I had found the nickel—was a crisp new five-dollar bill!

Sweet Jesus!

I HID MY TREASURE BETWEEN THE PAGES of my Catechism which, if you're not familiar, Adrian, is a summary of the principles of the Christian religion in the form of questions and answers, used predominantly, but not exclusively, by Catholics. It seemed a safe place to store my booty. The value of a five-dollar bill was incomprehensible to my young mind and I was reluctant to break it, fearing the change I received would run through my fingers like water.

Mid-week, as I lay in bed, I overheard a conversation between my mother and father. It was uncharacteristically civil, even tender. With a gasp, I learned that my mother was gravely ill and nearing the end of her life. She wanted only for her family to do a road trip, a pilgrimage back to the birthplace of her parents, a thousand miles away.

Marge, my father said, such a trip would cost five hundred dollars! We don't have that kind of money!

We'll find it, my mother said. Let us pray...

I imagined my mother and father kneeling side by side, their heads bowed. The following Sunday, with great expectations, I put my five-dollar bill into the collection basket and walked home imagining the joy on my mother's face when I gave her the gift of five hundred dollars and a trip home to the burial ground of her people, but on the magic spot that had yielded one hundredfold a week before...there was nothing. I waited days, weeks, months. Nothing.

OUTSIDE, THE TREES WERE CRUSTED in ice, the frozen mud frosted with snow. My mother packed her little suitcase and put on her little round hat with the little red feather, her long grey tweed coat, and her black boots and gloves. She gave my brothers and me and Sonia each a hug and said she'd be back when she felt better, and our father took her away in his car. I snuck two quarters from her change jar and bought a bag of apples at the A & P and put them in a bowl by her bed, where the sun lit them up and made her room glow. But she didn't come home to see them, not that day, nor the next. Soon, the apples were shriveled and dark. I shined my flashlight on them, but they wouldn't hold the light.

I WAS NOW A BITTER YOUNG BOY. I had been tricked by God, and by his emissary on earth, into believing if I gave I would receive one hundred-fold. But my money was gone and my mother was dead. I became a juvenile delinquent and Satan's pride and joy. Thereafter, when the collection basket came around, I pretended to give but took instead, determined to multiply my fortunes my own way. In due course, my sleight of hand failed me, and I was severely reprimanded by the church but excused because I had lost my mother.

In time, I lost everyone. My brothers left home as soon as they could. My father let them go. Bobby dropped out of school, had a brief affair with Sonia, and was drafted and sent to Viet Nam. Sonia came to my bedside with a tear on her cheek.

I have to go, Jordan, she said.

Her perfume smelled like the first day of summer.

She wore her dead mother's pearls.

In Chicago, she said, I'll have a life. There's nothing for me here. I mean, *you're* here, Jordan, but...you'll be alright, won't you? Say you understand! Say you'll miss me! You will miss me, won't you?

Yes, I'll miss you, I said, and I really would.

MY LIFE OF PETTY CRIME PERSISTED. I was busted for shoplifting and put on probation. The next year, I was busted for having organized a bicycle theft ring and given probation again. Two years later, I was arrested for burglary and sent to Juvenile Hall for six months, where I was abused by older boys and learned to fight.

Shortly after my release, my father's car spun like a top on a rain-slicked road and plunged into a swollen creek. I went to live with his brother, Atticus, in a secluded cottage in the woods a few miles outside of Columbia, Missouri. Out back of the cottage was a dilapidated barn. In front was a porch, and on the porch a swing, and beyond the porch a pond. I would sit on the swing and listen to the bullfrogs croak in the rushes around the pond and contemplate my next caper. Uncle Atticus shared with my father a fondness for alcohol and couldn't care less what I did with my life as long as I stayed out of his way and didn't come between him and his bottle. He did give me a piece of fatherly advice once, which I failed to heed: The law's gettin' mighty tired of messin with you, son, he said. You're not a little boy anymore, you're nearly a grown man. Any more funny business, you'll do a grown man's time!

PIGEONS PERCHED IN THE RAFTERS of the barn out back where I stored the stuff I burgled from houses in neighboring towns and sold at the flea market every Saturday on the lot of the abandoned drive-in movie theatre where they hadn't shown a film since *The Hoodlum Priest*. Uncle Atticus turned a blind eye to my escapades for a piece of the action. One fateful night, on the second floor of a house I'd broken into, I encountered its elderly owner. In my haste to escape, I pushed her aside. She tumbled down a flight of steps and broke a hip and three vertebrae and spent her remaining days in a wheelchair. I was apprehended. The property was searched and the booty in the barn discovered and seized. I testified that Uncle Atticus knew nothing of my business, and he was exonerated.

I LAY ON MY BACK UNDER a course blue blanket on a steel bunk in the County Jail and imagined Bobby's bloated corpse lying face down on the steaming floor of a jungle on the far side of the world. Better, I thought, than being a three-time loser waiting to be shipped to the Big House, the imponderable weight of thirty years on my narrow shoulders.

SONIA CAME DOWN FROM CHICAGO where she did who knows what for money. She had left her and Bobby's baby, Bobby Junior, with a friend. I thought her heels were too high, her skirt too short, her lipstick too red, but it was her life. She had brought me sympathy and a few dollars and a rosary. That night I lay on my bunk, and with no illusions that I was communing with a higher power, I fingered the beads.

Goddamn motherfucker, shit piss fuck, I said.

Goddamn, titty caca, fuck a duck, I said.

It helped the time go by bead…by bead…by bead.

IN THE MISSOURI STATE PENITENTIARY at Jefferson City, built in 1836 on the banks of the Missouri River, prisoner assaults were common. Time Magazine called it the "bloodiest forty-seven acres in America." I called it home for fifteen years. For the first five, the bitterness begot by my sense of betrayal by the Lord and his lackeys ruled my life. I railed against my fate, fought with my fellow prisoners, and with the staff, and spent thousands of hours in *the Dungeon*, subterranean cells beneath the prison's oldest building, where death row inmates, the violent and disorderly, and the mentally unstable, were consigned.

Racial tension was the order of the day. Though people of color represented only twelve percent of the population of Missouri, they represented nearly half the population of the prison system. White supremacist groups abounded. Caucasian inmates were pressured to pledge allegiance to one or another. I resisted. I bore no ill will to people of color. My grievance was with a more formidable adversary. Therefore, I made enemies on both sides.

I was assaulted on numerous occasions. Five years into my sentence, following the most brutal attack, I was taken for surgery to the Sisters of St. Mary's Hospital in Jefferson City, a Catholic facility whose stated mission is to reveal, through exceptional health care, the healing presence of God. Under anesthesia, I entered a realm of eerie blue light suffused with ineffable love and divine intelligence. The landscape was vast, the horizon impossibly far away. Here, the wisdom of the Holy Book—the only book we'll ever need, Adrian—was imparted by its vast panoply of elders, from Adam to Abraham, to students of every color and persuasion eager to know the Word of God. They spoke in the tongues of the Bible—Hebrew, Aramaic, and Greek—yet their lessons were intelligible to all. I sat at the feet of each Patriarch in turn and was imbued with the collective wisdom of the Old and New Testaments. An interesting aside, Adrian: none of the central figures of the Bible were blue-eyed and blond.

There was no dimension of time in this realm of light, no sense of its passing. I might have dwelt there a day or a thousand years. When I emerged, there was not a psalm in the Bible that was not readily on my tongue. Two were most pertinent, given my circumstances: *Get rid of all bitterness, rage, and anger, brawling and slander, along with every form of malice.* Ephesians 4:31. And, *For I know the plans I have for you, declares the Lord, plans to give you hope and a future.* Jeremiah 29:11.

I ROSE THROUGH THE RARIFIED AIR of anesthesia like a hot air balloon through layers of cloud. I blinked away the bright light. A woman in starched white linen stood at the foot of my bed like an apparition. Sister Anne, I soon learned.

Doctor, she said, your patient is awake.

I was told by the bespectacled young MD who had patched me up that, though no vital organs had been pierced, I had lain on the yard a long time and lost a lot of blood. There had been some anxious moments.

Someone was looking out for you, he said.

Amen, I said.

I spent a week in the care of Sister Anne, a short, florid woman descended of Irish Travelers. Despite our age difference of thirty-plus years, we became friends. We shared our love of Jesus and punctuated our conversation with the recitation of psalms. She was feisty and made a game of our exchanges, an amiable jousting of Christian Soldiers. Impressed by my knowledge of scripture, she counseled me upon release from her care: *Don't let anyone look down on you because you are young,* she said, *but set an example for the believers in speech, in conduct, in love, in faith, and in purity.* 1 Timothy 4:12

THE PENITENTIARY CEASED TO BE an arena for battling my fellow inmates and my personal demons. I embraced the lesson of Isaiah 41:10 and lost all fear for my safety: *Fear not, for I am with you; be not dismayed, for I am your God; I will strengthen you, I will help you, I will uphold you with my righteous right hand.*

I paid my first visit to the prison chapel, a non-denominational refuge from the horrors of prison life. The chapel was cool and dark and pungent with the aroma of incense. Candle flames swayed gently on invisible currents.

On the far wall, an array of framed symbols gave proof that in this sanctuary all beliefs were accommodated: a crucifix; the Star of David; the Islamic star inside a crescent moon; the Chinese Yin Yang; the Greek letters Alpha and Omega; the American Indian Thunderbird; the

Egyptian Ankh. And following the series of symbols, a framed print of the Laughing Buddha, plump and jolly, a sack of scant possessions slung over his shoulder.

I was astounded! How could I have gone five years blind to the existence of this oasis of tranquility and quiet meditation? But one must have eyes to see: *And immediately there fell from his eyes as it had been scales and he received sight forthwith, and arose, and was baptized.* Acts 9:18.

I requested an appointment with the Chaplain, The Reverend John Love, an African American Minister from St. Louis with roots in Haiti. Called affectionately by inmates, *Doctor Love*, and his chapel, *The Chapel of Love*, he was a colleague of Martin Luther King Jr. We had a long and fruitful conversation. Serendipitously, his assistant had been paroled and I was invited to replace him.

I spent the next ten years under the auspices of The Reverend Dr. Love. He would quote the scriptures; he would quote Martin Luther King; and as often as not, he would quote Malcolm X or Minister Louis Farrakhan. Wafting through the semi-dark of the chapel might be heard the Gregorian Chants of the Benedictine Monks; the choral music of Angelus Echeverry; or an angry Nina Simone singing *Mississippi Goddam*! I became known to inmates, white and black, as Brother Jordan. I was never again assaulted. From my dollar-a-day salary, I saved a dollar a week for ten years. Five hundred dollars. A year before my release I was notified that Uncle Atticus had passed. Six months before my release, I received a letter from my long-lost sister, Sonia. She had found God and forsaken her life of sin and moved with Bobby Junior to Jacksonville, where she was swept away by the powerful undercurrent of the love of Jesus. Upon parole, I would join her there. A week before my release, I received a letter from a law firm in Columbia, Davis, Gracey and Wall, instructing me to come to their office immediately upon release concerning an urgent legal matter. On the day of my release, I was given a Greyhound Bus ticket to Oregon and three days to get there; a two-hundred-dollar debit card courtesy of the state, known as *gate money*; and a check for the five hundred dollars I had saved from my dollar-a-day salary. I cashed the check and put the money in an envelope and took a local bus to the town I'd grown up in. I visited the little house by the levee. I was flooded with memories, none of them pleasant. I walked to the church where, fifteen years earlier, I had deposited first a shiny nickel, then a crisp five-dollar bill. With no expectations, I handed the envelope to the startled young Priest inside. A debt paid, I visited the

Law Office in Columbia to which I had been summoned, and the second of the minor miracles on the long and winding road to my Ministry occurred. Before Uncle Atticus entered a hospice to spend his final days, he sold his secluded cottage in the woods and left me the proceeds: fifty thousand dollars. You do the math, Adrian.

JORDAN CEASED HIS NARRATIVE and regarded me with a smile tinged with triumph. I was amazed at the twists and turns of his journey. Who would have thought so unassuming a man would have traveled so rocky a road to redemption?

Great story, Brother Jordan, I said. I like it. Your minor miracles certainly qualify as unlikely and inexplicable…although I think you'd say they're not inexplicable at all but work of a higher power whose thoughts are not our thoughts, whose ways are not our ways. We can agree on that. So…you came to Jacksonville twenty years ago. How has it gone for you?

I was welcomed into Sonia's circle of devotees, Adrian. They were devout but not organized. They seemed to be waiting for direction, which I provided. I bought ten acres on the banks of the Little Applegate River and founded The Little River Christian Fellowship. Together, with our hands and our hearts, and the money bequeathed by Uncle Atticus through the intercession of the Lord Jesus Christ, we built a facility second to none.

I had had my sojourn in the Timeless Blue Void, Adrian, at the feet of the Patriarchs, but had no formal credentials. I attended Pacific Bible College in Medford. There was little they could teach me that I didn't already know but I came away with a BA in Biblical Studies, and administrative skills, and took the helm of a Fellowship that has become the flagship of Christianity in the Valley.

And your sister, Sonia?

She was secretary to the Fellowship for a decade. She ran a popular vintage clothing shop in town. She gave her money freely to whatever cause she deemed worthy. She wanted nothing for herself. She ministered to the poor, the oppressed, the luckless, and the lame of spirit, of which, unfortunately, there are many. She embraced the truth of Philippians 2:3: *Do nothing out of selfish ambition or vain conceit. Rather, in humility value others above yourselves.*

You speak in the past tense…

She's with Jesus now.

I'm sorry.

We'll be together again.

And Bobby Junior?

Pot farmer. He has a hundred acres in the hills above the valley.

Is he a follower of Jesus?

Of Haile Selassie. You'll recognize him by his dreadlocks. *Many are called but few are chosen.* Matthew 22:1–14.

Brother Jordan, thank you so much! You've given me what I wanted and more. I'm honored to include the story of your long and winding road fraught with peril in my humble book. By the way, are your disciples aware of your history?

He smiled his wily smile.

No, Adrian, he said…but they will be.

OCTOBER

TRAVELING MAN

It is not that the girl is unfit for everything,
it is that she is not of this world.

– Gabriel Garcia Marquez
Of Love and Other Demons

Wednesday, October 2nd, 2019

IN A COMMUNITY OF CREATIVE TYPES like Jacksonville, Oregon, one or more will be wrestling personal demons in a struggle they are bound to lose. Darla, for instance. Not her real name. I'll grant the poor soul anonymity, and the tale I tell of her life will likewise be fictitious.

Yesterday, Sam, while I sat at my usual table at the Good Bean Café in the early morning hours knowing only that I would contrive a tale around an unstable character in a volatile situation, I composed crude limericks to stimulate my imagination:

> *Darla loved to get high*
> *Before the sun rose in the sky.*
> *She would nibble an edible*
> *That tasted incredible*
> *And say what a good girl am I!*

> *She got so high one day*
> *Her mind was blown away.*
> *She now believed*
> *The world was conceived*
> *By spirits at work and play.*

Dreadful stuff that likely made my muse, Miranda, cringe but it served the purpose: she delivered the model for my unstable character, Darla, who sat two tables over, watching me, one shoeless foot bouncing like she pumped the brakes of a runaway car, her disheveled hair channeling energy that coursed from an agitated mind. A fascinating and frightening visage. She caught me looking. Came over and sat in the chair opposite mine. Hers was a face once pretty, now ravaged from within. Her eyes burned bright. Her lower lip quivered.

Hey, she said.

Hey, I said back cautiously.

I'm Darla, she said.

Adrian, I said.

I'm in the business, she said.

I see. And what business might that be?

Her voice rose.

I'm a fireball! I do it all! I make it real! I seal the deal! I represent the rich and famous: Tori Amos. Nicodemus. Bella Lugosi. Nancy Pelosi. Mr. Magoo. The Wandering Jew. Do you have a clue who these people are, Mister Adrian Fuck Face? They are not landscapers. They are travelers! They have seen the world! There is nowhere they haven't been! And you? I can see you have what it takes by the way you don't look at me when you look at me. Clever! Here's my card.

She slid a card across the table. I noticed the hospital bracelet on her wrist.

Call me, she said.

She padded across the room in her bare feet and plopped herself down at the table of a bible-reading group. Their expressions said she wasn't welcome. She threw a bible on the floor and jumped up.

Pansies! she yelled. Posers and pussies! Sister fuckers!

Clearly, she was not a fan of the faithful. She glared around the room. A Barista approached. They were about the same age; they might have gone to school together. She put a hand on Darla's arm.

Be *nice*, Darla, she implored.

Darla shoved her hand away.

You be nice, shit-for-brains. I'm out of here!

She wheeled away and stormed out the door. Startled patrons watched her go. Through the window I saw her pace the sidewalk, muttering to herself. Pedestrians stepped aside. I read the card she'd given me:

DANNY MUELLER LANDSCAPING
Serving The Rogue Valley Since 2009

I now had the components I needed to contrive a tale around the life of Darla. It would not be pretty.

TRAVELING MAN

THE SUN STRUGGLES TO SHINE through smoke from the fire in the hills above the Applegate Valley. Darla is tired of the smoke. It wraps around her like a dirty blanket. It makes her angry!

She marches barefoot across the lawn between the white frame farmhouse on the edge of town she shares with her husband, Danny, and the studio he built for her when they married a dozen years ago, him a few years older, her straight out of high school. She is determined to finish her painting today, *Consumption,* a gruesome work inspired by Goya's *Saturn Eating His Son.* Sinister and dark, it befits her mood of late.

She stands before the canvas in the center of the room holding her palette knife aloft. She doesn't like what she sees. Who's been in my studio? she wonders. Who did this to my painting? She brings the knife down, slashing the canvas from right to left.

A tremor ascends her spine.

Shadows scurry in the corner of the room.

I know you're there, she says. I know you're there.

DARLA VISITS *LA MOTA*, her favorite cannabis dispensary in neighboring Medford. She is frustrated with edibles and their seemingly interminable onset time. She wants her high and she wants it now!

I recommend *dabbing*, Darla, the clerk behind the counter says.

Tell me about it, Mary, Darla says.

She and Mary are friends from way back. She has only recently come into the world of recreational marijuana in all its myriad manifestations, unlike Mary and others who were there at the gate from day one.

You dab a *concentrate*, Mary says. It's the essence of the plant containing all the *cannabinoids* and *terpenes* of the flower. They're found in the *trichomes*. Let me show you.

Mary takes a bud from a white plastic container and puts it under an illuminated magnifier. There's a ring on every finger of the hand that holds the bud. Fanciful tattoos emblazon her creamy white forearm.

Look, she says. See those glistening little bumps? Those are trichomes, where the cannabinoids and terpenes reside. They're distilled into a concentrate which you vaporize with a dab rig or pen. I recommend the pen. It's pocket-sized and portable. You can put it in your purse. Here—

She retrieves a silver pen-shaped device from under the glass-topped counter. She holds it out for Darla's perusal.

It's attached to a battery, she says. You put the concentrate into this little hole and press this button. Voila! The dab evaporates! Fumes rise! You inhale! The magic happens! You're high!

I'll take one, Darla says.

You'll have to choose a concentrate, Mary says. There's *Shatter* and *Badder* and *Budder* and *Crumble*. It's all about the texture. For my money, honey, *Budder* is best. It's soft and oily and easy to spread.

Hook me up, Darla says.

We're not through, girlfriend. We have three brands of *Budder*: Caked Oreoz; DBR Blue Monster; and Gelato 25 X Dosido Honeycomb.

What do you recommend, Darla says.

The Gelato 25, Mary says. It has the highest THC content. 73.34%. It'll knock your socks off...if you're wearing socks.

I'll take a week's worth, Darla Says.

How often do you get high? Mary says.

All day, every day, Darla says. And I'm going out of town.

Two grams of Gelato should suffice for a neophyte dabber like yourself, Mary says.

How would it be if I ate edibles for breakfast and lunch and dabbed throughout the day? Darla says.

Fine, Mary says—if you want your brains to flow like a molten river into the setting sun.

I'll have five grams of Gelato, Darla says. And a pack of Limeade Gummies and a ten-pack of Marionberry Edibles.

Mary rings her up and bags her goodies.

Do be careful, girlfriend, she says. You're playing with fire.

COME OUT TO MY SHOP, Darla, Danny says. I want to show you something.

Darla follows Danny across the lawn to his shop. The smoke is worse, the sky a sickly yellow. She blinks and brushes soot from her face and neck.

They step around his late model Ford F-150 pickup truck and the trailer it pulls, loaded with landscape machinery and supplies. They enter the shop, once a tumble-down barn, since retrofitted into a fine repository of tools for every conceivable landscape project. Darla had been thrilled to marry Danny back in the day. He was an apprentice landscaper in high school who took over his mentor's business when he retired, renamed his company *Danny Mueller Landscaping*, and moved them from a rental in Medford to a house on an acre on the edge of Jacksonville. He was a catch. A physical guy with a winning smile, a car and money, and big ideas. No one had been prouder to be at his side. Or in his bed.

Now she is merely bored.

Danny takes a tool off a workshop bench, a long flat appendage lined with tiny blades on either side like the teeth of a saw-tooth shark, attached to a shiny red motor. He holds it before him like a trophy.

Einhel! he proclaims. German engineering! Dual action with twenty-eight inches of diamond-ground, laser-cut blades delivering 2,700 cuts per minute! A swiveling ergonomic handle so you can trim at any angle without straining your wrists! Isn't it beautiful?

Beautiful, Darla replies with a note of sarcasm that is lost on Danny. She is repelled by his enthusiasm. He's as much a boy with his toys as when they met. She's simply evolved beyond him to a higher plane, while he remains mired in the mundane. She reads the great Theosophists: Blavatsky. Besant. Leadbeater. Hodson. She reads the surrealist fiction of Leonora Carrington. She reads the history of the occult. Danny reads instruction manuals.

She touches her fingertips gently to the tiny blades. Danny pulls the tool away.

Careful! he says. Those blades will go through your fingers like a hot knife through butter!

How do you turn it on? Darla says.

The push of a button, Danny says. It's cordless. It runs on two eighteen-volt rechargeable batteries. They're adaptable to all Einhel products. I can promise you, Darla, I'm done with Black & Decker and Dewalt and Makita and all the rest of those posers. I'm an Einhel man from now on!

Turn it on, Danny, Darla says.

Danny takes two hefty batteries from the workshop bench and slams them into the rear of the trimmer.

Step back, he says.

He presses a button on the handle. The blades come alive with a whir like a swarm of locusts. The motor hums in high-pitched unison. He holds the trimmer aloft.

See what I'm talking about, Darla? he says with a smirk that makes Darla recoil inside.

I do, she says. I do.

DANNY UNDRESSES SLOWLY while Darla watches. He is proud of his member. She was once impressed. He can pound like nobody's business but he does it the same way every time. Sometimes with his MAGA hat on backward. When she introduced him to the *Kama Sutra*, he'd said: To hell with those Punjabi ragheads, Darla! I'll show you the *American* way: *Cowboy Sutra*! He mounted her from behind and held her hair like a horse's mane. *Yeee ha!* he hollered when he got his rocks off.

She was not amused.

THE ROOM IS DIMLY LIT by a lamp in the corner. A ceiling fan turns overhead. Danny sits in his favorite overstuffed armchair. Darla sits across the room on the far end of the couch. Her legs are crossed.

Danny holds his tumbler up to the light.

Westward American Single Malt, he says. Distilled in Oregon! Pulled from the barrel and bottled at barrel strength. A hundred bucks a bottle. A gift from the crew.

They must like you, Darla says.

They love me, Danny says. I'm glad *someone* does!

Don't be dramatic, Darla says.

While Danny sips, Darla dabs. She declines his offer of a tumbler of Westward American Single Malt Bourbon. He declines her offer of a dab of Gelato 25 X Dosido Honeycomb.

I'm worried about you, Darla, he says. You're wasting away. I'll bet you're down to a hundred pounds!

I'm wasting away alright, Darla says. Wasting away inside! Becoming nobody!

Now who's being dramatic?

It's true! Darla said. I'm disappearing! I'm being sucked into the void!

She exhales a cloud of vapor into the room.

It's the goddamned dope, Danny says. If you don't get a grip, you'll be camping out on Bear Creek with the rest of the tweakers and losers!

Darla puts the pipe down on the coffee table between them. She looks at the floor, then at Danny. Her expression borders on outrage.

What's bothering you, Darla, Danny says.

They declined my application for a show at *Art Presence*, Darla says. The curator said my work was contrary to the *zeitgeist* of the community. What crap! She didn't even use the word Zeitgeist right. It's the spirit of an era, not of the local Podunk community. She's afraid of my message. The bitch needs to grow a pair!

Maybe she thinks your work isn't, you know, good enough.

Is that what you think?

You haven't been painting all that long, Darla. Just saying…

Darla stares hard at Danny.

Did you change my painting? she says.

What painting?

Consumption. Don't play dumb!

I haven't been in your studio, Darla. Maybe you changed it and forgot. You haven't been yourself lately.

Darla narrows her eyes.

I'm not who you think I am, she says.

Got that right. I don't know *who* the fuck you are anymore.

No, you don't!

Ah, you're making me tired, Darla.

She takes a long, deep breath. She would lighten the mood in the room if she could. It was sympathy she needed, not acrimony.

I'm tired, too, she says. I'm drained. I want to go to San Francisco. Let's go together. There's so much to see and do. And a breeze off the Bay to blow the smoke away.

Danny frowns.

San Francisco! I've got no use for the goddamned hippies and liberals in San Francisco! They're worse than the Yankees in Portland! Listen, Darla, I have friends in Bend. You remember Gary and Rika? They have a cabin on a lake. Two bedrooms. We'll hang out. Walk in the woods. Talk about old times.

Bend! Darla says. I don't want to hang out with your friends in Bend and talk about old times!

You used to like my friends, Darla. What happened?

Nothing happened. That's the problem. No one changes around here!

Why should they? What's the fucking point? Look at you! I want my goddamned Darla back!

Darla sighs.

Maybe it's the smoke, she says. It makes me crazy. When will it go away?

Danny leans forward. He puts his hands on Darla's shoulders. He speaks gently: There *is* no smoke, Darla. There *is* no fire. The fire was last year… okay?

Liar! Darla screams. Don't fuck with me, Danny!

He pushes up from his chair.

I've had enough, he says. Knock yourself out, psycho. I'm sleeping in the guest room.

Whatever! Darla says. I won't be here when you get up.

Suit yourself, Darla, Danny says wearily. Suit yourself.

DARLA BOOKS A ROOM at the Stanyan Park Hotel, a beautiful old Victorian on the National Register of Historic Places in the Haight-Ashbury District across the street from Golden Gate Park. She doesn't care about the cost. Danny will pay. The breeze off the bay has blown the smoke away. The sky is a powdery blue. The space inside her head is filled with sparkling light. She heads for *Hippie Hill*, a green expanse on the east end of the park that was once the haven of a host of 60's luminaries: Janis Joplin. The Grateful Dead. Jefferson Airplane. She lounges in the grass beneath a canopy of trees at the top of the hill. The heady scent of cannabis mingles with the rhythm of a dozen drummers. Young lovers lost to the world couple in the grass. Hula hoops twirl on supple hips. Frisbees float on invisible currents. She sings the lyrics of a Friends of Distinction song:

> Grazing in the grass is a gas
> Baby can you dig it?
> Everything here is so clear, you can see it
> And everything here is so real, you can feel it
> And it's real, so real, so real, so real, so real, so real
> Can you dig it?

Darla can dig it. She vapes a dab of Gelato 25 and wishes Danny could dig it, too.

GALLERY WENDI NORRIS ON OCTAVIA STREET exhibits the surrealist paintings of Leonora Carrington. Darla marvels at her great good fortune. She has only seen Carrington works online. She steps sideways from one to another and is pulled into the startling dream world each evokes.

An attendant approaches, an attractive fifty-something woman in a bone white pantsuit, with close-cropped hair and dangling earrings.

Are you a fan of Leonora, dear, she says.

Oh, yes, I'm in awe! Darla says.

She did some of her best work in an asylum, you know.

I didn't.

When she was twenty, she began an affair with a much older man, the artist Max Ernst. Do you know the work of Ernst?

No, I—

If you admire Carrington, dear, you will *love* the work of Ernst. He and Leonora bought a farmhouse in the South of France where they painted together and entertained fellow surrealists like Picasso and Kahlo and Duchamp and Miro. Theirs was an unconventional lifestyle by any standard. I would *love* to have been a fly on the wall of *that* farmhouse!

I can only imagine, Darla says.

Leonora's work flourished until 1940, the attendant says. Then her world fell apart. Ernst was imprisoned by the French as an enemy alien. He escaped to America with the help of heiress Peggy Guggenheim, whom he later married. Leonora had a breakdown and was sent to a psychiatric hospital where she underwent a brutal regimen of electroshock therapy and experimental drugs. But she continued to paint.

Good for her! Darla exclaims.

She was nothing if not resilient, the attendant says. The art world owes her an enormous debt. Are you a painter?

I've only just begun.

I'm sure you'll have a brilliant career. What is your name, dear?

Darla.

I'm Leslie, Darla. Here's my card. If you have a question, don't hesitate to ask.

Leslie wanders away. Darla resumes her perusal of the paintings of Leonora Carrington. She stops before the one entitled *Down Below* in which curiously clad women with disdainful expressions lounge in a sinister underworld. Darla is enthralled. She would be one of them. She pulls the dab pen from her purse and lights up. She exhales onto the painting. Smoke permeates the canvas and drifts in the very air the women breathe. Darla feels herself pulled in.

Darla!

Leslie approaches quickly.

No, no, no! she says. This will never do! I mean, are you fucking kidding me?

Darla returns the pen to her purse.

I'm so sorry, she says. I forgot where I was. I thought I was…somewhere else.

Which is exactly where you need to be right now, Darla—somewhere else!

Darla hurries out the door.

SHE HAS FILLED HER PHONE with photos of the landmarks of San Francisco. She takes one now, her last day in the city, of the street signs at the corner of Haight and Ashbury. She regrets she will not return home with something more substantial than photos by which to remember her trip. She hears a voice behind her: Pardon me, miss.

She turns. There stands a tall man in a yellow silk shirt with puffed sleeves over baggy crimson trousers tied at the ankles. His long black hair is parted in the middle. Gold hoops hang from his ears. His eyes are piercing. She could not have guessed his age.

Allow me, he says.

His voice is resonant, seeming to come from far away after a long journey. Darla feels compelled. She places her phone in his outstretched hand. She notices the profusion of black hair on his forearm and the mat of it on his chest where his yellow silk shirt hangs open.

Take a step back, he says.

Darla obeys.

Take a step to your left, he says.

Darla steps to her left.

Smile, he says.

Darla smiles despite herself. She has not smiled in a long time. The stranger returns her phone.

No picture is complete without you in it, he says.

Thank you, Darla says.

She feels flattered. Redeemed.

The pleasure is all mine, he says. Are you from out of town?

Is it so obvious?

Most residents don't take pictures of street signs, he says.

His expression is gentle. Caring.

Right, right, Darla says, feeling silly. Yes, I'm from out of town. I'm going home today.

Did you get what you came for?

Darla thinks a moment.

I had hoped to capture the spirit of '67, she says. The *zeitgeist* of *the Summer of Love*. But something is missing. Do you live here?

I come and go. I lived here during the Summer of Love.

Really! Darla says.

She calculates the years since 1967. Fifty-two of them. He is older than he looks. Or else he's lying. But she doesn't care. He has a certain dark charm.

How was it back then? she says.

There was the hippie mystique the media promoted, he says: flowers in your hair; music in the air; free love everywhere. But there was darkness, too. An undercurrent of evil. Charles Manson lived here with some of his girls: Susan Atkins. Patricia Krenwinkle. Squeaky Fromme. Do you know their story?

Barely…the news…you know.

Their impressionable young minds were so easy to manipulate…or so I imagine. Would you like to see his house?

Who's house?

Charlie's. It's a short walk away.

I would love to, Darla says.

She feels something is happening. She is being swept along on a wave. Presently she and the stranger stand before the *Charles Manson House*, an unremarkable beige Victorian with a gated portico at 636 Cole Street.

Did you know him? Darla says.

I was aware of his presence, he says. And he was aware of mine. Would you like me to take your picture?

Please, Darla says.

She hands him her phone. He takes her picture.

Perhaps you'll consider taking one of me, he says.

Of course! Darla says.

He returns her phone. She waits for him to hand her his but he doesn't. She feels foolish. He smiles apologetically.

I'm sorry, he says. I don't have a phone of my own. Perhaps we might use yours?

Darla thinks this an odd request. The man is nothing if not eccentric. But he is strangely irresistible. He stands tall and straight before the portico of the *Charles Manson House*. His arms hang loosely at his side. His eyes are hidden in shadow. She takes his picture. He approaches.

Thank you, my dear, he says.

His face is close. There is the heady scent of musk. And patchouli oil.

Perhaps now you've gotten what you came for, he says.

Darla doesn't know what this means. She feels his words conceal a great mystery.

Perhaps, she says uncertainly.

What is your name, Little One?

Darla likes that he called her Little One. She feels watched over by a higher intelligence.

Darla, she says.

Darla, he says, licking his lower lip as though tasting her name on his tongue. Darla. Very nice.

And yours?

I am called the Traveling Man. At your service.

He bends slightly at the waist and offers his hand. His dark eyes shine. His smile is sinister and beguiling at once.

She puts her hand in his. He puts his free hand on top of hers. He squeezes gently. It feels like a promise. A pact.

Until we meet again, he says.
He walks quickly away.
Darla watches him go.
She clutches her phone.
It is warm to the touch.

THE MARIONBERRY EDIBLES that served as breakfast and lunch have taken up residence in Darla's head. She dreads returning to the Valley of the Rogue. If she could be born again, she would be a contemporary of Leonora Carrington and Max Ernst. Not a fly on the wall of their South-of-France retreat—but one of them! They would talk about her work! Or she might be young and alive and full of light in 1967, the Summer of Love. When *he* walked the streets of Haight-Ashbury. The Traveling Man. She admires his absolute self-assuredness. His sense of the inevitable. He knows what he is about. As she does not. She knows only that she is more than Mrs. Danny Mueller. More than she has been or is expected to be by those who think they know her but don't. She is someone else…but who?

Danny is away. He left a note in his sprawling script on a paper bag from Ray's Food Place:

> *Darla, If I'm not here when you get back I'm up to Corvallis for supplies. Coming back tomorrow, Tuesday. I forgive you for leaving me alone for a week—and for running up $2,000.00 on my credit card! You're worth every dollar. I'm sorry I called you psycho. I can't wait to see you. Let's make it be like it was when it was good. Can we do that? Love you, Darla! Danny*

No, we *can't* do that! Darla shouts. She crumbles the note and throws it on the kitchen floor. Being like it was when it was good isn't good enough anymore! She is confused. Why does he have to be so nice?

She throws her suitcase on the bed, takes the dab pen from her purse, and marches across the lawn to her studio. The sky is metallic grey, the air thick with ash. She hurls the painting *Consumption* across the room and mounts another canvas. Pure white and waiting to be filled. She tokes from her dab pen and stares at the vast white emptiness. She opens her phone to *pictures* and scrolls through till she finds the one she wants. By midnight she has captured his image and likeness. He stands tall and straight before the gated portico of the *Charles Manson House*, 636 Cole Street, San Francisco. His arms hang loosely at his side. His eyes are hidden in shadow.

DARLA TOSSES AND TURNS. She wonders if she might have gotten too high too soon before bed. No, she decides, there is no such thing as too high. Nevertheless, she is anxious. She feels so alone. Danny's big dick would be a blessing about now. She pushes the sheet aside and slides her fingers between her legs. Before a moan escapes her lips, she feels a presence in the room. She sits abruptly: The Traveling Man lounges in the chair in the corner, draped in a black satin robe, his legs crossed at the ankles, his fingers laced in his lap. His expression is indecipherable. She pulls the sheet up under her chin.

You! she says. How did you get here?

You brought me, Darla, he says.

He takes her phone from the dresser beside the chair and holds it up. His unlikely assertion registers in a remote part of Darla's brain where anything is possible.

Umm, she says. You're not just any old hippie, are you?

No, Darla, he says. I am the Traveling Man. I have been to the far-flung corners of the world. To hidden temples and castle towers. To bat-filled subterranean caverns and steaming jungle villages. To Aboriginal outbacks and lonely shacks by railroad tracks. To the top of the tallest mountain. To the bottom of the sea.

Wow, Traveling Man, she says, you *have* gotten around. I want to hear all about it. Wait! Do you mind if I smoke?

Please yourself, Darla, he says.

His smile is generous and indifferent at once.

She takes the dab pen from the bedside table. The sheet slips into her lap. Her breasts are exposed. Her nipples are stiff. She extends the pen toward the Traveling Man. Her hand trembles slightly. He declines with a flick of his wrist.

I could not be *high*er than I am, he says.

Darla lights up. She exhales vapor into the room. It disperses like a cirrus cloud buffeted by the jet stream.

Traveling Man, she says, this is great. Tell me what you've been doing in all those far-flung places.

She feels on the brink of a rare disclosure. She feels privileged. The Traveling man uncrosses and recrosses his legs.

Developing my powers, Darla, he says. Becoming who I am: Master of Sorcery, Scientology, Theosophy, Anthroposophy, Wizardry. Of Alchemy, Necromancy, Voodoo. Of Santeria, Obeah, Isangoma, Mundunugu. Of

Sufism, Mysticism, Mumbo Jumbo, and Hocus Pocus! I've been the Consort of Cult Leaders. Conferee of the Charismatic. Mentor of the Mad Monk, the Medicine Man, the Black Magician. Dark Charmer of the High-Priest, the Low-Priest, the Shiite, the Shaman.

Darla shakes her head in amazement.

That *is* an impressive resume, she says. But what brings you to Jacksonville, Oregon, of all places?

You do, Darla, he says. Because you suffer so.

Darla feels the compassion in the Traveling Man's voice. He sees into her very soul. She teeters on the brink of tears.

I do! she says. I do!

Knowing who you *aren't* but not who you *are* is the source of your suffering, child. Be assured you are not alone. We feel your pain.

We…?

Fellow Travelers, Darla. We who have *arrived*. Who would have you pass from the outer threshold to the inner sanctum and join us there, to spend eternity in the Realm of Light.

Darla takes a deep breath. She feels on the brink of deliverance.

What do I have to do? she says.

She is willing to do *whatever* it takes to join the Traveling Man and his cohorts in the Realm of Light.

He announces with great solemnity: Remove the remaining barrier in your path to illumination, Darla.

She knows immediately to whom he refers.

Yes, he says. Danny. Know that he is not who you think he is, Darla, but rather an Agent of Change, an Enlightened Being sent to lure you into complacency, to test your will to be other than one of the sleeping masses who impede the evolution of mankind. With great courage and resolve you have passed that test, Darla. Now it is time for Danny to go home, where he will awaken and remember who he is, and *you*, Darla, must facilitate his return. Free him from his mortal coil. Once you have completed this noble task, your training will begin. You will be introduced to the curriculum of the occult. You will meet the Brethren one by one. Each is a Master in his or her own way. You will learn secrets known only to the chosen few. You will attain perfection in your art and create works to rival those of your idol, Leonora Carrington. Though she has departed this mortal plane, she yet resides in a higher place into which you will be welcomed as an equal.

Wow! Darla says. I'm ready for that! Hook me up!

Close your eyes, my child.

Darla closes her eyes.

Look deeply into yourself, he says. See what I see.

Darla looks deeply into herself. She sees what he sees.

Oh, no! she exclaims. I couldn't do that! I can't! I won't!

But you can, Darla. And you will. That he might return home and reawaken to his true self. He will be so grateful.

It will hurt!

It will pass.

Darla opens her eyes.

Alright, she says. I will do it for him.

Outside, a storm has commenced. Rain pounds the roof and thunder rattles the windowpanes. The Traveling Man stands.

It is time to seal the deal, he says.

He approaches her bed. His long black robe slips to the floor. His member is monumental, a warthog to Danny's weasel.

Look closely, he commands.

Nodules like the trichomes on a bud of cannabis line the shaft. They glisten with an interior light.

Take me! she pleads. Take me now!

He enters, and at once the yawning chasm of her desolation is filled. The atoms of her flesh are dispersed, and she is stardust, one with the Universe. After a seeming eternity, she reassembles on the material plane. She is alone in the room. She frees herself from the tangle of sweaty sheets and goes to the window. The sun has risen. The sky is blue. She sings her favorite Jimmy Cliff song:

> I can see clearly now
> The rain is gone
> I can see all obstacles in my way
> Gone are the dark clouds that had me blind
> It's gonna be a bright, bright
> Sunshiny day!

FUELED BY THE VISION she shared with the Traveling Man—and by a fistful of Limeade Gummies—Darla prepares for Danny's arrival. She changes the sheets on their bed from cotton to pale green satin; sprinkles the sheet with rose petals, white and red; places candles about the room, a circle of them on the bedside table; empties a quart of *Western American Single Malt Whiskey* into a crystal decanter; puts a CD of Andrea Bocelli's *Con Te Partito—A Time To Say Goodbye*—into the player; lights a coil of spicy Tibetan incense; and conceals a crotchless blood-red Teddy under her Levi's and flannel shirt.

DARLA AND DANNY EMBRACE at the door.
I missed you, Darla, Danny says. You made me a lonely man!
I'm back now, Darla says. I'm sorry I was a bitch.
Did you get what you went for?
I did and more. Do you want to see pictures?

AT THE KITCHEN TABLE, Darla dabs and Danny sips his whiskey neat. They peruse the photos on her iPhone.
Who's this dude? Danny says. He looks like Ronald McDonald in drag!
He wouldn't like to be called a clown, Danny. He's been to the top of the tallest mountain, and to the bottom of the sea. He's mastered the methods of Mysticism, Mumbo Jumbo, and Hocus Pocus.
You're crazy as a loon, Darla, but I love you—and I know what you need!
So give it to me, big boy. We're wasting time.
She takes Danny by the hand and leads him to the bedroom.
Wow! he says at the door. If this is some hippie shit, I'll take it!
Darla disrobes down to her teddy. She slides onto the satin sheets and spreads her legs.
Hot damn! Danny says.
He peels out of his Levi's and boots. Over his shoulder, Darla sees the Traveling Man in the chair in the corner. He wears the dark suit of an undertaker. His legs are crossed at the ankles, his fingers laced in his lap. His expression is indecipherable.

WHILE DANNY BANGS AWAY, Darla fantasizes partying with Leonora Carrington. With Max Ernst, Frida Kahlo, Pablo Picasso, Duchamp and Miro. They eat raw meat with their fingers and drink wine from the skulls of baby goats. Their laughter rises to the rafters. After Danny does his business, he rolls onto his back and is soon fast asleep. His lips are parted. The artery in his neck pulses like the heart of a baby bird. Darla reaches under the bed and retrieves the trimmer. She holds it aloft. She looks to the Traveling Man. He nods. She presses the button on the handle. The blades come alive like the whir of a swarm of locusts.

Einhel! she exclaims. German engineering! Dual action with twenty-eight inches of diamond-ground, laser-cut blades delivering 2,700 cuts per minute! A swiveling ergonomic handle so you can trim at any angle without straining your wrist! Isn't it beautiful, Danny?

She brings the blade down slowly.

MEANWHILE, 5,320 MILES TO THE EAST, flames leap from the burning roof of the Cathedral of Notre Dame. Silver-blue smoke billows upward as thousands of Parisians line the street and watch in horror and disbelief. A few blocks away, a young woman in designer jeans and *Denali Outback* hiking boots snaps pictures of the conflagration with her iPhone. She hears a voice behind her.

Excuse-moi, Mademoiselle.

She turns. There stands a tall man with black hair brushed back severely, in black trousers and a black leather vest over a shiny white shirt with puffed sleeves. He might be a waiter. Or a bullfighter. Or a handsome, charismatic con man. She doesn't care. He exudes a certain dark charm.

I'm sorry, she says. I don't speak French.

Ah, you are American.

His voice is resonant, seeming to come from far away after a long journey. He turns to watch the flames lick the sky.

Such a tragedy, no?

Yes, she says. So terrible!

They will say it was an accident.

I'm sure it is.

Please, allow me.

His words are compelling. She puts her phone into his outstretched hand.

No picture is complete without you in it, he says.

His expression is indecipherable.

DARLA PUTS THE SEVERED HEAD of Danny inside the circle of candles on the bedside table. He opens his eyes.

You didn't have to kill me, Darla, he says. You didn't have to kill me.

She closes his eyes with her fingertips. Kisses his parted lips. Puts his Maga hat on backward.

Shut up, Danny, she says. You're going home. You'll thank me when you get there.

She looks at the chair in the corner, but the chair is empty. Save for the severed head of Danny, she is alone in the room.

Traveling man? she says. Are you out there?

Traveling man?

Traveling man!

NOVEMBER

TEN THOUSAND HOURS
IN SHADOWLAND

Music is a strange thing. I would almost say it is a miracle.
For it stands halfway between thought and phenomenon,
between spirit and matter

— Heinrich Heine

Sunday, November 3rd, 2019

I HOVERED IN THE VOID between stories like the severed head of a Barbie Doll suspended in Jell-O in a Bell Jar. Good Bean patrons moved soundlessly on the other side of the glass. *Is anybody out there? Can anybody hear me?*

No one heard me.

Sometimes I get this way, Sam. Especially when feeling abandoned by Miranda. Where was she now? Who was she with? I was being a baby, I know. An insecure whiney brat. She told me early on I was not the only writer with whom she conjugated. Still, I couldn't help but feel she was laying her eggs in another bird's nest.

I went to the counter for a refill. Second of the morning. On impulse grabbed a copy of the *Jacksonville Review*. Read at random, searching for something, *anything*, to rekindle the dying fire of my creativity. I settled on the column *The Unfettered Critic.* It read:

> Hats off to The Craterian Theatre at the Collier Center for The Performing Arts for bringing to our beautiful valley the phenomenal Yama, the dynamic duo of Jane and Kenneth Yamaguchi. Hawaii-born Japanese American Jane Yamaguchi, ukulele Maestro non-pareil and a transcendent vocalist, has performed in concert halls coast to coast and in the major capitals of the world since she burst upon the scene in 1967. She has shared the stage with fellow ukulele masters Eddie Kamae, Israel "Iz" Kamakawiwo'ole, and Daniel Ho, among others; mentored rising stars Jake Shimabukuro and Taimane Gardner; toured with an array of rock luminaries from Jimmy Hendrix to Joan Jett; played an improvised ninety–minute duet with Ravi Shankar at Carnegie Hall to a standing ovation; and performed for President Barack Obama at The White House. She and her partner, viola virtuoso Kenneth Yamaguchi, formed the duo Yama in 1992 after they met on the stage of the Boston Pops Orchestra where Jane opened for Grammy Award-winning vocalist Bonnie Raitt and her father, John Raitt. Yama's repertoire is eclectic and far-ranging. To the driving beat of Peruvian percussionist and femme fatale Theresa Avila Estrada on Cajon box drum, expect to be regaled by a night of rock, classical, blues, folk, flamenco and

funk. You don't want to miss an evening of Yama, folks. They take the stage Saturday, November 2nd, at 8:00 p.m. Tickets are available at the box office at 16 S. Bartlett, Medford, and online at Ticketmaster.com.

The concert would be the next day. I was sure I wouldn't be there. I have always viewed the ukulele as not a serious instrument, but a toy, a prop for Tiny Tim. I turned the pages of the *Review*. Attempted to read the column about our celebrated cemetery, the Silent City on the Hill, but the words seemed as lifeless to me as the inhabitants of those hallowed grounds. Just as I closed the *Review* in despair, my cell phone rang.

It was my old friend, David. Not old because we go way back, but old because he's twice my age. He calls me son. He believes in me, and I'll take it. You can't have too much validation of your work. David is a retired jazz pianist of some repute. He put out a few platters over the years. Garnered a few awards. Played on the big stage. After fifty years touring, tickling the ivories coast to coast, he arrived in Jacksonville by a circuitous route, as had so many of the recently arrived, and settled in for the remainder of his days. Out of the limelight, into the twilight.

Adrian, he said, what are you doing tomorrow night?

Tomorrow night? Well, David, I'll be countin' flowers on the wall. But that don't bother me at all. Playin' solitaire 'til dawn with a deck of fifty-one, smokin' cigarettes and watchin' Captain Kangaroo. Now don't tell me I've nothin' to do.

You're too young to know that song, Adrian.

I know that song and a few that preceded it. What's up, David?

Yama's up, son. Are you hip to Yama?

Funny you should ask. I just read about their performance in the Jacksonville Review.

A performance not to be missed, my man. That the greatest Ukulele Lady of all time is gracing the stage in Medford, Oregon, is a miracle. I have tickets. Front row seats. I'm proud to call Jane Yamaguchi a friend of mine from back in the day. *Way* back! We jammed together in San Francisco in the '60s. She's staying at my house after the show. I'm hosting a reception. You're invited. There'll be lots of folks you know and some you don't. Are you on board, young man?

Hook me up, old man.

I'll swing by at seven.

I'll be here.

AS YOU KNOW BY NOW, SAM, I don't believe that events are ever random. I prefer Carl Jung's concept of *synchronicity*, that events with no evident cause and effect are related on a deep level, woven into a cosmic tapestry by a superior intelligence behind the illusion of the manifest world. David calling and inviting me to attend a concert about which, moments before, I had read and dismissed, is a perfect example of synchronicity, and the likeliest representative of the intelligence orchestrating this meaningful coincidence—is Miranda! If the performance of Yama, and the reception after, are the genesis of my next story—well, I will apologize profusely to Miranda for having doubted her fidelity!

THE CRATERIAN THEATRE is a jewel in the crown of Rogue Valley venues. They brought a gem to the Valley when they booked Yama. *Incredulous* would describe my reaction to their performance, especially that of Jane Yamaguchi.

David and I sat in the first row a dozen feet from the lip of the stage. Jane Yamaguchi was an apparition, a diminutive fairy in an emerald-green pantsuit that shone under the lights. Her body moved with supple grace to the rhythm of the music. I could see her face. Youthful despite her seventy-plus years. Intense and full of joy. Rhapsodic one moment, playful the next. Her fingers were a blur, notes cascading from her instrument like water over a cliff's edge. She employed a device David later informed me was a *loop*, or *looper*, whereby a musician accompanies him or herself by playing and recording a passage of music, then playing over it, and recording again, then playing over the composite thus far, et cetera, until there seemed to be not a single instrument playing but half a dozen. A veritable orchestra!

And what a voice! Sometimes delicate as a leaf in the wind, seeming to drift down to our world from another time and place, at other times throaty and unrestrained in the manner of Edith Piaf. Midway through her set, she sang the Piaf standard *Non, Je Ne Regrette Rien—No Regrets—* in flawless French. Where had I heard that before?

Pieces from every musical genre are found in their repertoire. I present here their playlist as I remember it: Queen's *Bohemian Rhapsody; The William Tell Overture; Hotel California; El Condor Pasa; Orange Blossom Special; Ghost Riders in the Sky; Nights in White Satin; Hallelujah; No Regrets; Somewhere Over the Rainbow; Sukiyaki* in Japanese; the Hawaiian standards *Ukulele Lady* and *On the Island*. They finished with a spectacular rendition of *Flight of the Bumble Bee* that brought the house down and garnered a two-minute standing ovation.

I came away with a brand-new respect for the ukulele.

DAVID LIVES ALONE in a rambling Victorian house on a hillside at the edge of town. His wife of forty years, Eileen, passed shortly after they arrived. We had never met. David is most often melancholy and spends days on end in solitude playing and composing. Occasionally, as though to resurrect a life, he entertains. Tonight, there is a mix of guests from out of town, and luminaries from the local community of artists and intellectuals: poets, painters, and entrepreneurs; pot farmers and politicians. They circulate around the Grand Piano in his spacious living room, meeting and greeting, holding finger food courtesy of Jefferson Farms Kitchen in one hand, a glass of wine courtesy of South Stage Cellars in the other. There is the director of the Britt Festival Orchestra talking with Kenneth Yamaguchi. There is the curator of Art Presence. The publisher of the *Jacksonville Review*. The authors of *The Unfettered Critic*. The proprietor of *Rebel Heart Books*. There is Paul the Potter, tall and stooped, chatting with Bennie Esposito, formerly known as Dominic De Luca, and before that Nobody Number Ninety-Nine, and his wife and fellow former Nobody, Ginna. I wonder who else among the revelers were once Nobodies who became Somebodies.

I see Jane Yamaguchi in a cluster of admirers. She has switched out her green pantsuit for a blue and pink floral-print wrap-around dress and low heels. Guests clamor to meet her, but I don't presume to be one of them until David takes her gently by the elbow and steers her away from the pack in my direction. Her long silver hair is pulled back severely and gathered in a bun held fast by a long wooden stick pin. Tasseled earrings dangle from delicate lobes. Her face is smooth, her eyes dark, her make-up artfully applied. She is beguiling. I am beguiled. David introduces us and wanders away.

An honor to meet you, Ms. Yamaguchi, I say.

Jane, she says.

Jane, I say.

She holds out her hand. I take it in mine. Her fingers are slender and smooth, save for their calloused tips. There is an aura of timelessness about her. I feel in the presence of a superior being with an uncanny depth of understanding.

Our conversation is brief and perplexing. I tell her I was in awe of her performance, and immediately feel foolish, sycophantic. She's heard it all before. She thanks me politely. I ask how long she practiced before her first public appearance.

For only a moment, she says. For as long as it takes to blow out twenty-one candles on a birthday cake.

Her smile is enigmatic. She does not explain.

David speaks highly of you, she says. That you're writing a book about unlikely and inexplicable events and how they impact our lives.

Yes, I say, I am.

Very good, Adrian, she says. Tell me: What are the *parameters* of an event?

The parameters...?

Yes. When does an event begin and when does it end? What is its *duration*?

Duration? Well, I—

She answers her own question: When time and space collapse, she says, there *are* no events. Neither beginning nor end. No duration. Only *simultaneity* when everything happens at once. I have some experience in these matters, Adrian. I have something to tell you that might be of interest. Can we meet again?

I was stupefied. The Diva wants to meet me in private?

Of course! I say. When and where?

Tomorrow, she says. Early. I have a flight out in the afternoon. You decide the time and place.

There's a coffee shop in town where I write, I say. The Good Bean Café. How would eight o'clock be?

That would be wonderful, Adrian. I'll be there. Until then...

She offers her hand. I wonder how many hours of practice are behind those leathery fingertips.

ON A GIVEN DAY THE GOOD BEAN CAFÉ at eight in the morning is bustling and likely minus an empty table. I arrived at six and claimed my usual two-seater against the far wall with a view of the room and the front door. I spent two hours tweaking last month's story *The Traveling Man* and wondering with what disclosure the Diva would entrust me.

She arrived promptly at eight. She was not alone. I recognized her partner, Kenneth. She introduced us. Apologized for the intrusion and said his presence would add dimension and credibility to her account. I was pleased.

It's an honor and a privilege, Mr. Yamaguchi, I said.

Call me Kenneth, please.

Kenneth, I said.

Our table for two would never do. I scanned the room. Against the back wall was an empty table with four chairs. How serendipitous! Had it been reserved for the occasion? I imagined a sign: *Lomachenko. Party of Three.* While I packed my laptop and relocated, Jane and Kenneth queued up for coffee and soon joined me.

Jane was dressed casually in white denim trousers, open-toed shoes, and a black satin blouse. Her hair was freed of its bun and hung to her shoulders. She seemed more human to me today, more down-to-earth, a welcome perception that lessened my awe and allowed me to relax. Kenneth Yamaguchi gave an impression of hipness that belied his age, in faded Levi's over zippered black velvet boots with heels, and a white linen blazer over a pale blue t-shirt. His Asian features and long white hair brought to mind the professor of theoretical physics, Michio Kaku. His expression was reserved. He seemed to be waiting for the conversation to begin. I asked if there was a stringed instrument he was not a master of.

Of course, he said with an impish grin. There have been countless clever stringed instruments around the world for thousands of years—and I'm only master of half of them!

His smile faded. He looked down, as though embarrassed by his sudden expressiveness. His shyness was endearing.

Adrian, Jane said, what are some of the unlikely and inexplicable events contained in your stories?

Well, I said…a man drives alone across the desert under a clear blue sky and a body bounces off the windshield of his car. A man awakens with no knowledge of who he is and is free to become whoever he wants. A disturbed young girl snaps a picture of a mysterious stranger and takes him home in her camera. A man and a dog trade places and romp for an evening around the fireplace. A youth encounters himself in the wilderness, they have a contentious conversation and go their separate ways. And other improbable scenarios, Jane, I said.

Very good, Adrian, she said. And how far along are you?

Just finished story ten of twelve, I said. One for each month of the year. I'm through October.

Have you chosen the subject of number eleven?

No. I'm awaiting inspiration. Something always seems to come my way. Once a month a story idea is delivered like a parcel.

Perhaps what I've come to tell you will qualify as unlikely and inexplicable, and merit inclusion in your book as the November story. Would you like to hear it?

Would I ever! Do you mind if I record it?

Please do, she said.

I placed my phone between us and turned on the *record* function.

Where should I begin? she said.

At a moment in time preceding your event, I said. You can't go wrong with *I was born...*

She smiled and related the following:

TEN THOUSAND HOURS IN SHADOWLAND

I WAS BORN AN ONLY CHILD in Honolulu in 1946 to an alcoholic Japanese father and a paranoid schizophrenic Hawaiian mother. It was a marriage made in hell. My childhood was challenging, as you might imagine, Adrian. My father was a good man who did his best to raise me despite his penchant for booze and his tragic marriage, but I was unruly and rebellious. Drugs and brushes with the law were the hallmarks of my adolescence. I managed to finish High School by the slimmest of margins and had no prospects. My father, bless his soul, saved enough money to send me to Tokyo to study Namikoshi Shiatsu under the grandson of the founder, Toru Namikoshi. My fingers were strong yet nimble, and I became a skilled masseuse. I returned to Honolulu and was kept busy by the tourist trade but my heart wasn't in it. Truth is, I only studied Shiatsu to please my father and to get away from Honolulu. When I heard through the grapevine that a grand hotel and spa, the Radisson Miyako, was opening in San Francisco's Japantown and needed authentic Shiatsu practitioners, I packed my bags. I said goodbye to my father. He cried and gave me money, probably the last of his savings. I visited my mother at her care home. She didn't know me.

My last night in Honolulu was fateful. As a parting gift, a girlfriend took me to a performance by ukulele master Herb Ohta. I was blown away. I had always regarded the ukulele as a counterfeit instrument that went plunk, plunk in the hands of jolly fat Hawaiians. Little did I know! From that day forward I knew what I wanted to do, and it was not Shiatsu.

The Miyako took me on. I was the quintessential Asian masseuse they were looking for. The money wasn't great but I could afford my share of the rent on a two-bedroom apartment with a fellow masseuse in the Fillmore District and saved enough to buy a ukulele. I practiced incessantly but despite my dexterity and determination my progress was slow. I couldn't *hear* the music. Melodies were elusive. Chord changes befuddled me. There was a disconnect between my ears and my fingers. Practice doesn't make perfect, Adrian, if you continue to do the same wrong things over and over. You merely get better at being bad. I needed mentoring but couldn't afford lessons.

Then I met Freddie. Not his real name, Adrian. You would recognize his real name because he's still out there in the public eye but I won't say his name because it is not my practice to cast aspersions on my fellow human beings—but if it were I would cast them on Freddie!

We met at the Miyako. Freddie was a lead guitar player in a rock and roll band of some notoriety. It was 1966 and San Francisco had launched a rock music revolution. The West Coast sound. I'm not telling you anything you don't know, Adrian, but I was there, and it was special. On any given night you might see Grace Slick and the Jefferson Airplane at the Fillmore Auditorium. Or Sly and the Family Stone. Or Big Brother and the Holding Company. Santana. Steve Miller. Credence Clearwater Revival. The Grateful Dead. Or Freddie's band. I won't say their name. You would recognize the name. For our purposes, we'll call them *Freddie and the Fucktones*. I see that amuses you, Adrian. But I haven't always been the proper Diva, you know. I can be down and dirty with the best of them. I've been around the block.

I do find it amusing, Jane, I said. And refreshing. You've let your hair down, literally and metaphorically, and become accessible to me. I appreciate that. You have another side, too: student of metaphysics. You spoke last night of the collapse of time and space and the duration of an event. I've been intrigued ever since.

We'll come to that, Adrian. I'm not finished with the Fucktones. Freddie was in town. He was staying at the Miyako. He called for a massage. I went to his room. He wanted more than my strong nimble fingers. He was sexy and beautiful and wild but I was strictly business. He asked me out. We became lovers. I had no one else. My mother died of an undisclosed illness shortly after I left Honolulu. My father took his own life a month later. I was alone in the world. I accompanied Freddie and his band on tour.

The road was exciting for a while. I met the megastars of rock but midway through the tour I tired of the drugs and the late nights. And I began to see Freddie for what he was: an egocentric asshole and a middling musician. He was content to be an ordinary rock star. He had promised to improve my technique on the ukulele but wearied of the effort. Given my ineptitude, it was more of a challenge than he cared to meet. Besides, he couldn't care less if I played well or not at all. *He* was the musician in the house, and it was *me* he was playing. I was his trophy girlfriend. His personal Yoko Ono. His naughty little Nip. When he offered to share me with his band mates in the spirit of free love, I declined and knew our affair was coming to a close.

I practiced the ukulele on my own when I could, on the tour bus and in hotel rooms coast to coast. I was determined against all odds to excel and perform.

In June of '67, we arrived back in San Francisco. It was the Summer of Love: Flowers in your hair. Music in the air. Free love everywhere. It was also the month I turned twenty-one. Freddie decided we would have a birthday party in Golden Gate Park. He wanted to show me off. I said I wanted to play ukulele at the party for all assembled. He tried to discourage me. Said I would embarrass myself. I said I was playing, goddamn it, if only *Mary Had a Little Lamb* or *Happy Birthday to Me!*

Freddie and I and the boys in the band booked rooms at the Stanyan Park Hotel in Haight-Ashbury. We set off for the iconic Golden Gate Park locale, *Hippie Hill*, laden with instruments and amplifiers and food and wine, and a birthday cake with twenty-one candles. Tens of thousands of flower children from across the country had converged on the park. We set up camp in the grass beneath a canopy of trees at the top of the hill. The heady scent of cannabis mingled with the rhythm of a dozen drummers. Young lovers lost to the world coupled in the grass. Hula hoops twirled on supple hips. Frisbees hovered on invisible currents. Local musicians, now famous, gave free concerts. On this day, my twenty-first birthday, Grace Slick and the Jefferson Airplane were there. Jerry Garcia and the Grateful Dead were there. Ken Kesey and the Merry Pranksters were there, distributing LSD-laden punch, *electric Kool-Aid*. You can be certain we had our share.

Freddie broke out the cake. He lit the candles. Make a wish, he said. I wished for two things: that I would have the strength of character to persist in my practice until I had mastered the ukulele, and that I would get out from under Freddie and the Fucktones.

I took a deep breath, closed my eyes and blew, and when I opened them—I was somewhere else. Gone was the green grass of Golden Gate Park and the milling hordes of hippies. Gone were Freddie and the Fucktones. I was alone, immersed in eerie blue light. Before me stretched a vast horizon impossibly far away. Approaching was a cluster of shadowy figures. They seemed to float above the ground. They stopped before me. Truly featureless. Naught but hovering shadows. I was amazed but fearless. Strangely calm. A voice came from their midst. I heard it in my head.

Welcome to Shadowland, Jane, it said. We're so pleased to have you and look forward to your stay. Please come along.

They drifted away. I drifted behind them. It seemed a most natural thing to do.

Adrian, now begins the account of how Yama came to be. It would take the length of your book to tell you what transpired in Shadowland. I don't want to use more than November's share of words, so I'll try to keep my account down to what is essential.

Don't worry about it, Jane. It's my job to pare each story down to an optimum length. You just tell yours and I'll do the rest.

Very good, Adrian. Shadowland. It's a kind of a university beyond time and space where people are brought to be mentored in their chosen endeavors. Their art. The length of their stay is the time it takes to practice for ten thousand hours—ten years at the rate of twenty hours per week, after which one would presumably be a master. Each student of Shadowland is assigned a *shade,* a sort of Faculty Advisor. Shades are amorphous, without a body to call their own. They may appear in one guise or another, but one always recognizes them. They are whoever one wills them to be at a given moment. For example, if you spent the morning mulling over the veracity of the oft-quoted phrase *I think, therefore I am*, or the meaning of E = MC squared, your Shade may appear as René Descartes or as Einstein, but you immediately recognize it for what it is: your Faculty Advisor. Your shade.

Shades have personalities. Some are formal and aloof, others playful and mischievous. All have names. Mine was a feisty nymph named Miranda—

Miranda! I exclaimed. Jane! Are you kidding me? Miranda…?

Yes, Adrian, Miranda. Why does that surprise you?

Umm…it's nothing, Jane. The name is familiar is all. Do go on…

Thank you, Adrian. Upon arrival in Shadowland, one is informed that he or she would spend ten years deeply immersed in his or her art, ukulele in my case. At the moment of my arrival, I had felt no anxiety or alarm, only total acceptance of my suddenly altered state. Likewise, when informed I'd be there for ten years, I had no misgivings. There was a radiant intelligence in the eerie blue light that imbued a calm acceptance of what was. I was further informed that at the end of my sojourn in Shadowland I would be returned to the exact moment in time and space from whence I had come—blowing out the candles in Golden Gate Park with my eyes closed—and would have no memory of having spent ten years in Shadowland, though I would retain the skills I had honed for ten thousand hours. You may wonder, Adrian, if I would not remember my ten-year hiatus, how I can relate my story to you now. I'll get to that soon enough.

The role of a shade was to plan a curriculum for the newly arrived and to keep them on track for the duration of their stay. To assign to them a cadre of mentors in his or her principal art, as well as a supplemental field, a *minor*, if you will. A mentor is an incarnation of a deceased master in a particular field who, upon his or her demise, is recruited into Shadowland. They have the option of declining, but none do, as it is an honor to pass on one's skills to an eager apprentice in Shadowland. I was taught ukulele by the masters Roy Smeck, George Formby, Arthur Godfrey, Israel Kamakawiwo'ole, and Jake Shimabukuro. You might protest, Adrian, that at the time of my *extraction* from Golden Gate Park, 1967, Smeck and Godfrey and Kamakawiwo'ole and Shimabukuro were not deceased but were very much alive. Such is the paradox of Shadowland, which lies outside the boundaries of time and space. Curiously, though I was mentored by Jake Shimabukuro, following my return to the so-called *real world*—I mentored him!

I was further instructed by masters of string instruments other than the ukulele: flamenco guitar by Ramon Montoya, Sabicas, Paco De Lucia and Vicente Amigo; banjo by Roy Clark and Earl Scruggs; jazz guitar by Earl Klugh, Pat Martino and Lee Ritenour; rock guitar by Jeff Beck and Eddie Van Halen. I *minored* in voice, learning from the likes of Jenny Lind, Maria Callas, Edith Piaf, Billie Holiday, Barbara Streisand and Bonnie Raitt.

Shadowland is the ethereal birthplace of prodigies, Adrian. You might wonder how a child with no prior instruction can emerge as a gifted practitioner of a certain art. Take Wolfgang Amadeus Mozart for example. He composed his first piece of music at the age of five. He performed before the Royal Court at the age of six. How could this be? I will tell you. It is a mere footnote in history that at the age of four, Mozart became ill with a high fever in Salzburg, Austria. He slept for twenty-four hours, during which time he was transported to *Shadowland* where he spent ten years studying music. And who was his principal mentor? Himself! Yes, Adrian, the fledgling Mozart was mentored by an older incarnation of himself. Such is the paradoxical nature of Shadowland, where the laws of physics are suspended. When the younger Mozart finished his ten-year apprenticeship, he awakened from his slumber in Salzburg an accomplished musician and composer—a prodigy! Likewise, prodigies throughout the ages, in every discipline—musicians, painters and poets—have been nurtured in Shadowland and emerged fully formed.

Shadowland is home to countless artists of every persuasion from every era of history, all present at once. I became acquainted with the likes of Michelangelo, Raphael, and Pablo Picasso. Despite the differences in our eras, our cultures, and our language, we understood one another. Goethe would address me in German, and I understood. Edith Piaf would sing to me in French, and I understood. Homer would recite passages from *The Odyssey* in Greek and be understood.

We were a social lot, assembling for long conversations about the meaning of art and life, and performing for one another under the approving gaze of our Shadows. We were proud to display our evolving skills. I made many friends, chief among them—Kenneth Yamaguchi.

JANE PAUSED HER NARRATIVE and looked at her partner. They smiled into one another's eyes.

Kenneth! I said. You were in Shadowland, too?

So I'm told, Kenneth said. Though I have no recollection.

But how could you not remember, if Jane does? I said.

We're coming to that, Adrian, Jane said. Allow me to continue.

Please do, I said.

Kenneth and I fell in love. We spent the better part of our ten years together, playing crazy, complex off-the-cuff duets, sharing details of our pre-Shadowland lives. There was little we did not know about one another. Alas, I had arrived in Shadowland before him and completed my ten thousand hours first, and it was time for me to return. For each of us, there was a graduation ceremony. Fellow apprentices and shades alike gathered around. I was given a cake with a single candle, symbolic of the first year of my new life to come. My heart ached. I knew when I blew out that candle, I would immediately return to a moment ten years prior with no recollection of Shadowland, nor of my beloved Kenneth. I closed my eyes, inhaled, and blew.

TENDRILS OF SMOKE SPIRALED UPWARD from twenty-one blown-out candles. The Fucktones clapped and hooted. Freddie strummed his guitar and played Happy Birthday. I spied my ukulele in the grass. Felt the dread of anticipation. Why ever had I committed to playing at my party? But I was determined. I picked it up.

Plug me in, I said.

Freddie hooked me to an amplifier. Faced two speakers toward the masses milling on the hillside. I chose a chord and strummed. My fingers came alive. They were not my own. My left hand raced up and down the fretboard with blistering speed. The fingers of my right were a blur. I blew that hillside away, Adrian. Freddie and the Fucktones tried to keep up but I left those slugs in the dust.

I was as amazed as anyone. A moment before, I was a tone-deaf dufus who couldn't carry a tune, now I'm playing an electric version of *Night on Bald Mountain* on the ukulele! A thousand people gathered around. Two thousand. Three thousand. I wowed that crowd for ninety minutes straight. By chance Rock Impresario Bill Graham was among them and my career was launched. Freddie tried to take credit for my skills. Said he would manage me. Take me to the top. I told him to fuck off. I would get there without him.

I played local venues until a tour could be arranged. I shared a stage periodically with our mutual friend, David, at the dawn of his career. Our paths continued to cross.

A decade following my emergence from Shadowland, my career in full force, I began a series of recurring dreams wherein I had long and pleasant conversations with notable intellects and artists throughout history: Tolstoy, Whitman, Vivaldi. They were so vivid! I would awaken remembering every word! I had never been a proponent of reincarnation, Adrian. It had always been enough for me to manage the life I was living, but the reality of my dreams was compelling. Had I lived before? I engaged the services of a renowned Past-Life Regression Hypnotherapist. I was skeptical but during our very first session, my sojourn in Shadowland returned in a flash of eerie blue light. I recalled every detail. Remembered every face. The mystery of my implausible breakout performance on Hippie Hill became clear.

I kept my revelation to myself. It was nobody's business. The media would make a circus of it that would disrupt my career. I didn't need the aggravation. I did wonder why the Overseers of Shadowland would permit this breach in their security. Was it deliberate or a rift in the tapestry of time, space, and memory? I will never know.

For the next dozen years, I toured the world. Periodically I would see a familiar face, a former fellow student of Shadowland. He or she would not recognize me. I would say nothing. In 1992 I opened for Bonnie Raitt and her father, John, on the stage of the Boston Pops Orchestra. I couldn't take my eyes off the viola player. Despite twenty–five intervening years, I could not fail to recognize my Shadowland lover, Kenneth. I whooped across the stage.

Kenneth! It's me! Jane!

He was startled.

Kenneth, I said, quite stupidly, don't you know who I am?

You're Jane Yamaguchi, he said. The Ukulele Lady. Of course, I know who you are.

No, no, we were lovers in Shadowland!

He was mystified. He remembered nothing.

There's something incredible I have to tell you, Kenneth, I said. Please indulge me.

We arranged to meet at a local bar after the show. I told him everything. He shook his head in disbelief. I said did you not have a sudden unlikely and inexplicable improvement in your playing twenty-five years ago? He agreed he did. I told him intimate details about his life before 1967 that even he did not remember. He was convinced. He left The Boston Pops and we formed Yama…and here we are, Adrian. The rest is history.

Wow, Jane and Kenneth, that is one of the most incredible accounts I've ever heard. It certainly merits inclusion in my book as the November story. Thank you both for sharing. Say, Jane, I wonder, since you can recognize your fellow Shadowland students, do you recognize me?

I wouldn't tell you if I did, Adrian.

No worries, Jane. I would know if my writing was prodigious. It's not. I'll be getting my ten thousand hours the hard way, one hour at a time, and I'm fine with that. I'd say I'm five down, five to go, and I'll get there. What's next for you guys. You're no spring chickens. You can't tour forever.

Funny you should ask that question, Adrian. We do have plans. Last night's reception at David's, seeing how dense this lovely little town is in talent and creativity, made up our minds. In fact, I recognized a few faces from Shadowland, though I won't say who. We're retiring from full-time touring at the end of the year. We're buying a house in Jacksonville. We'll maintain our residence in Honolulu and commute. Kenneth was offered a position with the Britt Festival Orchestra. Yama will play wineries for fun, and I will write my memoir, featuring my Shadowland experience. Inclusion in your book as the November story will serve as a precursor… and I'll want your assistance, Adrian. I've not written a book before. Will you help me?

Whoa, Jane! I can't believe I'm hearing this. Of course, I'll help you! It will be an honor. And welcome to Jacksonville, Jane and Kenneth!

Thank you, Adrian.

What do you intend to call your memoir, Jane? Wait, don't tell me: *Ten Thousand Hours in Shadowland.*

She smiled.

Great minds think alike, she said.

She gathered her purse.

We have a plane to catch, she said. I'm so glad we had this conversation. I look forward to reading your book, Adrian, and to working with you on mine.

Likewise, Jane. One more question, if you don't mind.

Of course.

What became of Freddie and the Fucktones?

Only Freddie and the drummer survive. The other players are subs. They play the casino circuit, and low-rent venues where the marquees are cracked and missing letters. Do I sound like I'm gloating? I'm not. Well, maybe I am just a little…

Who are they, Jane, really? Just between you and me.

She pursed her lips and reflected.

Just between you and me, she said.

She came around to my side of the table. Whispered in my ear.

No! I said.

Yes, she said.

Well, I'll be damned, I said.

She rose to go.

We'll be in touch, she said.

She offered her hand. I took it. Her fingers were cool and smooth, save for the calloused fingertips. I shook hands with Kenneth. I watched them go. They passed through the door and were gone.

Yama, I thought. My November story.

I turned my gaze to the ceiling.

I know you're there, Miranda, I said. Forgive me for having ever doubted you. Mea Culpa, Mea Culpa, Mea maxima Culpa.

Amen.

DECEMBER

WHEN THE TRAIN LEAVES THE STATION

Our duty as storytellers is to bring people to the station.
There each person will choose his or her own train...
but we must at least take them to a point of departure.
                                    – Federico Fellini

Tuesday, December 31st, 2019, 11:45 p.m.

ENSHROUDED IN A CLOUD OF UNKNOWING, that's how you would have found me the first two weeks of December, Sam. Notice today's date, the last of the month. When this day is over, the year is over. Where have I been? I had sat at my usual table at the Good Bean Café on Sunday morning, December 1st, feeling good about myself, maybe a little smug even. Eleven months and eleven stories into a twelve-story series—what's not to feel good about? I was confident the twelfth would come in a flash of inspiration, or yield to my methods of evocation, or else be narrated by a stranger who would introduce himself and ask what I was writing and I would tell him I was writing stories around unlikely and inexplicable events and he would say he had one for me, would I mind if he shared, and I would say, no, not at all, please do and he would have a seat and tell me his story…but, no, on December 1st I sat alone without a clue what my next story would be. I might as well have had a brick for a brain, such was my inability to think. For the first two weeks of the month, my muse, Miranda, was absent without leave. Then the unexpected occurred.

I'D FIRST SEEN THE FUNNY LITTLE MAN in September. He wore lime green leather shorts held up by yellow suspenders. Hiking boots and rainbow-colored stockings to his knees. A Swiss Alpine hat with a perky red feather. He carried a walking stick. Walked up one aisle of the café and down the other, nodded when our eyes met and left the cafe.

Such was his routine several times a month, coming and going, never buying coffee, never sitting, never saying a word. A nod of recognition, then out the door.

Until Sunday, December 15th, when he came in, caught my eye, and came straight to my table.

You'll be needing a final story, he announced. And artwork for your cover.

I was too astonished to respond. Indeed, I'd been pondering the artwork for the cover of my book since I began to write it. Would I have a publisher thousands of miles away determine what imagery best represented the soul of my work? I didn't think so. I would design it myself. But how did this odd fellow know I needed artwork—and know, too, that I was in want of story number twelve? I didn't ask. It had been a year filled with surreal moments like this one and the year wasn't over. I thought of a favorite quote by the poet Kay Ryan: *As for reality, I don't even have any interest in that word.*

I can provide both, he said. May I join you?

Please do, I said.

He sat and faced me. His expression was mischievous, yet I perceived a grievous life. Sorrow sat on his shoulders like a sandbag.

Richter, he said. Conrad Richter.

He did not offer his hand.

Adrian, I said. Adrian Lomachenko.

Pleased to meet you, Adrian, he said.

Despite his name and his odd attire, he had no discernible accent.

Conrad, I said, you have a famous namesake: Hans Richter. A principle in the Dada Art Movement. Any relation?

An uncle twice removed, he said. My great great grandfather married his mother.

Really! I exclaimed, surprised because Richter is a common German name. I had only asked to make conversation.

He reached into the side pocket of his leather shorts and pulled out a gold watch, elaborately engraved. Flipped it open and noted the time. Noticed my admiration for the piece.

Junghans, he said. German engineering. My father's watch, and his father's before him. And a good place to begin my story, Adrian, with my father, in Germany, long ago…if I may.

Absolutely, I said.

He returned the watch to his pocket. I put my iPhone between us and pressed the *record* button without asking his permission. He began.

WHEN THE TRAIN LEAVES THE STATION

I WAS BORN IN THE RESORT TOWN of Baden-Baden, in the Black Forest of Germany, in 1940. My father was the proprietor of a small hotel and spa, *The Gasthaus Richter.* He was a neophyte painter, an amateur with no formal training and no recognition, but a true *appréciateur* of the arts, especially the Surréaliste Movement. Are you a fan of Surrealism, Adrian?

As a matter of fact, I am, Conrad. As a boy, I was gifted the *World Book Encyclopedia.* I went straight to the heading of Art. I fell in love with the Surrealists. I look for their work now wherever I go. I'm not a true scholar, Conrad, but I do sometimes drop the name of an artist into a story, to make myself appear more sophisticated than I am.

A frank admission, Adrian, which I can appreciate. And you would have appreciated growing up in our household. The surrealist painter Max Ernst came often with his writer and painter girlfriend, Leonora Carrington. They were joined by their contemporaries: Marcel Duchamp, Marc Chagall, Giorgio De Chirico, Yves Tanguy, the young American, Darla Mueller—

Darla Mueller! Conrad, you say there was a young American painter named Darla Mueller in this group?

Yes. She was a minor figure, Adrian. A mediocre painter. I doubt if any of her work survives, but she provided a bit of drama. It's said she competed with Ernst for Carrington's affection. How do you know of her?

Umm…heard the name, is all. Or maybe I imagine I have. Please continue.

Ernst was sympathetic to my father's lack of skill. He coached him on technique. My father was resigned to never being great but appreciated their friendship. Ernst painted a picture for him that hung over the fireplace of the Inn. It was admired by guests from far and wide. There was altogether an atmosphere of historic and cultural significance to Gasthaus Richter, and my father was determined to keep it afloat, for posterity's sake, and to support his family: my mother and I and my older sister, Heidi, whom I loved dearly.

The hotel was a fiscal challenge in the best of times; in 1944, tragedy struck: we were set upon by a horde of rats. Heidi was bitten as she slept and succumbed to a rare form of meningitis. We became known as a House of the Plague. My father moved the family to New York, where a friend managed a luxury hotel. He gave my father a job. The Ernst painting came with us and graced our modest apartment. I went to public High School. I wanted to be a painter. My father wanted me to be a lawyer. As much as he loved art, he did not want me to grow up in romanticized poverty. I graduated Cornell University School of Law and became an Associate in a prominent firm. I married my High School sweetheart, Nancy. We had three children. My parents died within a year of each other. I inherited the Ernst painting. It hung in the living room of our townhouse in Tribeca.

I took my family to Germany, to Baden-Baden, on holiday. We visited the ruins of Gasthaus Richter. We stayed at a grand hotel nearby. Troubled by the proximity of the ruins of my childhood home, and haunted by memories of my dearly departed sister, I left my wife and children in our suite of rooms and ventured out to a nearby ratskeller where I drank shots of Jagermeister until they closed. While I drank myself silly, there was a terrible fire at the hotel. My family perished, save for my youngest daughter, Sharon, who lingered in hospital for a month before dying. Their charred remains are buried in the same graveyard as my sister. I have not been back to Baden-Baden.

Conrad fell to silence. I assumed he wanted an expression of condolence. I didn't know the man. I obliged him with a stock phrase: *I'm sorry for your loss, Conrad.*

Thank you, Adrian, he said.

He resumed his narrative.

I took a month's sabbatical from my firm. Traveled Europe by train with no particular destination. At each stop, I would take a room at a local Inn. Do a walking tour of the town. Engage people in conversation and inquire about their lives. Imagine them vividly. Each life I embraced would supersede a facet of my own, which had become torturous. When I boarded the train the following day and departed for the next destination, my grief had been lessened by degrees. Have you traveled by train, Adrian? No? Then you don't know the pleasure one feels when the train leaves the station. The past recedes, the future unfolds. When a dozen stations were behind me, the present had become bearable.

I returned to New York. Moved out of my memory-filled townhouse in Tribeca and rented a brownstone on the Upper East Side, my Ernst original in tow. I began a whirlwind of superficial relationships with an array of women. Wary of commitment, I would love them and leave them. I thought I would never marry again…until I met a most unusual woman: Hannah.

Hannah was a Russian supermodel with a PhD in mathematics, related distantly to the Imperial Romanovs. I see you're as dubious as I was, Adrian. Such a combination of brains and brawn and pedigree is a rarity even in Manhattan. And she wanted me! Said she would give up her career on the red carpet to have my children! I prayed to the spirit of Nancy for approval and married Hannah.

We had two children, twin girls. They were bright and inquisitive, long limbed and lissome as their mother.

When the girls were five, we took a ski vacation to the Republic of Kabardino-Balkaria, on the Northern flank of the Greater Caucasus Range. Hannah's mother, Olga, from the nearby capital of Nalchik, joined us there. Three days into our holiday, weary of skiing, I sat on the deck of the bar drinking Yorsh, a traditional mix of beer and vodka. Hannah and Olga coached the twins on the bunny slope. A tremor deep in the heart of Mt. Elbrus triggered an avalanche. Ten thousand tons of snow and ice like shards of broken glass roared down the slope at a hundred miles an hour. My family was swallowed before my eyes. Their bodies were never found.

I wired my firm that I would take an indefinite leave of absence. I traveled north to Moscow via Russian Railways, thence from Moscow to Vladivostok via the Trans-Siberian Railway, a distance of 5,772 miles. I disembarked along the way at Yaroslavl, Chelyabinsk, Omsk, Novosibirsk, Ulan-Ude, and dozens of lesser towns and villages, and spent a few days in each. I became addicted to the release from the fetters of grief I felt each time the train left the station.

I was gone six months. Manhattan had become a foreign place to me, bleak and inhospitable. I accepted a position with a law firm in Columbia, Missouri: Davis, Gracey and Wall. I purchased a secluded cottage in the woods a few miles from town. There was a porch. And on the porch a swing. And beyond the porch a pond. And around the pond, in the rushes, croaked a chorus of bullfrogs. When the sun went down, heat lightning silent as prayer slid across the darkening sky. Swallows soared and dipped in the damp air, feasting on fireflies. Forgive my flowery description, Adrian, but the atmosphere was truly mystical, the solitude a balm to my troubled soul.

Our firm's secretary, Ronit—wholesome, diminutive, and shapely as an hourglass; I called her *Petite Ronit*—was a recent graduate of the local university. She'd never been east nor west of Missouri and was impressed by my relative sophistication. I hadn't lost my regard for a winsome lass and though I was twice her age I took advantage of her naiveté and seduced her. I made it clear I was a ship in the night: we would never marry; we would never have children.

It is what it is, she said with feigned nonchalance, though I perceived she wanted more.

Six months into our affair, she was diagnosed with stage IV Acute Myeloid Leukemia and given a month to live. I was told by her doctor she was pregnant and the fetus would not survive. I knelt by her bedside in hospital and asked her to marry me. *Ronit Richter*, she whispered. *It has a nice ring.* A month later, I said farewell to my third wife and sixth child.

Conrad paused. His story was a greater litany of love and loss than I was prepared to commiserate about. We were silent together for a moment.

Did you marry again? I said at length.

No, he said. Even had I wanted to, I wouldn't have. Marrying Conrad Richter had become a death sentence. I left Missouri and went into private practice in Philadelphia. I threw myself into my work for thirty-five years, and for one month out of each of those years, I rode the rails: the Ghan across Australia; the Shongololo Express across the African countries of Eswatini, South Africa, Namibia, Zimbabwe, and Mozambique; the Rocky Mountaineer across Canada; the Danube Express from Istanbul to Budapest; the West Highland Railway from Glasgow to Mallaig; the Darjeeling Himalayan Railway from the plains of Jalpaiguri to Darjeeling…and dozens more excursions, Adrian, each a journey out of myself into the unknown. My annual leave sustained me until I could walk away from the demands of my profession and do what I had spent a lifetime waiting to do: painting. It's been said that ten thousand hours of practice are required to master an art. I did not have ten thousand hours left and would never be a master, but never mind, I was sure I had one good painting in me and set about producing it. Which I have. And now—

Conrad pulled his watch from his pocket and glanced at the time.

—now it's time to go, he said. Take this, Adrian. I won't be needing it.

He reached his watch across the table. I took it, too surprised not to. He stood and bowed at the waist. His voice was solemn.

Auf Weidersehen, Herr Lomachenko, he said. Until we meet again.

He turned and strode away, clopping his walking stick on the hardwood floor as he went.

SAM, I IMAGINE YOU'RE AS FRUSTRATED now as I was at that moment. I had waited two weeks suspended in the null and void for a December story to materialize when along comes a man who says he has one for me, and a book cover to boot, and I listen to his tale of woe, of incidents certainly unlikely but not inexplicable, because they could be explained, and he walks out the door without providing either.

I resolved to use what Conrad told me and to fabricate the second half of his story. As for artwork, I had wielded a fair brush back in the day; perhaps I would do it myself. Such were my thoughts when I walked home with Conrad's Junghans watch in my pocket and found in my mailbox a letter from the Philadelphia law firm of Taube, Roberts and Roberts

informing me of an unspecified inheritance from an unidentified bene-
factor. I was to go to Philadelphia to receive it. Travel and hotel arrangements would be made for me, paid in advance. I called and spoke to the
secretary, Desiree—yes, Sam, Desiree—and booked an appointment with
Attorney Roberts.

MY SUITE ON THE 55TH FLOOR of the Four Seasons Hotel in downtown Philadelphia was extravagant. The bar was fully stocked. The floor-
to-ceiling window opened onto a view of City Hall, the Delaware River,
and the greenbelt and pedestrian walkway alongside it. Philadelphia,
birthplace of the nation. I popped a cork from a glistening green bottle of
Champagne and took a bubble bath, reflecting that a few short years ago,
Nobody Number Ninety-Nine had done the same.

The next morning, Desiree, in a green silk blouse and black skirt over
thigh-high black stockings, led me down a long corridor to the office of
Attorney Roberts. I admired the sway of her hips and the way her calves
bunched beneath her stockings with every step.

Felicity Roberts was reserved and courteous in a charcoal grey pantsuit
over a pale cream button-up blouse.

My condolences, Mr. Lomachenko—

Adrian.

My condolences, *Adrian*, and my apologies for the circumstances under
which you are receiving your inheritance. It was Mr. Richter's stipulation
that his identity not be revealed until now. He was nothing if not peculiar,
as you know.

Mr. Richter…?

The deceased. Conrad Richter.

I was dumbfounded.

Where? When? How? I said.

Three months ago, Adrian. The day before his passing he delivered a
parcel to our office and an addendum to his will. The next day he died in
his sleep. Peacefully, I like to think.

Felicity and I shared a moment of silence.

How did you know him? she said.

There was no alternative but to relate my version of events.

We'd only spoken once, I said. In a coffee shop in Oregon. Two days
ago. He told me his life story, how he was born in Germany and became a
lawyer in New York and traveled the world by train and had three wives
and six children and lost them all in an unlikely series of tragic events.

I could see the wheels turning as Ms. Roberts processed this contra-dictory information. Cognitive dissonance would describe her state. She came to a resolution.

I don't deal in enigmas, Adrian, she stated flatly. I deal in facts. Mr. Richter was a lifelong friend and I can assure you he's never been married. He's never had children. He was not a lawyer. He was a plumbing contrac-tor in Philadelphia his entire professional career and has never been out of the country. Certainly, never to Oregon. And the fact is—he's been dead for three months!

She pushed a button on her intercom.

Desiree, she said, bring Mr. Lomachenko's property and your notary book.

Desiree brought in a narrow crate, securely fastened, three feet square with a handle. I signed for receipt of it. I would open it at home.

I SAT ON THE COUCH IN THE LIVING ROOM of my small apartment drinking a Napa Valley Pinot, as had Paul the Potter the night before his fateful venture west into the labyrinthine chambers of his acid-fueled mind. Outside, the winter rain tapped pleasantly against the roof and the windows, and the sound of windblown branches scraping the walls mingled with the voices of playful spirits taunting me: *Come on! Come on! Open it!*

INSIDE THE CRATE ARE TWO PAINTINGS, each eighteen by twen-ty-four inches. The first an alien landscape signed in the bottom right corner, *Max Ernst, 1941.* The second a somber work in blue that parrots the sinister, unsettling images of Leonora Carrington's work. From windows in buildings left and right protrude five women in various attitudes of distress, five anguished women wailing, representing, I presumed, three wives, a sister and a mother-in-law, all dead. On the lower right, on a ledge, sit a row of six skulls, one for each of six deceased children. On the top of the wall to the left is written the German word for Departure: *Abfahrt.* On the opposite wall, a clock reads five minutes to midnight. At the end of the alleyway, under an arch, sits the Laughing Buddha, amused by it all. On the right side of the picture, the complex of buildings and the alleyway are transformed, by some trick of perspective reminiscent of MC Escher, into a train bound for a distant horizon. In the window of the foremost car is the forlorn face of Conrad Richter. I recognize it at once, a startling resemblance. The title of the painting is written on the back of it: *When the*

Train Leaves the Station. Though technically flawed—*an uneven work*, the critics might say—the devotion and tenacity that produced it are admirable. Nice work for a plumbing contractor from Philadelphia.

I had the second half of my December story and the artwork for the cover. What more could I want?

IN ANOTHER UNIVERSE, SAM, A READER ARRIVES at the end of a story I might have written but didn't. Thank you for being here at the end of the one I did. Twelve stories in twelve months! You and me and Miranda—what a team!

Outside, the rain and the wind have ceased. I look at my newly gifted, elaborately engraved Junghans pocket watch. It is 12:01 a.m. on Wednesday, the first day of January, in the year 2020.

Happy New Year, Sam!

EPILOGUE

AND THEN WHAT HAPPENED

*This is the end of a story that even people who are not usually
amazed at anything may refuse to believe.
But I am armed in advance against human incredulity.*

– Jules Verne

Friday, May 15th, 2020

EVENTS UNFOLDED QUICKLY IN THE NEW YEAR. Not having the same sentimental attachment to the Ernst painting as had Conrad Richter, I took it to Sotheby's. They confirmed its authenticity and arranged a sale. It is now in the private collection of Gallery Wendi Norris on Octavia Street in San Francisco. My share of the proceeds: 2.7 million dollars. I paid off my student loan, bequeathed to Art Presence an amount equivalent to their annual budget, gifted a tidy sum to The Little River Nondenominational Christian Fellowship, and purchased the two-bedroom cottage next door to Paul the Potter, known to the locals as the *Bledsoe House*. I sleep in the room where, on August 1st of 2017, Hattie and Ordell died in bed together, spooning like lovers. Above the fireplace hangs the only Richter original known to exist. I rescued a dog at the pound and named him Conrad. He leads me around town at the end of a leash with a smile on his face and a tail that wags like windshield wipers on high. He romps and stomps with his doggie pals, Dada and Jack. I sit on my porch in my rocker and contemplate my next book, about what I haven't a clue, but an idea will come, they always do, and when it does, my friend, I hope to see you there.

Au revoir, Sam. Until we meet again…

THE END

AUTHOR'S NOTE

Early versions of *Geometry of the External World* were published in the magazines *Common Thought* and *ShabdAaweg Review*.

Early versions of *The Migration of Plastic Pink Flamingos* were published in *Opium Magazine* and *Rhodora Magazine*.

Portions of *One Hundredfold* were published in the anthology *Stories That Must Be Told* under the title *Bead by Bead*, and as *Luminous* in *The Del Sol Review*.

Ten Thousand Hours in Shadowland is an elaboration of the unpublished story *The Amazing Zachary's Fantastic 10th Birthday Experience*.

ABOUT THE AUTHOR

 A prolific short story writer, EA Luetkemeyer's fiction has appeared in the literary journals *Sou'wester, Opium Magazine, Del Sol Review, Perversion Magazine, The Ilanot Review, Cerasus Magazine, Rhodora, Centrifictionist,* and *The ShabdAaweg Review.*

His flash fiction piece, *The Southwest Chief,* was named a finalist in The Wild Atlantic Writing Awards, and his story *Bead by Bead,* a finalist in the anthology *Stories That Must be Told,* a publication of Tulip Tree Press.

He is the author of the memoir *The Book of Chuck,* and the novels *Inside the Mind of Martin Mueller* and *Penitentiary Tales: a Love Story,* a finalist in the 2020 *Wishing Shelf Book Awards.* He has been a martial artist, a long distance runner, an outlaw, a fugitive, an inmate, a husband and father, and, by his own admission, sometimes a fool.

Awarded an MFA in Creative Writing from Lesley University, Cambridge, MA, in 2015, he lives and writes in the picturesque Rogue Valley of Southern Oregon where, with inspiration from his capricious Muse, Miranda, he is at work on his next novel, *The Life and Death of Louie Amato.*

For excerpts and reviews of his work, visit **www.ealuetkemeyer.com**.

ALSO BY EA LUETKEMEYER

THE BOOK OF CHUCK

A memorial compilation of poetry and prose honoring the life and legacy of the author's late brother, an intractable poet and malcontent whose abiding tenet was the transient nature of the material world. Disdaining the attachment of others to form and appearance, he became cynical, bitter and belligerent, but never despaired of knowing, though he searched in drunkenness until substance abuse ended his life. An intimate portrait of life on the ragged edge of the sixties, seventies and eighties.

INSIDE THE MIND OF MARTIN MUELLER

Martin Mueller is a man of wealth and taste whose mission in life is to reassemble the scattered shards of the shattered Over-soul of mankind. Who believes the penitentiary he's an inmate of is in the basement of his country estate. Daily he discards the fine clothes of a retired billionaire, dons the blue denim of a prisoner, and takes an elevator down to his cell where he toils obsessively at his masterpiece, which he believes will alter the course of the evolution of mankind, and earn him a high place among his brethren-to-be, the Illuminati. Is he delusional? Which is real, the mansion or the cell block... or both? The reader must decide. *Inside The Mind of Martin Mueller* is a Rorschach inkblot test of a twisted tale: what you see is what you get.

"a luminous, far-fetched, existential mind-trip with a freaky twist ending"
– Onlinebookclub.org

PENITENTIARY TALES: A LOVE STORY

Dean Davis, an educated, straight white male from the affluent community of Sausalito, California, is sent to an Illinois prison dominated by a racially diverse population of inmates from the mean streets of Chicago. How does he do his time? How does the experience affect his social and political awareness? *Penitentiary Tales: a Love Story* is a serious inquiry into the minds and hearts of the marginalized and the oppressed, and a bit of a romp, for readers who appreciate a literary walk on the wild side.

"an insightful and at times darkly disturbing glimpse into an institution rarely entered by most readers"
- Dr. John M. Coggeshall, Clemson University